STARTING OVER

By the Author

Secret Sanctuary

An Alaskan Wedding

Cowgirl

Starting Over

STARTING OVER

by

Nance Sparks

2023

ISBN 13: 978-1-63679-409-9

This Trade Paperback Original Is Published By
Bold Strokes Books, Inc.
P.O. Box 249
Valley Falls, NY 12185

First Edition: May 2023

Credits
Editor: Barbara Ann Wright
Production Design: Stacia Seaman
Cover Design by Tammy Seidick

Acknowledgments

First and foremost, I'd like to thank my readers. Your encouragement keeps me at the keyboard.

I'd also like to thank everyone at Bold Strokes Books. You are all so enjoyable to work with, and I'm constantly amazed by what you do to support and encourage your authors. You make my work shine in a way I never knew it could.

I'd like to dedicate this novel
to those who find themselves starting over.
May you find happiness and peace.

CHAPTER ONE

It had been more than a year since Sam'd had a full night's sleep. Without fail, her eyes popped open somewhere around two forty-three in the morning to the imaginary sound of relentless pounding on the front door. The grim reality of that single moment in time had since become a recurring nightmare. Like a bad habit she couldn't seem to break, regardless of how late she forced herself to stay awake the night before or what over-the-counter medication she took.

Sleep never used to be an issue. Prior to that fateful night, she would have been sound asleep as soon as her head hit the pillow and would remain that way until the alarm sounded. She squeezed her eyes shut and tried to picture a black canvas. She'd read that doing so could help insomniacs fall back into a peaceful slumber. Desperate for a solution, she was willing to try most anything at this point.

An hour later, it was clear that picturing the canvas wasn't working. Her eyes refused to stay closed, so she went back to staring at whatever caught her attention. The bright light of the full moon cast shadowy silhouettes of naked tree branches onto her bedroom walls and ceiling. It was beautiful and eerie at the same time. The image reminded her more of Halloween and less of late winter. She half expected to see fluttering shadows of bats or an outline of a black cat or a witch.

The tree limbs were swaying wildly in the wind that lingered after the previous night's snowstorm. The scene from the movie *Poltergeist* came to mind when the young boy was watching the storm whip the branches just outside his bedroom window. Lightning and thunder had been the least of that kid's problems. Just like the swaying branches were the least of hers. Could spirits become stuck somewhere in this realm like they had in that movie? Was Kara stuck somewhere? If so, would she ever come and visit?

Sam flipped over on her side for a change of scenery. This was worse because now she was staring across her huge king-size bed. Every single day, she woke up with the hope that it had all been a nightmare. Over and over, she was met with the realization that it was indeed a nightmare but one she'd never wake up from. Kara's side of the bed was still cold and empty. Her pillows didn't smell like her anymore, and the scent of her perfume on its own did little to capture her essence. Sam had realized over time that it was the combination of Kara and her makeup, blended with her multitude of hair products, and her perfume that created the complete olfactory addiction. Every attempt at a recreation had been futile. The scent couldn't be recreated because the primary ingredient was missing.

She closed her eyes and tried once again to focus on the black canvas. One of these days, it had to work.

The experiment of forcing herself to stay in bed until the alarm sounded continued to be an abysmal failure. Her mind wallowed less when she had something to focus on. Lying there, her eyes refused to stay closed, and staring at a void on the other side of the bed wasn't helping her heart heal. She wondered if it ever would, or was she destined to be broken forever?

Everything she'd read said that she should have been back to normal within a year. It had been thirteen months, eight days, one hour and—she looked over at the clock—twelve minutes, and nothing felt close to normal. Tomorrow, she'd allow herself to get up when her eyes popped open. In other parts of the house, she could be pathetic, sad, and lonely, but at least she'd have coffee.

Finally, after what seemed like an eternity, the alarm clock clicked, and the soft and sultry voice of her favorite morning DJ filled the quiet void. "Good morning, my Minnesota peeps. Bundle up well before braving this bitterly cold morning. Hard to believe it's almost April with last night's snowstorm. Sadly, we now have another eighteen inches of fresh powder dumped on our world. The temps were expected to fall after the snow clouds made their way east, and boy howdy, was that forecast ever spot on. It's now a not-so-balmy negative fifteen degrees outside. This cold snap is expected to stick around for a bit. Someday, spring will arrive, I hope. So while you're waking up and deciding whether or not to call in frozen, I'll grace you with some classic Melissa Etheridge. Go grab some coffee and bask in the warmth of her seductive, sexy voice."

Melissa's rasp blessed the tiny speaker of the alarm clock. Sam instantly recognized "I Will Never Be the Same," perfectly appropriate for this melancholy morning.

Oh, sing it loud and proud, girlfriend. Sam belted out the lyrics while she made the bed. Music had a way of expressing what she couldn't begin to put into words. Just as the song finished, the coffee pot beeped, announcing that the carafe was full. Thankfully, the insomnia torture was over, and it was time to trudge through another day. At least there would be plenty of distractions at work.

Would this profound emptiness get any easier? It hadn't so far, but her thoughts of joining Kara in the afterlife, whatever that looked like, had become a little easier to ignore.

Thirty minutes later, with a jumbo YETI mug of coffee in the cupholder, Sam was on her way to work. The roads were quiet, and her favorite DJ continued to keep her company. The commute typically took about thirty minutes, but on this frigid snowy morning, it took closer to an hour. It was a good thing she'd left early. *Slow and steady for the win.*

The local snowplow gal, Heather, had just finished the parking lot when Sam pulled in. Her parking space had been salted too, as was the sidewalk to the office doors. It wasn't Heather's first rodeo. Sam had worked for Mike Walsh for the past twelve years, and Heather had cleared the parking lot for almost as long.

Heather lowered her window and waved emphatically as Sam pulled in and parked. She was wearing her trademark Carhartt hoodie, zipped up to her neck, and a matching knit hat pulled over her ears. When she turned her head sharply, her long ponytail curled around her neck like a wildcat's tail. Sam had no idea what kind of clothing she wore beneath the winter wear. In all the years they'd shared this exchange, she'd only ever seen Heather in that tattered, faded hoodie. She imagined Heather to be a no-frills kind of gal and pictured a rotating stack of T-shirts with funny and slightly off-color phrases on the front or back. When it came to women who lived in the country, it was sometimes difficult to guess who was a lesbian and who was simply a rough-and-tumble Minnesota gal. Sam still wasn't sure which it was for Heather, but everything about her attire and her beefed-up beast of a truck with huge gnarly tires made it clear she could likely handle anything thrown at her.

Sam rolled down her window and waved back. "The lot looks great. Thank you for getting here so early."

"I know you arrive around five, so I make sure to start my day here. Have a great one, Sam."

"You too. Stay warm," Sam said and waved again.

She liked to arrive at the office as early as possible. She enjoyed the few hours of solitude before everyone else showed up with their incessant chatting. A quick scan of her badge and she walked through the front door that automatically locked behind her. The security system was programmed to unlock at eight o'clock sharp each morning, which meant she had another three hours all to herself. It was her favorite part of the workday.

The majority of the building was dark, except for a few security lights that dimly illuminated the path to her office. She unlocked her door, flipped on her office lights, and powered on her bank of wide-screen monitors. She launched the streaming app on her computer, and her favorite DJ poured from the speakers. She was on the air until nine o'clock, companionship that didn't include the need for small talk.

She glanced at the server resource utilization webpage. Her breath caught, and her chest tightened when she saw that the servers hosting their clients' primary business application were about five minutes away from full system alarms. She sat on the edge of her seat, ignored her racing heart, and got to work on the issue. The electronic health records application, designed by her employer, had developed some kind of glitch in the last few versions and now periodically consumed server resources to the point of a server crash. It was an issue that was increasing in frequency and without an explanation from the programming team.

She checked the connected sessions, and there were only six users logged into the environment. It was designed to support several hundred. With this light a load, the server farms should be contently purring, not crashing. She quickly downloaded the system logs and took screenshots before she urged the few users off the systems and rebooted the servers. It was a temporary fix at best, but if the past few weeks were any indication, it would get them through a few days before it started to creep up like that again. When the crisis was averted, Sam sat back in her chair. She took a sip of coffee and tried to breathe through the effects of the strong jolt of adrenaline still coursing through her body. Her aching heart didn't need any additional strain.

She spent most of the day trying to isolate the issues for the analysis report that would be sent to the clients in an effort to explain why their staff had been—once again—kicked off the application. It gave her something to dig into and get lost in. She sent off the email with the documents attached and hoped that Mike, the owner, would see the urgency of the situation. They had already lost one client to the issue, and the other clients would only tolerate being bumped off for unscheduled reboots for so long.

Two quick raps on Sam's office door interrupted her thoughts. She glanced at the clock on her monitor. Shit, it was almost six at night. Where had the day gone? She paused her playlist.

The door pushed open slightly, and half of the office admin's face peeked through the opening like a one-eyed jack-in-the-box. "Hey, hey, it's FriYay! Should we save you a seat at Tally's bar?" she asked.

Once upon a time, Sam would have led the charge to FriYay happy hour. "Thanks, Kelly, but I'll pass."

"I had a feeling you'd say no again, but I'll just keep bugging you until you say yes again." Kelly's one visible penciled-on eyebrow wiggled up and down. It was a finely detailed border between her glistening blue eye shadow and her wavy auburn bangs. Ever since Sam had come back to work, Kelly had started making all sorts of goofy facial expressions in an attempt to make her laugh. So far, it still wasn't working.

"You do that. Someday, I might surprise both of us and feel up to socializing again." She doubted that. Everyone wanted her to go back to being the fun-loving life of the party. No one understood that cracking jokes and laughing was hard when the source of her happiness, the sun that she'd revolved around for most of her adult life, was gone forever. "Oh, hey, do you know if Mike's hired a new programmer yet?"

"He's interviewed a few but felt like they lacked the skills to dig into the issue. He even tried to poach a few from rivals, but they declined unless he brought in a team with experience, and we can't afford that kind of financial hit."

"It's a no-win situation, isn't it? He can't afford the talent because the clients are bailing out, and he can't afford not to bring in the experience, either. I hope he can sort this out before there are no clients left." The last few words all but stuck in Sam's throat. There was no doubt that this job gave her a reason to keep going. Quite honestly, it was all she had left, and the realization that they were in danger of closing the doors hit with the swinging force of a wrecking ball.

"Us too, believe me. If things get much worse, we may have to look at a second mortgage on the house to keep the company afloat. Mike said that Brent made a mess of things, and he feels pretty useless because he hasn't coded in so long. He's worried he'd do more harm than good. I think he's talking with a consulting company. Losing the Eastman account definitely got his attention."

Sam let out her breath. A consulting company should offer some seasoned talent. It gave her hope. At least he was working on some sort of a solution. "Expertise would be a welcome change. He can't keep hiring fresh college grads and expect them to work miracles. I've been able to keep us limping along, but it's a short-term solve."

"He knows and appreciates all your efforts." Kelly disappeared from the small opening before reappearing like the guy from *The Shining*. "Are you sure you don't want to join us at Tally's? I'll buy you a round."

Sam shook her head. Tally's Bar was so much more than FriYay happy hour. It had been Kara's favorite hangout. They'd always sat on the same two stools. They'd had their own cues for pool, kept safe in a case in Sam's truck. Neither of them was rock-star awesome, but they had enjoyed playing in the league. It was something fun to do. No one seemed to understand that hearing the clack of the balls on the table and smelling the food and stale beer was just another reminder that Kara wouldn't come busting through the doors announcing that the party could now commence.

"Thanks, but I'm really not up for it."

Kelly nodded and pulled the door closed. The light in the hallway clicked off, and Sam was, once again, the last one in the office. She didn't have the energy to pretend to have fun at happy hour, and that was exactly what her coworkers would want. She could hear it all now: "Come on, Sam, lighten up, laugh a little. You need to move on."

If they only knew how much easier that was said than done. Sam checked on the servers' resource usage one last time, undocked her laptop, and packed up to head home.

The grocery store wasn't too busy for early Friday evening, and over the past year, she'd finally figured out how to shop for one person. A rotisserie chicken from the deli and three quarters of a pound of ham would offer both dinners and lunches for the next seven days. A three-pack of romaine lettuce hearts, one container of cherry tomatoes, and a couple of cucumbers easily made a week's worth of salads. Lastly, she sought out some cheese and eggs and a loaf of bread. It was surprising how little she needed to live on. She and Kara used to pile one of the big carts high. Kara had enjoyed elaborate meals and entertaining, and Sam had enjoyed seeing her shine. They'd complemented each other. They had been the couple everyone wanted to be around. The couple everyone wanted to emulate.

Sam shook off the thought and pushed her tiny cart to the front of the store. "Excuse me. Can I sneak by?" she asked someone blocking the path to the checkout line.

The tall, broad-shouldered woman was wearing a knee-length, brown herringbone Nili Lotan wool coat. Impressive winter wear. Sam recognized the designer instantly because she owned one herself, although hers hung in the closet unused, along with the rest of her dress clothes. She could picture the blurb on the website: "Created for the professional man" *or masculine woman*, she remembered thinking when she'd purchased hers. Dress slacks and a pair of cap toe oxford dress shoes were the only other items she could see from her current position behind the cart. Either the wearer had great taste in clothing, or someone loved her very much.

"Oh, I'm sorry. My wife just remembered like ten things, and here I thought we were all done shopping." Sam recognized the voice at the same time the woman turned and looked her in the eye. "Sam? Holy crap, is that you? We've been wondering how you were doing. Are you okay? You don't look so good. Have you been sick?" Pat Adams. Sam hadn't talked with her or her wife, Angie, since the funeral. Sam had pushed her entire group of couple friends away by ignoring texts and calls until the attempts had finally stopped. She couldn't take conversations that always started with *remember when*.

"Hey, Pat. I'm fine. Can I get by? It's been a hell of a day."

"You don't look so fine, my friend. We're all really worried about you." Pat lifted her arms and stepped forward for a hug. Sam kept her cart positioned as a barrier. She didn't need to turn into a blubbering idiot in the main aisle of the grocery store. Pat lowered her arms. "Oh, hey, we're all getting together at our place tomorrow night, you should come. Everyone would love to see you. The parties aren't the same without you and…" Pat stopped talking, and the unspoken name hung in the air.

Sam swallowed the lump in her throat. "Thanks, but I'm not up for it."

Pat tilted her head slightly to the side. "I thought we were friends. What happened?"

"I wouldn't say we're not friends. Jesus, Pat, I haven't been up for socializing."

Why couldn't anyone understand what it was like to exist without your one true love? Pat still had Angie. Kelly still had Mike. Everyone who wanted her to be more social and move on still had their person. She didn't expect them to really understand—she wouldn't wish that pain on anyone—but they could at least try.

Pat stepped around Sam's tiny cart and stood next to her. "It's not about socializing. You pushed us all away. I'm guessing you pushed everyone away. You don't answer texts. You don't answer calls. Dude, it's like you're tumbling down the rabbit hole. Is it depression? Have you talked to your doctor or tried counseling or grief group?"

She'd never heard of grief group. Her mind conjured up an

image of a bunch of people sitting in a circle holding foam cups of coffee, sharing their woes, and dabbing at tears streaming down their cheeks. *Yeah...no, hard pass, thank you very much.* There was nothing she could say that would express what she felt inside. This was exactly why she didn't answer texts and calls. Everyone wanted her to feel something besides numb, broken, and alone. She had no idea how to do that. "I'm managing fine. I still get up and go to work every day."

"That's not fine. It's like you've completely shut down. How long has it been since you had a haircut?"

Sam sighed. "Give it a break. So what if I'm a little overdue?"

"A little overdue? Ya think?" Pat cocked her head and rubbed her chin. "Dude, with your hair long like that, you look like Frodo Baggins from *The Lord of the Rings*. All you need for Halloween is a pair of hairy elf feet and those pointy ears."

She knew Pat wasn't trying to be an asshole. She always used humor to lighten things up. Another time, a lifetime ago, the Frodo comment might have been funny, but today, it felt a little like a sucker punch to the gut. Sam had a mirror. She knew what she looked like. The truth was, over the past year, she'd stopped caring. The faded jeans and flannels she'd used to wear while doing yard work had replaced the items that required ironing or trips to the dry cleaners.

Pat rested her hand on her shoulder. "I'm sorry. I thought the Frodo thing would make you laugh."

"Yeah, no, not today." Sam tightened her grip on the cart. She tried to breathe through the emotion that was stuck in her throat. No way was she going to allow herself to cry. Not here and definitely not in front of Pat.

"Sam, it's like you're barely existing. Can't you see that? Listen, pal, I'm here if you ever want to talk. If not me, talk to someone because it's like we lost both of you in that car accident and, news flash, you weren't even in the car. I miss ya, buddy." Pat squeezed her grip on Sam's shoulder and tried to turn her so they would be facing each other.

Sam wasn't prepared for Pat's blunt honesty, though she should have expected nothing less. It was something she'd always admired about Pat. She'd gotten used to the comments on her appearance.

She had ignored them well enough, but Pat's words were like a harsh slap. *It's like we lost both of you in that car accident.* There were times she'd wished that was the case. Tears welled up in her eyes and threatened to spill over. She released her tight grip on the handle of her shopping cart, turned, and walked right out of the grocery store without buying a single item.

CHAPTER TWO

Jennifer Delgado sat in the back corner of the hotel restaurant in Taos, New Mexico, sipping coffee and watching the news. The people all around her had become familiar faces, offering unspoken comfort with a simple sympathetic smile. Sympathetic because they were all in the same situation while awaiting the same news, and being together was much better than sitting alone in individual hotel rooms.

The air, even inside the hotel, was heavy with smoke. Once upon a time, forest fires in the late winter months were almost unheard of, but times had changed with the prolonged drought in the Southwest. She'd been evacuated from her home for almost two weeks. The Cross Canyon fire, ignited by a lightning strike in early February, had been burning for almost two months. Over three hundred thousand acres had already been consumed, and the monstrous inferno was only twenty-six percent contained. At this point, she had no idea whether or not her house was still standing. The hill behind the homes at the far end of her subdivision was already ablaze when they had sounded the evacuation alarms. Hotshot crews had positioned themselves between the hill and the homes, hoping to cut a fire break. She'd stuffed all she could into her car with the time she'd had and had gotten the hell out of there. This fire marked her third evacuation in two years, and with the severity of this blaze, whether her house survived or not, it felt like it might just be her last.

"How far are you from home?"

Jennifer looked up into soft brown eyes. The woman was older, perhaps her early to mid-seventies. Her streaked gray hair was pulled back into a bun. She held a cup of tea in one hand and fidgeted with the tea bag tab with the other. "My place is about a hundred and thirty miles from here. Almost due east of Santa Fe. This was the nearest hotel with vacancy. You?"

"Twenty-five miles. Do you know if the fire took your house?"

Jennifer shook her head. She couldn't bear the thought of losing her home to the fire. The house itself could be replaced, but she'd forgotten a few treasured keepsakes from her grandmother, and the thought of losing those was what she couldn't bear. "There's been no word."

"Me too. I was so grateful that they let me check in with my cat."

The hotel was running amok with household pets. There was an especially upset poodle in the room next to hers. It yapped off and on throughout the days and nights since she'd arrived. Earplugs and headphones were the absolute best inventions ever.

"I saw someone with a guinea pig cage when I was checking in." She closed her laptop and slid it into her briefcase. "My name is Jennifer. Would you care to join me?"

"I'm Maura. That's very sweet of you, but I don't want to disturb your work."

Jennifer motioned to the seat across from hers. "You would be a welcome distraction. Besides, I was just checking email. I'm actually between contracts at the moment and trying to figure out where to go next. A lot depends on whether I have to file an insurance claim. Please, join me. This is a big table for one."

"Well, okay. I don't mind if I do." Maura pulled out the chair and sat. "To be honest, I don't know a soul here, and it's weird to feel lonely when you're surrounded by people. Especially being that we're all in the same boat."

Jennifer couldn't agree more. She felt the loneliness too. It was something she'd been feeling more and more lately. Her skills were in high demand, and she attributed it to being on the road so much, not that she had friends or a social life at home. Still, home was where she recharged on her breaks between contracts, and she missed not being there now. If she was home right now, she'd probably be cooking one of her grandmother's recipes and listening to music as loud as she wanted to, without the need for headphones. That was one of her favorite ways to recharge.

"It's very nice to meet you. What's your cat's name?" Jennifer sipped on her coffee. She'd used a variety of questions as an icebreaker when meeting new colleagues. Consultants weren't always welcome, but a simple, light, non-work-related question always seemed to put people at ease.

Maura chuckled. "I adopted him as Manny, but I've only ever called him Asshole because as a kitten, he destroyed my furniture with his tiny razor claws. Now that he's older, he's more of a couch potato than anything else, but he doesn't know who I'm talking to if I call him Manny."

Jennifer thought about Maura's neighbors and wondered if they'd ever heard the cat get outside and need to be called back by name. Certainly, with a cat named Asshole, Maura could come up with a colorful collection of words if he was like most cats and taunted her from the edge of the yard. The collective string of profanity would be something to witness.

"What does that say about me?"

Maura's question interrupted her thought. "That tells me that you are a no-nonsense kinda gal. You say it like it is without mincing words. I bet your friends all come to you for advice."

Maura cocked her head. "I'll be damned. You know what? They do come to me for advice."

"So it's just you and the cat?" Jennifer swirled her last sip of coffee around in the bottom of the cup.

"Yep. How about you?"

"I travel too much to have an asshole of my own." Jennifer winked. While her comment was light, the pangs of loneliness were becoming more and more difficult to silence.

Maura chuckled. "Do you travel all over the country?"

"Most of my work is in the Southwest, but I've been as far north as San Francisco."

"Do you enjoy traveling for work?"

Jennifer sat back. She used to enjoy the carefree freedom that came with her profession. For the longest time, traveling had been fun and exhilarating, but anymore, it felt like she was packing up and starting over every six to nine months. A new city, new hotel room or temporary apartment, and a new contract that came with new colleagues. None of that allowed for friendships or companionship beyond the random one-night stand.

"I once enjoyed it more than I do now. I think it's wearing on me. I find myself craving the stability of home more and more. I hadn't realized that until this very moment."

"And then you're evacuated." Maura's expression shifted to the empathetic glances she'd seen all morning. "What do you do?"

Jennifer sat up taller in her seat. Her confidence blossomed when it came to her career. "I'm a software engineer, but because I'm a consultant, I'm frequently the engineer, developer, and the programmer in one compact package. It's all about a speedy, stable solution for the client."

Maura's eyebrows furrowed, and she tilted her head slightly to the side. "You're such a dainty thing. I pictured you in a softer profession."

"What do you consider a softer profession?" She'd fought against those stereotypes and expectations all her life. Dainty didn't have to mean meek, and small didn't mean less than. She didn't need to look like Xena, Warrior Princess to be an intelligent, kick-ass developer. She was one of the most sought-after software engineers in the Southwest. Her designs were sleek, and her code was efficient and elegant.

Maura fidgeted with her tea bag tab again. "Poor choice of words. I meant a more social profession, like social work or education."

"Really? Because I'm such a dainty thing?" Jennifer expected this conversation from men. After all, she'd been reminded time and again throughout her career that programming was a man's job. There was one at every company she'd contracted with who'd insisted on telling her that she belonged in a social or educational profession. Even her parents had jumped on that bandwagon. But Maura's comment surprised her. It wasn't expected from someone she'd assumed to be a strong, independent woman. She bet that Maura could handle a direct answer without feeling insulted. "I may be tiny, but have no doubt about my mightiness. I've had to compete with two dominating brothers all my life, and I hate coming in second. I'm good at what I do, and I can hold my own in life and in a male dominated profession."

Maura nodded and smiled. "I bet you can do more than hold your own. I bet you show them how it's done and with class."

"You know it." Jennifer tapped her coffee mug gently on the table in emphasis. She'd enjoyed the visit. It was honest without the fluff. She didn't need fluff. She didn't appreciate fluff. Straight shooter was always the preferred.

"Hey, everyone, quiet." A man stood and clapped. "There's an update."

Jennifer focused on the TV.

"Strong winds and dry conditions have fueled the Cross Canyon Fire. It's consumed more than three hundred and fifty thousand acres in mountainous terrain, and because of this, we're back to less than twenty percent contained. That said, the following areas have been cleared for residents to return..."

Jennifer held her breath. Maura let out a *woot* of celebration when the town Vadito was called out with zero structures lost, but the broadcast finished without mention of Jennifer's tiny town. She looked across the table into Maura's tear-filled, smiling eyes. So much gratitude within that expression, all without speaking a word.

"Congratulations. I'm so happy for you." And she genuinely was.

"Thank you, dear. I hope your home is spared too. And thank you for the conversation and the company. It's been a pleasure. I should go pack up and get on the road before it gets dark."

Jennifer stood and hugged her. "Safe travels."

"I wish you well in your next adventure, whatever that might be," Maura said, and she turned and disappeared through the crowd.

Jennifer didn't want to assume the worst, but with each update, it was more and more difficult to remain positive. Each evacuation had lasted longer than the previous, and the unknown awaiting her was unnerving. The longer she'd been forced to stay in the hotel, the more New Mexico felt less and less like home. One way or another, she needed a change.

It was another few days before Jennifer's little town was on the list, though "no structures lost" wasn't part of the announcement. Closed roads and active spot fires took her on detours more than a hundred miles from the mapped route. At times, visibility was limited to the taillights of the car in front of her, and smoke leached inside the car, even though the ventilation system was turned off. Her expensive Italian clothes had all been dry cleaned before she'd left her last contract, and now, everything in her car smelled like campfire. Would she ever get the smell out of her clothes or, better yet, out of her nose? She wasn't so sure anything could cleanse her senses of the charred landscape before her. The view through the windshield felt eerie, almost apocalyptic. She drove miles and miles through a smoldering charcoal wasteland.

One detour took her through a neighborhood that had been completely consumed. Driveway after driveway led to a blackened outline of someone's home. Skeletal remains of vehicles and barely recognizable bicycles were all that remained where garages once stood. Lot after lot bore witness to the same kind of devastation. The families affected by this fire would all have to start over from scratch. Some interviewed on the news left with not much more than the clothes on their backs. Insurance aside, everything they'd worked for had been devoured in an instant.

It was heartbreaking. Guilt washed over her for feeling like she was starting over with each new contract, because she traveled with everything that was important to her; well, almost everything. Even if her home looked like the skeletal remains surrounding her, her nomadic way of life made her better equipped to handle the loss because for her, it would be an inconvenience and not complete devastation.

It went on for miles before there were spotty signs of life again. A few homes here and there had somehow been spared. A large brick home with a metal roof was the lone survivor in one neighborhood. The tree in the front yard was blackened and devoid of leaves. The bushes against the house were also charred and lifeless, but the house stood like a soldier who would carry on.

Eventually, Jennifer made it into her tiny town and later, to her own subdivision. The hill that had been a glowing orange inferno was now charred and bare. Stubby, blackened tree trunks dotted the landscape where towering ponderosa pines had once swayed gently in the breeze. While the hotshot crew had performed miracles and saved the homes, the little neighborhood was an ash-covered oasis in the center of complete devastation. The surrounding desert landscapes that had once taken her breath away now looked like something out of a doomsday movie.

Ever since her visit with Maura, she'd thought about what might be next for her. The need for friendships and community were tugging at her, but was this where she wanted to build any of that? Could this ever feel like a full-time home instead of base camp? She already knew the answer. She didn't know where home was, but she knew in her heart that this wasn't it. There wasn't much left surrounding this tiny town. There was so much to rebuild. All of it was more than heartbreaking.

Jennifer pushed the button on the visor to open the garage door. It didn't engage. She should have expected that, given the burned power poles alongside the road. She parked in the driveway and left her luggage in the car. With a chance to organize, she had room in the car for a few more things, and she had some daylight left to be selective. Each step she took on the concrete driveway left an imprint in the ash, as if she was walking in an inch of snow.

The lack of any other tracks surprised her. Like she was the only person left alive. Logically, she knew better, but still, it had taken her all day to get here; surely, someone else had returned to check on their treasures. The street revealed only one set of tire tracks, hers. Her front yard was blanketed in ash. The cactus, the rocks, even the metal Kokopelli cutout that she kept by the front door. Everything was covered in ash. Every rooftop she could see lacked shingles, and all were the same ashy gray. She'd had enough of being outside all alone. She half expected zombies to come around the side of the house. Eerie was an understatement.

She unlocked the front door. Her decision to start over somewhere else was cemented the moment she stepped inside. This house held no more warmth than the countless hotel rooms she'd stayed in over the years. This wasn't a home, or at least, it no longer felt like her home. Instead of the expected lavender scent from her diffuser, the house smelled like a stale campfire. She wasn't so sure opening a window would help, so she left them closed and locked. None of the prints on her walls warranted the limited space in the car. They weren't personal or meaningful. They were generic prints that she'd purchased from Pier One and hung up because it was what homeowners did to decorate. Same went for the furniture and knickknacks. She passed all of it by and walked into the kitchen. There were two personal items she had kicked herself for forgetting. She pulled open the bottom drawer, picked up her grandmother's recipe box, and held it to her chest. She couldn't imagine losing this treasure to the fire. It was one of her most valuable belongings, even though it lacked any monetary value.

The small tin box contained years upon years of cherished memories. Memories that she'd relived time and again while creating the culinary masterpieces encased on each card. It was the only thing she'd asked for when her grandma had passed away. Time spent with her, working through the list of ingredients and creating the most incredible dishes, were some of Jennifer's fondest childhood memories.

Her grandmother was a gift from the heavens. She'd lifted Jennifer up when others had knocked her down. Jennifer's parents had never hidden the fact that she was an oops baby. Her parents and brothers were so much older when she was born that she was often an afterthought, but her grandmother always made her feel wanted and special. She felt it the most when her grandmother would invite her to help in the kitchen.

She found programming to be almost as comforting and soothing as cooking. Both were an art form, and sometimes, cleanup was a bitch. Programming could be a leftover mash-up where things were randomly tossed together and somehow managed to work. It could also be simple and effective like scrambled eggs or intricate and elegant like an enchilada feast from scratch. Jennifer relished all things intricate and elegant.

She kept hold of the small tin box and pulled the oven door open. The second most cherished item in the kitchen was her grandmother's cast-iron tortilla pan. Her mom had shipped it with the recipe box. Jennifer set the two items by the front door and set about collecting the last of her clothing, shoes, and a few other favorite things.

Lastly, she sat on the couch and pulled out her cell phone. A headhunter had reached out with a job offer in the Midwest. She'd told herself that if her house was still standing, she'd take the opportunity as a sign to do something different and hit the road.

There was nothing left for her here. She wanted a place to put down roots and call home. She opened the map app and looked at the satellite view of what would be her new town. It looked lush and green and fireproof. She clicked on the photos and swiped through. One was of a lake with fireworks igniting above. The reflection in the water was just as brilliant as the display. She'd never seen fireworks in person. The Southwest desert was too dry, and fireworks were banned. Another photo was of a quaint town square. The Zoom call a few days ago with the headhunter had gone well, as had the call with the company owner. She was certainly qualified for the role. She closed her eyes and drew in a deep breath. Maybe this could be her last new beginning. The last time she'd have to start over. It felt right. She needed a change. She was ready for a change. She opened the email and sent off the draft that she'd typed up earlier at the hotel, accepting the contract. Who knew, it might just be the change she'd been looking for.

Chapter Three

It's like we lost both of you in that accident.

It had been a little over a week, and Pat's words hadn't stopped replaying in Sam's mind. She stood outside the community center and watched as people went inside. No one looked like they were tumbling down a rabbit hole. No one looked consumed with grief. No one looked stuck. Instead, they looked like, well, normal people. Did she look normal to each person walking by? Well, if they looked past the long hair and the baggy clothes. Maybe she did. Maybe if she'd just get a haircut, things would turn around for her, and she'd want to be more social again. Somewhere, deep inside, she had a feeling that it wouldn't quite work that way. *Nope, that'd be too easy.*

She'd researched the options Pat had mentioned at the supermarket. She'd dug into all sorts of ways to cope with long-term grief. She didn't want to be stuck, yearning for what she could never get back, and at the same time, she didn't know how to become unstuck, either. She had no idea how to snap out of it or where to start.

The thing that scared her more than anything was, what if the efforts paid off? What if it worked, and she did become unstuck? The mere thought of moving on and letting go made her chest tighten up as if she would be betraying her marriage vows. Kara was a beautiful ball of light, a once-in-a-lifetime love, and while she understood that she should be healing, she couldn't imagine waking up and not missing her. Did her death negate the promise to love, honor, and cherish? It was hard to figure out what to do when she felt like she was trying to exist while underwater. So all of those thoughts and all of that research had her standing in front of the community center on a Sunday afternoon, debating whether to join the local grief group.

The door swung open, and an older man leaned out. Water from a dripping icicle splashed on his head. His warm breath puffed a cloud of steam in the brisk air. "Are you here for grief group?"

Sam nodded.

"Well, the meeting is about to start. Are you coming in?"

It was just the nudge that she needed. Sam swallowed her fear and pushed away from the handrail. She followed him through the door, pausing to stomp wet snow and salt off her boots. The small room was much like she'd imagined: several chairs set up in a circle, coffee and hot water for tea on a side table. She skipped the refreshments and sat in a chair just outside the circle. This way, she'd have her own observation post without being so far away that she drew unwanted attention. A way to test the waters and see what this group was all about.

The man from the door leaned back in a chair. He wasn't much taller than she was. He looked fit, like his career was in a physical profession. His hands were the most telling: calloused and scarred. The long stubble of his white goatee and his two white bushy eyebrows were all the hair he had on his head. He wore a classic ragg wool sweater. The Henley style offered a view of a pressed flannel shirt beneath the sweater. Only a particular-minded person would press a flannel shirt. Even as particular as she was, well, had been, about her clothes, she'd never pressed a flannel shirt. His jeans were pressed too, with a crease down the front. Interesting.

"For those of you who don't know me, I'm Bill. I started this group six years ago when my sweet Cathy passed away. I found that being around others who were working through loss helped me accept my own loss, and I hope it helps you too." He rested his hands on his thighs, leaving his torso exposed. Unlike crossed arms, this body language suggested openness. She'd learned that in a class once. "Would anyone like to share today?"

The door banged open, and a tall redhead ran to an open seat. "So sorry I'm late. I was at the cemetery paying my respects and lost track of time."

"Quite all right, Bethany. We were just accepting volunteers for sharing," Bill said.

"Oh, I'll start." Bethany hung her fluffy coat on the back of her chair, adjusted her slacks, and sat.

"Please, no," another man said, "not unless you show us where the off button is."

"Oh hush, George."

Sam followed Bethany's glare to George. He was a stocky man with a bushy, unkept beard. A knit hat hid most of his dark brown hair. He wore a frayed and faded hooded sweatshirt with the pocket ripped slightly at the top seam. His jeans were threadbare and tattered at the cuffs, as if they had been walked on. He had his legs stretched out and his feet crossed at the ankles. The soles of his leather work boots were worn through to the honeycomb inner sole. Sam imagined that those boots had quite the story to tell, as George likely did too. Was that what she looked like to other people: tattered, unkept, and worn?

"We have a few new people this week. Why don't we give them a chance to contribute?" Bill looked at two other people and then at Sam. "Would any of you like to share why you've joined us today?"

Sam stiffened at the thought of sharing. She wasn't going to open up to this group of strangers. She hunched down, avoided eye contact, and tried to disappear in her Carhartt hooded winter jacket.

"I'm bettin' it's because someone died." George leaned back in his chair and folded his arms.

Another time, not too long ago, that would have tickled Sam's funny bone. Hell, it would have brought on a deep belly laugh. While a tad inappropriate, the comment was just dry enough to be funny as hell. It had been a while since she'd had a good belly laugh. George was a character. She settled in her seat and relaxed a bit. It would be interesting to watch what he came up with next.

"Let's try to be a little more considerate to one another, all right, George?" Bill said and turned back to Sam. "How about you? I bet you have a story to tell."

Sam froze like a deer caught in the headlights. Her breath caught, and her heart rate shot up. She had no intention of participating today. Hadn't she made that clear by pulling her chair out of the sharing circle? One of the other newbies started to talk and pulled Bill's attention away. Thank goodness.

"I'll go. My name is Kim, and I lost my mom last month to a heart attack. She was only sixty-two." Kim pulled a tissue from her jeans pocket. "It was so out of the blue. I didn't expect it to hit me like it did. I didn't expect it to pull the rug out from under me. Sometimes, my chest tightens, and I wonder if it might be my last breath too. What if that happens to me or my husband or, God forbid, my children? How do I keep living with so much uncertainty? I mean, I guess I always knew she wouldn't live forever, but I didn't expect—" She began to sob.

Others pulled tissues and started to dab at tears of their own. Sam felt like she would drown in everyone else's sadness. Hell, she had enough sadness of her own without piling more on. She certainly had sympathy for their losses, but she wasn't about to sit there and soak in even more sorrow. How would that help anything? There was no way she was going to waste an entire hour in this den of despair. She stood and walked out without saying a word.

She pushed the heavy metal door open and squinted against the sun's reflection on the snow. Her truck was parked a couple of blocks up. She stuffed her bare hands in her coat pockets and made her way along the sidewalk. When she was almost to her truck, the scent of burgers and fries teased her nose, and her stomach grumbled. Talley's Bar took up the entire block just beyond where she'd parked. It had been a long time since she'd had a burger and fries. Instead of grief group, maybe a better first step would be a lunch and a beer at Talley's.

She tucked her keys back into her pocket and passed her truck. She hoped she wouldn't bump into anyone she knew. She wasn't up for the "so glad to see you're getting out" conversations because that was always followed by questions she wasn't in the mood to answer. Questions that would most certainly bring her heartache back to front and center and ruined her appetite.

Compared to the blinding white snow, the bar was dark, and it took a moment for her eyes to adjust. She heard the distinct clack of a cue ball striking its intended target, followed by the thump as the ball tumbled down into a pocket. The familiar sounds weren't as painful as she expected. Sure, the *woot* of celebration in the back room conjured up memories of Kara beaming because she'd sunk the eight ball, but so far, she didn't feel the urge to bolt back to her awaiting truck. She'd consider that progress.

The main bar area was surprisingly quiet, especially when compared to the insanity of five o'clock on any given FriYay. Sam had her choice of barstools and picked one at the opposite corner of their usual seats. There was a Vikings game on. It had to be an old game since the season had already ended.

"Hey, Sam, long time, no see. What can I get ya?"

"Hey, Steve." Sam was glad he was tending bar. He wasn't much of a talker, and that suited her just fine. He was an eighties throwback, still wearing stonewashed jeans and Def Leppard concert T-shirt that were two sizes too big. At least he'd let the mullet go a few years back. She ordered without looking at the menu. "I'll have a Talley Burger with cheddar, everything on it, thick-cut fries, ranch on the side, and a Fulton Lonely Blonde."

"Bottle or tap? I'm sorry, I don't remember."

"Tap, thanks for asking."

He filled a frosted mug to the brim, slid it down to her, and disappeared into the kitchen. So far, so good. She couldn't imagine a better way to ease back into a social life than a quiet Sunday afternoon at Talley's. The beer was so cold that ice crystals floated on the surface. It was exactly how she liked it, and that first sip hit the spot. *Yum. Absolute perfection.*

The click of high heels on hardwood stopped directly behind her left shoulder. "That must be some beer. I'll have to order one and see if it makes me moan like that too." The woman's voice was sultry, with an unfamiliar accent.

Sam froze and squeezed her eyes shut. She hadn't realized that she'd moaned in her beer. Grief group shouldn't have ended already. The voice didn't sound familiar, but then, she'd only heard two of the women at the community center speak. No, the woman behind her sounded too chipper to be from the grief group. It would be rude not to acknowledge her comment. Besides, there was something about her voice that sounded teasing and playful. Curiosity got the better of her, and she twisted to the left. One quick glance and she couldn't look away. The stranger was captivating, a petite woman with a deep brown complexion complemented by a cascading mane of wavy, dark brown hair. Her smiling eyes were light brown with flecks of darker brown, or so it seemed in the dim bar light. She looked like an elegant ray of sunshine, and for reasons Sam couldn't explain, she had the urge to bask in the warmth of those rays. She'd always thought that some people had a knack for taking the ordinary and wearing it extraordinarily. The way certain pieces were combined said a lot about the person wearing them. Sam had a closetful of tailored suits and had always admired fashion. Not so much the over-the-top runway stuff but rather fashion that showed off a sense of classic elegance, and the woman standing next to her was first-class feminine fashion personified: tasteful, high-heeled, brown leather boots were detailed with three leather straps wrapped around the ankle and buckled on the side. They showed off beneath form-hugging dark blue jeans. A delicate, cream-colored blouse peeked out from beneath a double-breasted, six-button, navy wool blazer. Sparkling gold earrings and a necklace completed the outfit. She looked as if she'd stepped out of a Saks Fifth Avenue catalog. Her clothing consisted of simple, timeless pieces, but the way she'd combined them screamed elegance. She carried herself with a calm confidence and a dazzling smile.

She walked up to the stool around the corner from Sam's and tapped the backrest with her finger. "Do you mind if I sit here? I've had about all I can take of eating alone. It's lonely and depressing."

Eating alone was absolutely lonely and depressing. She wanted to ask why the stranger was lonely but didn't want questions in return, so she simply smiled. "I don't mind at all. The chair's yours," Sam said and realized that, for once, she really didn't mind, not at all.

"Thank you." She smiled back and hung her black leather tote on the hook and hopped up onto the barstool. "Is it always this cold here in April? I thought it would be warmer."

Sam chuckled. She was definitely not from around here. "April is known for extremes. Next week, it could be seventy. You never know in April. We're halfway to May. It'll warm up soon."

"That's welcome news. I'd take seventies over this bitter cold any day. Brr, it'll be July before I thaw out."

"What can I get you?" Steve asked.

"I'd like exactly what she's having."

He raised an eyebrow, looked at Sam, then back to the stranger. "You want a third-pound Talley Burger with cheddar and everything on it, thick-cut fries, ranch on the side, and a Lonely Blonde?"

The stranger glanced at Sam with a smirk on her face. "Tell me, was it the Lonely Blonde that made you moan?"

Sam felt the heat rise in her cheeks and knew her face had turned beet red. She was grateful when Steve started talking:

"Minnesota's finest. It's a blond ale made from German hops and American malt. It's one of our most popular on tap. It's so good, in fact, that some small town in Wisconsin imports it over for a beer festival each year."

"No way. I didn't know that," Sam said. "Brilliant idea, a festival for beer. I might have to look that up."

"Indeed, that does sound intriguing," the stranger said. "The entire order sounds perfect. Thank you."

Sam tapped her fingers on the bar. "I have a ten says she can't eat half."

"Oh, you're on." Steve smacked the counter. "Because I think she's gonna take you down, and I can always use some extra cash. You still have to tip like regular too." He filled a frosted mug, set it in front of the captivating stranger, and disappeared back into the kitchen.

"Haven't you heard the saying that great things come in small packages?" There was that smirk again. "That goes for appetites too." She took a sip of beer and let out an exaggerated moan. "Oh, now I get it. I never knew how much I'd enjoy a lonely blonde." She set her beer on the cardboard coaster and offered her hand. "Hi, I'm Jennifer."

It felt good to joke around, and Jennifer seemed like a great sparring partner. She gave it right back. "Hi, I'm Sam." Jennifer's hands were soft, and her nails were perfectly manicured.

Jennifer slid off her stool and walked to the dartboard. She picked up two sets of darts and held one out. "Would you like to play a game of 301 while we wait for our food?"

Sam sighed. The last few minutes of visiting with this beautiful woman had been light and fun, but a game would inevitably lead to icebreaker questions. So do you live close by? What do you do for a living? How long have you been married? What does your wife do?

And, *boom*, the fun would be over, and the pitiful looks would come out to play, followed up with the litany of questions about how she was holding up and adjusting to being alone. She wasn't adjusting, and she didn't want to talk about it. Not at grief group and not over lunch.

Sam shook her head. "Nah, thanks, though." She stared into her beer. This was exactly why she'd been avoiding FriYay happy hours.

"Come on. I'll give you a chance to win back the ten dollars you just wasted betting against me." Jennifer shook the dart cup.

Pat's voice sounded in Sam's head again: *It's like we lost both of you in that car accident.* She shook her head, knowing that nothing would change if she didn't start doing something different. Who better to practice on than a stranger that she'd likely never see again?

Sam sighed. "Yeah, okay, why not?" She spun her stool and stood. "Are we doubling in or playing straight in?"

"Let's play straight in. Otherwise, my food will be ice-cold by the time I hit a double and can start deducting points."

"Fair enough. You go first." Sam stood back and watched Jennifer throw her three darts. She hit a double twenty on the first throw, a nineteen, and finally, a five. The electronic dart board deducted the sixty-four points from her starting score. "Uh-huh, your food will be cold by the time you hit a double? Somehow, I think I'm going to be out twenty bucks before I even pay for lunch." Sam stepped up to the line. She took aim and threw. The dart struck the metal divider between the one and the eighteen and ricocheted across the floor. Smooth, real smooth. Heat flushed her cheeks, and she shook her head.

Jennifer retrieved the dart and handed it back. "Consider that a practice shot."

"Oh no, I intend to win on the up-and-up." Sam threw her second and struck a triple thirteen.

"Ah, so it's going to be like that." Jennifer laughed. "Just my luck, I ask the dart shark to play."

Sam's third dart deducted another eighteen. She wasn't too far behind. The score went back and forth until Jennifer finally nailed the six she needed to win. The game had been fun. There wasn't a litany of probing questions, just easy, enjoyable banter. Sam put the darts back into the cups just as Steve arrived with their food. She ordered another beer for each of them, and they continued chatting while they ate.

The conversation was light and effortless. Before Sam knew it, she was stuffed. More than half her burger sat on the plate, and she'd barely dented her pile of fries. Her appetite wasn't what it used to be. Jennifer, however, had cleared every morsel.

Sam pushed one ten-dollar bill to Steve and another to Jennifer. It didn't matter. The laughs and jeering were worth the extra twenty dollars. Sam couldn't remember the last time she'd laughed and joked around. It dawned on her that for just a few hours, she hadn't been consumed by grief. She was able to forget about the sorrow and enjoyed the tiniest taste of what it felt like to feel alive again. For the first time in a long time, she wanted more of that feeling. She let the fun of the those few hours keep her company on her drive home.

CHAPTER FOUR

Jennifer stepped out onto the patio of her small, furnished apartment that overlooked the town square. The temperatures had dropped dramatically overnight, and the air was colder than anything she'd ever experienced. The inside of her nose burned, and she was certain that her lungs crackled when she drew in a deep breath. It wasn't long before her exposed skin started to sting as if sunburned. There had to be several inches of snow on the ground, but instead of it being pristine, fluffy, white, and picturesque, it was dingy and dirty from being mixed with salty road glop that splattered everywhere with each passing car.

What had she been thinking to accept a job in Minnesota? She'd thought for sure that it would have warmed up in the time it took her to drive across the country, find an apartment, and prepare to start work. With any luck, that woman from the bar, Sam, would be right, and next week, it would be seventy. She could always hope.

It had sounded so romantic when the headhunter had presented the opportunity: "Miss Delgado, just picture yourself in a quaint Midwestern town. It will be like a working vacation in a Lifetime special." Now that she'd spent the last week getting settled, it was difficult to imagine that she had left the warmth of New Mexico for this. The need for a change of scenery had been nagging at her, but she wasn't so sure she was prepared for such an extreme shift.

The office building was only a few blocks away. If it had been warmer, she would have enjoyed the short walk, but there was no way she was walking in this arctic tundra. Besides, she didn't own a pair of snow boots and refused to ruin any of her shoes, especially her Jimmy Choos. She loved how the Anouk pumps looked and felt on her feet. She had a closetful of nice shoes, but this pair was an exceptional splurge that made her first day outfit a statement that couldn't be denied. Bonus, the sexy stiletto heel added almost five inches to her five-foot-two, which kept most of her colleagues from literally looking down at her.

She arrived at eight forty-five and was surprised to see only a few vehicles in the parking lot. She slung the strap of her black Varenne tote over her arm and picked up the leather portfolio that held all of the necessary paperwork. She'd worn her warmest professional suit over her tailored blouse instead of the typical first-day skirt and blazer. Although, with or without the lining, the suit didn't offer all that much in the way of warmth. Once out of the car, she walked on the balls of her feet and did her best to avoid salt with every step. Thankfully, the walk to the door wasn't longer because it felt even colder than when she'd left the apartment. She pulled on the door and stepped into the brightly lit lobby.

"Hi, may I help you?" a young man asked from behind the reception desk. He was wearing a fluffy, hooded flannel jacket. Typically, Jennifer wouldn't consider a jacket like that, but today, it looked like toasty warm heaven.

No matter how seasoned she was at contract gigs, the first day was the worst. She never knew how her presence would be perceived. Would she be welcome for the experience she offered, or would she be resented for being there at all? Jennifer shook off the cold and channeled her most confidant inner diva. "I certainly hope so." She smiled her best smile. "My name is Jennifer Delgado. I have a nine o'clock appointment with Mike Walsh."

"I'm sorry, he hasn't arrived yet. You're welcome to wait here if you like, or I can see if Kelly's available. She's our office admin."

"I'm happy to wait here if you don't mind the company."

"No, not at all," he said and returned his focus to his computer screen.

"Wonderful, thank you." Jennifer turned and admired the huge ficus in the corner. The short wait offered her a chance to thaw out, but before her teeth had a chance to stop chattering, cold air whooshed all around her, and she was chilled to the bone all over again. She turned and found a mammoth of a man.

He had to be close to seven feet and looked like a linebacker. A full beard and mustache covered most of his face. His brown eyes were warm when he smiled, and his expression was welcoming. A fuzzy knit hat was pulled down over his ears, and he wore a red-plaid flannel. Did everyone in Minnesota own a flannel?

"You must be Ms. Delgado. I'm Mike Walsh. I was hoping to beat you here, but my truck didn't want to start this morning."

"Perfectly understandable given the frigid temps. I had no idea that Minnesota would be this cold."

He smiled warmly and removed his knit cap, revealing neatly trimmed dark brown hair. "This is just a freak cold snap. Before you know it, the snow will melt away, and spring will arrive. The beauty of the area will make you forget all about the snow and cold."

Jennifer smiled. "Is that how you make it through the winter?"

"Yeah, well, that and alcohol." He chuckled while kicking salt and snow from his boots. "Ah, once you get used to it, winter isn't so bad. Follow me. Let's get you set up in the system."

An hour later, Jennifer was ready to jump right in. Mike led her on tour of the small office. He showed her the break room, the shared office for the staff who rotated through when not traveling to various client sites, and a small cubicle farm for those managing the phones. Finally, he led her down the last hall that looked to end just outside of the lobby where she'd started.

"Over here on the left is the IT department, or as Sam likes to say, the hardware side of the equation. The local server room is behind this first door. We have physical servers for our development environment and file storage. Our clients are hosted on a separate, cloud-based server farm. This next door is Sam's. She's our IT administrator and probably your best resource if you need additional information beyond the root cause analysis documents that are waiting for you in email. Truth be told, she authored those documents as well."

"Good to know." Jennifer wondered if this could be the same Sam she'd met the day before at the bar. She hoped so. She'd enjoyed her company and the easy conversations they'd shared.

There was something about Sam that had made her feel seen and not objectified.

Mike knocked on the glass and opened the door. Jennifer followed him in. The gentle scent of eucalyptus greeted her the moment she crossed the threshold. The walls appeared freshly painted and were decorated with a variety of landscape prints. A large desk sat in the back corner, positioned like a barricade. She caught a few notes of one of her favorite Sade songs before the music paused. Jennifer smiled when familiar unruly black hair with silver highlights peeked above the three very large monitors on adjustable arms that made a fortress out of the desk and side table. The wheels of the chair made a soft *whoosh*. Jennifer's hopes were confirmed when she saw striking blue eyes staring back at her.

"Sam, I'd like to introduce you to Jennifer Delgado. She's here to solve all our programming problems."

Sam smiled and stepped around. Her extended hand was warm when Jennifer shook it. It was so warm that she didn't want to let go. "Hello again. Welcome aboard. I'm excited to have you here. I had a chance to review your résumé this morning. Impressive."

Jennifer hoped she didn't look as dorky as she felt, but she couldn't stop the smile from spreading across her face. It wasn't often that she had an instant ally when starting a new role. Better yet, not only was her expertise welcome, but Sam was impressed. For some unexplainable reason, impressing Sam mattered and felt great. "Thank you. I'm looking forward to digging in." Jennifer reluctantly released her hand.

"Well, now you know where to find me if you have any questions." There was that smile from the bar that made Jennifer feel seen as a person.

She nodded. She still felt like a grinning idiot, but she couldn't stop herself. She tried to think up some questions, but her mind was blank. She'd think of something and circle back once Mike finished the tour.

He turned toward the door. "On that note, let me take you to your work space in what is affectionately called the programmer's cave. I'm sorry we don't have the space for you to have your own office."

Jennifer followed him into a space that could easily serve as a midsize conference room. The walls were covered in whiteboards. Shadows of several raunchy games of hangman had been partially erased. A desk sat in front of each of the four walls so that the occupants faced the center of the room.

Jennifer brought her finger to her nose to ward off the stench of what could only be described as a filthy college dorm. It stunk of old food, body odor, and dirty socks. Two young men stood and removed earbuds the moment Mike cleared his throat.

"Tom, Christian, I'd like to introduce you to Jennifer Delgado. She's contracted with us to help isolate the software issues." He looked from Jennifer to the young man just inside the door. "Jennifer, this is Tom. He's been with us for a couple of months. And this is Christian. He's been with us for three months."

Jennifer stepped into the room to shake their hands. Tom's was cold and sweaty. She released his grip as quickly as possible and stepped over to Christian. She glanced down and noticed that his big toe was sticking out of a mottled gray sock that looked like it had started out white once upon a time. Wet, salty rubber boots sat next to his desk. One was standing tall while the other had tipped over onto its side like a fallen plastic army soldier.

Well, that explained some of the odor. An open and half-empty jug of cheeseballs sat on the corner of his desk next to a can of Mountain Dew. Apparently, that was the breakfast of young champions. The garbage can next to the desk was full of snack wrappers and empty pop cans, some of which had overflowed onto the floor. He wiped orange dust from his fingers onto his shirt and extended his hand. She shook it quickly and made a mental note not to touch her clothing until she'd thoroughly washed.

"You can use that desk over there. It's the lead programmer's desk." Christian pointed to the spot next to his.

"Guys, please keep the distractions minimal. I'd like both of you to continue working the client tickets in your queues. Let me be very clear, at this point, Jennifer is not the new lead. She's here for a very specific purpose, and I need her focused on that task, so please come to me with any work questions. Well, welcome aboard, Jennifer. I'll let you get to it. You know where to find me if you need anything at all." He turned and walked away.

Jennifer walked to her work space for the foreseeable future.

The top of the desk glistened. She tentatively ran her fingers across the surface. It was gooey. She pulled her hand back, but remnants stuck to her fingertips. The desk chair looked to have started out as light blue fabric. The armrests, however, were now a dark brownish blue, and there was a mystery stain on the seat. There was zero chance that her clothing would touch that chair.

"That used to be my chair, but when Brent bailed, I swapped. One of the wheels is smaller than the rest, and it teeters. You can have this one back if you'd like," Christian said.

She looked over at the better chair, and it was every bit as filthy, especially with the fresh layer of orange dust on the arms. She'd find an office supply store and buy a new chair…if she returned at all. "Thank you, but you should keep it." She looked from Tom to Christian. "Would you please excuse me?"

Careful not to touch anything with her right hand, Jennifer marched directly to the restroom. She was grateful that this room looked and smelled clean, at least. She pulled out a few paper towels and wiped drops of water off the counter before she set down her handbag and portfolio. She pumped three shots of soap onto her hands and scrubbed them beneath hot water until they were clean. The warmth felt wonderful. She added one more pump of soap and washed again for good measure. Hell, this room would make a better office than the one she was assigned. She must have been out of her mind to think that small-town Minnesota could be a place to call home. It didn't escape her that she was the only one in the office who wasn't wearing a ratty T-shirt or a crumpled flannel or both, and it wasn't even casual Friday. The Southwest might have been in the midst of a twenty-year drought, but at least Santa Fe had some class.

She pulled a few more paper towels from the dispenser and dried while contemplating what to do next. Perhaps she could get a laptop instead of a workstation. Even if she sat in the break room, it would be better than sitting at that nasty desk. Or she could call up the recruiter and look for something closer to a big city. Just as she was retrieving her items from the counter, the bathroom door pushed open.

Sam nodded as she walked by and stepped into a stall before closing the door. She had shared how impressed she was with Jennifer's résumé. Something about seeing her again kept Jennifer from quitting on the spot. She was the IT administrator. Certainly, she could configure a laptop to connect remotely. Not wanting to hover but certainly wanting to talk, Jennifer collected her things and made her way to Sam's office. The door was closed and locked. Crap. Tom must have caught movement out of the corner of his eye because he spun his chair to the side and stared at her.

"We're on this side." He pointed at her desk in the back of the room.

Jennifer had to think of something quick. She was not going back into that office. "I forgot something in the ladies' room."

Sam was standing at the sink washing her hands. Her eyes met Jennifer's in the mirror, and her smile had an instant calming effect. "How's your morning going so far?"

Jennifer searched for words that would convey what she needed without being insulting. "Honestly? I'm not sure that I'm the best fit for this organization. I may have bitten off more than I care to chew."

"Is the code that bad?" Sam's smiled faded, and her expression showed concern.

Jennifer answered quickly. She didn't want to be the cause of that sad expression ever again. "I haven't looked at the code yet. It's more, um, the atmosphere in my assigned office. I'm not entirely sure that I complement their vibe."

Sam shook the water off and pulled a few towels from the dispenser. "I wondered about that when I realized that the résumé I saw this morning was for the same Jennifer I shared a beer with yesterday. It's not every day that Saks Fifth Avenue visits our little Carhartt town."

Jennifer wasn't entirely sure what she was saying. Was being called Saks Fifth Avenue a good thing, or was Carhartt preferred? Based on Sam's flannel-topped attire, it was likely the latter. But she remained professional and waited for her to continue.

Sam nodded to the tote on Jennifer's arm. "Easily an eighteen-hundred-dollar handbag. I'll bet a week's wages that I'll find the same logo on the sole of your shoes. Your suit…" Sam stepped back and looked her up and down. "A blazer that gives the appearance of a traditional Alexander McQueen but, given the embossed DG logo on the eight-button design, it's clearly Dolce & Gabbana. Your matching wool slacks are hemmed to cover your ankles and still show off the details of your shoes. Head to toe, expensive Italian excellence. A tailored fit and most definitely a different vibe than the two young men currently working in the programmer's cave."

Jennifer beamed. "Your accurate observation surprises me."

"Despite my appearance, I can appreciate elegant fashion."

Sam's Ugg Kennen boots were the only hint that she had any fashion sense at all, and that wasn't saying much, but Jennifer didn't want to insult the one person who'd called out each and every designer she was currently wearing. "I do like to make an impression on my first day."

"Impression made. Question is, can you code as eloquently as you dress?"

Jennifer thought that maybe Sam was flirting until she wrapped her up in a bear hug of a smile. It was a much warmer smile than Jennifer had seen the previous day at the bar. She wasn't at all sure about Minnesota, but one thing was for certain, Sam had some kind of magical powers. If a heart and a soul could express feelings, it would no doubt be done with Sam's eyes, Sam's smile, and Sam's expressions. The effect was profound.

Jennifer mentally shook herself and channeled her inner diva again. "I've earned a strong reputation for my skills."

"Have you already talked to Mike about canceling your contract?" Sam asked.

Something about Sam still had her a little wobbly. Jennifer drew in a breath with her nose and let it out quietly through her mouth. "Not yet. I was debating my options when you first walked in."

"Is there anything that would encourage you to stay long enough to take a look at the software? Our clients are growing impatient for a solution. From what I saw on your résumé, I believe you can help."

Sam's expressions could melt ice; hell, they could melt stone. Her eyes pleaded for help, and her expression emphasized the plea. Jennifer would walk through fire to bring back the bear hug smile.

"Perhaps, if I had a laptop instead of a workstation, I could be a bit more flexible with my work space. Maybe there's an open table I can sit at, or I could work remotely?" It wasn't necessarily the contract that she wanted to honor. She was willing to stay because Sam had asked her to.

Sam tossed the paper towels into the trash. "I gather that the boys didn't tidy up?"

Jennifer felt understood. "Not even a tiny bit."

"Personally, I would have made them clean that room top to bottom. For that matter, if it were up to me, it wouldn't look or smell like that in the first place, but I've been asked not to approach them anymore. Apparently, I come off as crass and scary." She rolled her eyes and shook her head.

Jennifer couldn't imagine that side of Sam, although, it wasn't like she knew her that well. Yet, something deep inside said that Sam was everything she'd expect her to be beneath those meaningful expressions.

"I'm sure remote will work once we ensure you have all the access you'll need, but on-site would be best initially. Let's see, Stacy and Jeff just finished up an implementation, so they'll be occupying the shared office for a month or so. We're fully staffed for the customer support people, so none of the cubicles are open. I can't think of any other desks that aren't occupied. What if I talk to Mike, and we make the boys clean up the cave? You can try a second first day tomorrow?"

Jennifer watched Sam work through each scenario. It was as if her expressions were guiding her words. One sentence was hopeful, and her eyes would sparkle, and then the realization was such a letdown that Jennifer wanted to hug her. All of it pointed to one resounding point: Jennifer would figure out a workable solution… for Sam.

She pictured the different offices she'd seen on her tour and had an idea that should have been obvious from the beginning. "If I may suggest something?"

"What's that?"

"You're my point person on how the code is affecting the environment, correct?"

Sam nodded.

"Well, would it be okay if I sat at that small conference table in your office? It would only be until I had a handle on things. After that, I can do most everything remotely. You wouldn't even know I was there. I'd make sure to supply you with dinner and a couple of Lonely Blondes as a thank you." Jennifer winked and smiled.

Sam scratched her head and looked at the floor. It was the first hint of doubt and uncertainty that Jennifer had seen from her all morning. "How long does it typically take for you to get up to speed?"

Jennifer tried to keep her answer light. She wanted to help, and she wanted to help because Sam had asked. "That depends entirely on the documentation and the complexity of the code. Short answer, I won't know until I dig in."

"Ballpark?"

It was the first time, in the short time they'd known each other, Jennifer couldn't read Sam's expression. She wasn't sure about Minnesota, but she really wanted this to work because for reasons she didn't yet understand, she was drawn to Sam. "A couple of weeks to several months. Again, it depends on the—"

Sam exhaled and shook her head. Jennifer's heart sank. It was over. Sam didn't want anyone in her space. She had a life here. What did she need with a stranger from New Mexico? "That little conference table is wobbly. It will drive you insane. I can swing my side desk around. That way, you'll have space for a few monitors. Yeah, okay. I'll make it work if that's what it will take to get you to stay and take a look at the code. I think Mike has a decent office chair at his conference table that I can snag. Come on, let's get you a laptop." Sam turned and walked out of the restroom.

Jennifer's spirit instantly lifted, and she was shocked by the response. Based on Sam's expression, she hadn't expected a yes. She turned and followed Sam to her office. For the first time all morning, Minnesota wasn't looking so cold and dreary. She had an ally, and based on the previous day at the bar, maybe even the potential for a friendship, and that would make all the difference.

Chapter Five

A few days later, Sam pulled into the parking lot and sighed when she saw the car with New Mexico license plates already parked in the spot next to hers. Jennifer had asked for extended access so she could dig in and map out the software architecture, but for some reason, Sam had expected her to work late, not super early. Sharing her office for the short term was one thing, but losing her treasured three hours of quiet time was an unexpected hit, to say the least.

Jennifer couldn't have been in the office all that long because the scent of her perfume lingered in the lobby. It was a fragrance Sam didn't recognize, solely associated to Jennifer. She followed it all the way to her own office door. The light was on, and she could see Jennifer seated in the newly rearranged office, typing away. Sam pushed the door open.

Jennifer spun her chair. "Good morning, I started a pot of coffee in the break room. It should be done any minute."

"Good morning. Thanks, but I bring coffee from home." Sam held up her dark blue YETI mug.

"Well, if you need a refill..." She smiled. "Quick question for you. The application that I'm here to help with is a complete electronic health records application, correct?"

Sam sighed. It was too early for questions. She'd say as much if she weren't so eager to see the issues affecting her servers resolved. Well, that and Jennifer was the one who was asking, and for reasons Sam still couldn't explain, she got a free pass. "Yeah, that's right. Why?" she walked to her desk and set her coffee cup on the coaster and her laptop bag in her chair.

Jennifer leaned back in her chair and crossed her legs. A sure sign that this was going to be a conversation and not a quick question. Her outfit, while still a professional suit, was a touch more casual: a deep purple turtleneck had replaced the silk blouse. Sam doubted she ever really dressed down. Seeing Jennifer's style for the past few days did have her trying on one of her own suits earlier, although she'd need to have it tailored or put on a good twenty pounds if she wanted any of them to come close to fitting. She opted for baggy jeans and a sweater instead. A small step up from the heavyweight flannel that had become her daily extra layer since the funeral.

"Well, I've been reading through the documentation, and I'm not seeing what I'd expect to see in a typical EHR application. Are the clients that use the application hospitals or doctors' offices?"

"Neither. Mike found an underserved niche in the market. Our clients are insurance companies that offer health plans to supplement Medicare. They use our software to keep track of their members and their members' providers, and the claims module was added to process and pay the providers' claims. There's a team out in the cubicle farm that does the data entry for that part once the claims are scanned in." She hoped Jennifer didn't need much more detail because she wasn't involved in that part of the business. Now, if Jennifer had asked about servers and infrastructure, she could talk until her eyes glossed over.

"That's exactly the part that I was missing. I couldn't figure out why claims were being paid, and there was a lack of invoice generation for services rendered, like a doctor's appointment. It also explains why there weren't fields for insurance information other than Medicare. It's not needed if the user of the application is the insurance company. Thanks."

Sam was confused. Jennifer should have already known all of this. The whole point of hiring her was to solve the issues that were causing the servers to crash. "I'm surprised that Mike didn't explain all this when he brought you in."

"It's really not an issue. I'm adaptable. I just need to know what I'm working with." She flicked her wrist in a dismissive wave. "He focused more on my level of expertise in the programming languages used and glossed over the business model once he learned that I had experience with electronic health records." She uncrossed her legs and stood. "One last question and I'll let you get to work. Where would I find the supply closet?"

"It's in Kelly's office, which is currently locked. She'll be here around eight. What do you need?" Sam wanted to wrap this up. Her favorite DJ was on, and she was missing the morning show.

"A couple of legal pads and a few dry-erase markers. That is, if you don't mind sharing your whiteboard."

She couldn't remember the last time she'd used her whiteboard. "It's all yours. I have a smaller one I can hang if you need more space. I always have a few extra legal pads in my desk too. You'll want to hide the dry-erase markers in the back of your desk drawer. Otherwise, the boys across the hall steal them instead of going to Kelly."

Jennifer started around the front of Sam's desk.

"You don't need to come back here. I can bring the stuff to you." Sam quickly grabbed a handful of markers and three blank legal pads, but Jennifer was already behind the desk. Sam froze when she realized what Jennifer had picked up. She closed her eyes and waited for the questions that were sure to come.

"Oh my, is that you?" Jennifer placed her fingertip on Sam's chin in the photo.

"Yeah. Here's everything you asked for." She offered the markers, hoping to exchange them for the photo. This was her sacred space. Those who entered her office were welcome to look at the prints on the walls, but the photos on her desk were personal and private. After the funeral, she'd purposely set up the space so there wasn't room for anyone but her behind the desk. Back then, she'd had to set boundaries. Too many people in the office wanted to come in, pick up a photo, and reminisce as if she hadn't just brought her wife home in an urn.

Jennifer stared at the photo, seemingly oblivious to Sam's discomfort. "When was this taken?"

Sam swallowed and dared to look at the photo. For that event, she had worn one of her favorite tailored Sharpe suits, a black three-piece, with a dark red shirt and pocket square to match Kara's dress. It had been a magical evening. They'd danced all night and had gone home and made love. "I think…" Sam cleared her throat. Her mouth was so dry that her tongue stuck to her lips. "I think that was Mike and Kelly's eldest's wedding. Maybe two years ago."

"Mike, the owner? He's married to Kelly?"

Sam was grateful for the topic change. "Yeah, the kids are from her first marriage. Mike's shy, a typical introvert programmer. Kelly keeps this place going. I was the first employee when they started the company. They invited all of us to the wedding."

Jennifer made no effort to exchange the framed photo for the markers and paper. "Why'd you let your hair grow out? You rock the fade. And look at that suit, wow, very dapper. It fits you perfectly. Did you have it tailored?"

Clothing. Another safe topic. Sam could talk clothing. "Told you I could appreciate a nice outfit." She forced a bit of a smile.

"You weren't kidding. I can't get over how different you look." She looked up from the photo but kept it securely in her hands. "The woman you're with must be someone very special. I don't know anyone who doesn't dream of having someone look at them the way you're looking at her. What's her name?"

She knew it would have come up eventually. After all, they were sharing an office for the time being. Sam looked at her desk and took in the several other photos scattered around her monitors. A knot formed in the pit of her stomach, and her throat tightened up. She cleared her throat so she could speak. "My wife, Kara."

"She's one lucky lady. How long have you been married?"

It was a sweet statement and an innocent question. Still, Sam wanted to bolt, but Jennifer was blocking her escape. Why'd she have to put the stupid conference table between the two desks? Seemed like a better idea the other day when it was supposed to act as a buffer, not a trap. Pat's voice boomed in her head. *If not me, talk to someone because it's like we lost both of you in that car accident.* She wished she'd never bumped into her at the grocery store. Things had been so much easier when she could be oblivious to how stuck she apparently was.

She cleared her throat again. "We were together for thirty-four years. We married the moment it was legal."

"Were? You're no longer together? Why keep all of the photos?" There was no judgment. The expression in her eyes was tender, and her tone was sincere. "I'm divorced too. Sometimes, love just isn't enough."

Sam hadn't even noticed the diamond ring on Jennifer's left hand until just that moment. Had she become so focused on avoiding difficult conversations that she'd forgotten how to behave around people? She used to be the one who'd noticed things and asked questions. Jennifer had been sitting at the table next to her for the last few days, and she'd never once asked her about family or anything outside of work. It appeared that they were talking now; might as well ask a question in return.

"You're divorced, and yet you still wear your wedding ring?" Sam hoped Jennifer would talk about herself instead.

"Everything about being a consultant is easier if I wear a wedding ring, especially declining unwanted advances. It's not my actual ring from the marriage. That's in a box somewhere. This one belonged to my grandmother. It fits perfectly, so I wear it every day." She looked at Sam's hand. "You're still wearing your ring too. Why do you stare at all these memories when your marriage ended after thirty-four years?"

Sam sighed. She hadn't spoken about it since everything was finalized after the funeral. Could she get the words out and keep it together? If she didn't tell Jennifer, someone else in the office would. No, for some reason, that felt wrong. Jennifer should hear it from her. She gently pulled the photo from Jennifer's hand. She looked at it for a moment and returned it to its proper place on her desk. "I'm not divorced. Kara was killed in a car accident a little over a year ago."

Sam exhaled a shaky breath and looked at the ceiling. This was a lot to deal with before she'd finished her first cup of coffee.

"Oh, Sam, I shouldn't have assumed. I am so sorry for your loss. Your entire world must have been turned upside down." She rested her hand on Sam's forearm. The touch was surprising and oddly welcome.

"It still is…upside down." It felt good to admit that tiny bit of truth.

"Do you have a support system, or are you trying to trudge through all alone?"

"Humph." Sam thought back to those first few weeks after the car accident. There had been plenty of people who had wanted to be part of her support system. Several who'd claimed they were there to be helpful. Helpful was the last thing Sam would have called their presence. Her dad had passed on two years before the accident. He would have been a welcome, grounding presence. Instead, her mom and sisters had come to stay so they could help with the funeral.

That visit hadn't gone well. Her younger sister, Becky, and her flavor of the month boyfriend had consumed every drop of liquor in the house and were sauced most of the time. Her older sister, Karen, who was a stay-at-home mom to college-age kids, had asked to borrow five thousand dollars. She'd blamed the financial need on that trip. Sam would have believed it if she hadn't already bought everyone's plane tickets, and it wasn't like they'd had to pay for a hotel or food. Karen had thrown a fit when Sam had declined and suggested she might want to look for a job. Then there was her mom, who'd insisted that Sam's house was too big to live in all alone. She was so completely out of touch. She'd said that it shouldn't be that hard to find a new roommate, even though she'd been in the front row at their wedding. Kara had never been just a roommate.

That comment had been the last straw. Sam had lost it in an explosion of emotion. She'd put each and every one of them on a flight home right after the funeral. Everything about that visit had been a mess.

"I'd say trudging is probably a safe bet. I bumped into an old friend a couple of weeks ago at the grocery store. Pat and her wife, Angie, were friends of ours for as long as I can remember. Angie and Kara shared a dorm room in college. Pat and I always got along fine. I hadn't seen them since the funeral. It's not to say they haven't reached out. They have. It's me. I can't bring myself to spend time with any of them without Kara."

Sam stared at the fistful of markers. Her urge to bolt had subsided. "Anyway, Pat told me that I was stuck and just going through the motions. She called it tumbling down the rabbit hole, whatever that's supposed to mean. I don't know, maybe I'm not trudging. Maybe it's like Pat said, and I'm stuck." She was surprised that she'd admitted that to someone she barely knew. Yet, for reasons she still couldn't explain, talking with Jennifer felt comfortable, almost comforting. Maybe it was because Jennifer hadn't known Kara. There were no shared memories to overcome.

"Based on what little I know," Jennifer said, "I'd say it means you were deeply in love for most of your adult life, and now, you don't know what to do without her. It's perfectly understandable. My husband and I never looked at each other the way you were looking at Kara in that photo. Our divorce was amicable, but still, I felt a sense of loss and failure. It's never easy to say good-bye and start over." Jennifer barely knew her, and yet, her words resonated. It was the first honest conversation Sam'd had about Kara's death, and Jennifer seemed to be able to explain what she could never quite put her finger on.

Sam felt a little lighter, like she had on Sunday at Talley's, and was surprised by her own willingness to share before she'd even had her first cup of coffee. "Why did you feel failure?"

"You don't want to hear about my marriage."

Feeling failure and loss was kinda like loss with guilt, which was a stone's throw from grief. Sam felt guilt. Sam felt loss. Jennifer had felt both and come out the other side. She appeared to be a happy person. "You started this conversation. Come on, out with it," Sam prodded with the hope of discovering Jennifer's secret to success.

Jennifer gave her a slight nod. "I was raised in a household where women had children and served their husband's needs. Success was being a good wife and a good mother, period. My mom and grandmother took great pride in how well they ran the household. I moved out of my parents' home directly into an apartment with my husband. A few years in, he started talking about moving out of our apartment in the city into a house in the suburbs so we could start a family. He was up for a promotion and wanted me to quit my job. He wasn't controlling or dominating, just wanted to be a good provider. That said, it didn't take long to realize I was not cut out for the housewife life. I wanted to dive into my career." Jennifer paused for a breath.

The words were something Sam could relate to. She'd grown up with a mom who had a career of wife and mother. There was never an issue while running a household with Kara, but being a dedicated housewife with children? *Hard pass.*

"Like I said, sometimes, love isn't enough. I felt like a failure because I didn't want to be a good wife and mother. I wanted to be a kick-ass software engineer and programmer. After the divorce, it took some time to adjust. I had to figure out who I was on my own. Maybe it's kind of the same for you."

What part of that was similar? Sam replayed the words in her head. She came up empty. "What do you mean? We weren't divorced. I was happy and in love."

"That wasn't the point. Who are you without your wife? Tell me, what kind of stuff do *you* like to do?"

Sam tried to think about things she did alone. She plowed the snow in the winter and mowed the grass in the summer, but those were tasks. She cut and split wood for the stove, but Kara had helped most of the time, unless she was traveling. She'd follow Kara around the greenhouse and load up the cart with annual flowers and help with the planting and mulching each spring, but she hadn't done it last spring and likely wouldn't do it this spring, either. The answer slowly became obvious. "Would you believe me if I said I don't have a clue? I like my job. Is that enough? If I wasn't at work, then I was with Kara. I can tell you what she liked to do. I can tell you her dreams and passions. I guess I wanted nothing more than to be with her and see her happy. God, I sound pathetic." The reality of that statement added new weight to her shoulders. Not only was she stuck, but she was stuck without her own identity outside of work. Shit, she was doomed.

"Did you have fun playing darts on Sunday?"

"Yeah. It's the first bit of fun in a long time."

"That's a start. I enjoyed it too, especially your company. If you'd like a friend while you're figuring it out, I happen to be available." Jennifer rested her hand on Sam's arm again. It was a soothing touch.

"Thanks." Sam nodded and smiled. It wasn't too in-depth, but the talk had helped her feel just a little bit better. "I should probably dock my laptop and check on the servers. The rolling reboots when no one is logged in are helping, but it's not a fail-safe. Here's the stuff you needed."

Jennifer accepted the markers and paper. "Thank you. I hope our conversation didn't upset you."

"You definitely gave me some things to think about," Sam said. "Would music bother you?" She had switched to earbuds for the last couple of days, but they hurt the inside of her ears.

"Not at all, especially if it's what you were listening to on my first day."

Sam watched Jennifer make her way back to her spot on the other side of the room. She pulled her laptop out of the bag, docked it, and set her briefcase beneath the conference table between them. Sam felt like she should say something more, but she was out of words. She opened the site to her server monitors and was relieved there weren't any alarms. To complete her morning routine, she opened the app to stream her favorite DJ, who finished the weather report and announced ten songs in a row. Sam recognized the first few notes of Sting's "Brand New Day." It was a light, upbeat song. She tapped her foot with the music. Jennifer looked over, smiled, and sang along with the chorus. Maybe sharing the office wouldn't be such a bad thing after all.

Chapter Six

Weekends were the worst for Jennifer. Consulting in a new town and, more importantly, an entirely new state wasn't too bad during the week when work kept her busy, but weekends were a boring and lonely affair. Especially when it was too gloomy outside to enjoy a walk around town. In the few weeks since she'd started work, the temperatures had climbed up to the mid-sixties, which meant that the snow finally melted, but today's steady rain made everything a sloppy mess. Some of the trees were beginning to bud, a sure sign that spring was around the corner. Yet despite the grass greening up, it all still looked very gray and bleak.

She could log in and work some more. That was typically how she passed the time, but while her work was often rewarding, working seven days a week was becoming much less so. She'd put so many hours in on the last job that she was already bordering on burnout. Not to mention, she'd missed her recuperation time at home due to the fire. If she'd been at home, she'd have spent the day cooking, but her small, semi-furnished apartment was much like Mother Hubbard's cupboards, at least, when it came to kitchen supplies. Everything was pretty bare, not so much as a set of measuring cups.

She wondered what Sam was doing. There was something about her that Jennifer found intriguing. She'd found herself drawn to her and enjoyed their conversations every day at lunch, so much so that the lunch hour was never long enough. Last weekend, Jennifer had spent way too much time at Talley's, hoping Sam would come in for lunch and a game of darts or dinner and a game. Sam hadn't stopped in, but Jennifer hadn't actually invited her, either. Eventually, she'd made her way home, disappointed that Sam hadn't shown. She had no idea what to make of her feelings. If she didn't know any better, she'd swear she had a crush. She couldn't recall feeling like this about another woman. Then again, she'd never met anyone like Sam before.

Instead of another day of hanging out at Talley's and hoping Sam would walk through the door, she decided to reach out and invite her over. She grabbed her cell phone and typed a short message: *Hey, what are you doing today?*

She sat at the dining room table, sipping her fifth cup of coffee and nervously waiting for a response. Time together outside of work would give them a chance to get to know each other better. Who knew, time together outside of work might help her figure out if she was experiencing amazing new friend feelings or something entirely different. Whichever it was, it was so much better than the typical loneliness of consulting, and she welcomed it.

Finally, bouncing dots appeared next to Sam's name, then her response popped up: *I haven't decided yet. It's a toss-up between painting my toenails pink or cleaning the bathroom with my toothbrush. How about you?*

Jennifer laughed. She could picture the mischievous twinkle in Sam's eye when she'd sent that text. *Exciting stuff! I want pics of the toenails. How about something a bit more fun? Do you like Mexican food?*

What, like tacos? Sure.

Jennifer shook her head as if Sam could see her. *More like homemade enchiladas. I am craving a taste from home. I'll cook if I can borrow a few supplies.*

What do you need?

A large saucepan, a set of measuring cups and measuring spoons, deep-sided cookie sheet, bowls...pretty much a fully stocked kitchen. Given my six-month contract, I may have to buy some supplies.

Dots flickered and disappeared and flickered again. Finally, Sam's response popped up: *It just so happens that I have a fully*

*stocked kitchen, and there's a better chance that I'll remember
everything if you just cook over here. I have a fully stocked bar too
and beer, oh, and I can make a mean pitcher of margaritas.*

Jennifer: *You had me at fully stocked kitchen and bar. I'm in.
I'll stop at the store and pick up a few things on my way. Do you
need anything?*

Sam: *A lime, if you'd like margaritas, otherwise, I'm all set. I
live about thirty minutes outside of town. I'm at 43275 Shady Oak
Lane. Your idea is much better than mine, and bonus, you saved my
toothbrush. See you in a bit.*

Jennifer smiled and shook her head. The day was already
looking less gloomy.

An hour and a half later, just after two in the afternoon, she
turned at the dead end of Shady Oak Lane and crept up a long
blacktop driveway. She tried to imagine how beautiful the area
would be in the summer when the landscape fully came to life.
It was already quite beautiful, even if the trees were still wooden
skeletons.

Sam's house was perched high up on top of a bluff with huge,
majestic trees scattered throughout the yard. Jennifer had never seen
such tall trees. There was nothing like this in New Mexico. When
she looked beyond the trunks, there were views that went on for
miles and miles. She felt like she could see forever, even with the
haze of steady drizzle fogging the horizon. Jennifer parked in front
of one of the three garage doors.

The center garage door lifted just as she was stepping out. Sam
ducked under the door before it was all the way open. "Hey, there.
Welcome to the middle of nowhere. There's a secret shortcut to the
kitchen from here. What can I help carry?"

"Hey, Sam. Thank you for offering up your home. It's absolutely
beautiful up here." Jennifer stood in the driveway taking it all in. A
nervous flutter tickled her belly. It was showing up more and more
often when she stood close to Sam.

"Thanks. Our little slice of heaven." Sam shook her head. "My
little, anyway. The views out back are pretty great too."

Jennifer wasn't sure what to say. Here she was batting down
butterflies, and Sam was still grieving the loss of her wife. She

needed to get the teenage jitters under control and be Sam's friend. After all, that was what she'd offered, to be Sam's friend while she figured out who she was without her wife.

Okay, was it better to ignore or acknowledge what Sam must be feeling? She decided to let it go for now and see how the day played out. She wasn't sure how long it had been since Sam had entertained. Based on a few of their chats, it had been quite some time. No doubt she was still reeling from being widowed after thirty-four years. "Everything's here in the back." She pressed a button on her fob and opened the hatch of her SUV.

Sam walked around the car. "Holy crap, is there anything left at the store? Better question, are you staying all weekend to help eat all this food?"

Jennifer could handle a full weekend at this beautiful retreat from reality. Time spent at a place like this could recharge even the most worn-out soul. She already felt better, and she'd just arrived. "I might have gone a little overboard. I wasn't sure what spices you had, so it looks like more than it really is." She grabbed the rest of the bags before pressing the button to close the hatch. She followed Sam into the house and was greeted with the same eucalyptus scent from Sam's office. The fragrance instantly put her at ease. "Wow. I'd definitely call this a fully stocked kitchen. I think I just died and went to heaven." She squeezed her eyes shut. What a poor choice of words. Jesus, could she get any more insensitive? "I'm sorry. That was an asshole thing to say."

"It's okay. I don't like it when people tiptoe around me. I'm not made of glass." Sam set the groceries on a large island.

"Fair enough." Jennifer placed her grocery bags next to the others. The spacious horseshoe kitchen was a culinary oasis. She loved the way the countertop on the island overlapped on three sides. It offered seating for kitchen gatherers but kept the work space open. She was glad that Sam had suggested she cook here instead of bringing everything to her small apartment. She felt much more comfortable in this space, mostly because it reminded her of her own, slightly smaller kitchen in New Mexico.

She started unpacking and setting things aside for the fridge. "I cheated and grabbed a roasted chicken from the deli so we didn't have to wait for the meat to cook." She pulled the warm container out of a bag and set it on the counter. "A little deboning and dicing, and it will be ready for the enchiladas."

"I can debone and dice up a bird with the best of them."

"Just a few more things to toss in the fridge, then maybe you'll give me the nickel tour?"

"Absolutely. Follow me." Sam led them through the kitchen to a spacious eating area with a counter-height dining table that sat four. Extra chairs sat in front of a large bank of windows on the left, next to a door that went outside. There were more windows on the other side of the door all along the back wall.

Jennifer looked out the windows to an expansive yard and a large pond. She couldn't get over the views. It wasn't difficult to imagine fun summer barbecues on that deck. Warm sunny days filled with laughter and friends. The pang of envy that popped up was an unexpected surprise.

"This is the dining room. They called it a breakfast nook, but what they labeled as the dining room had no view, so we put the table here. That door heads out to the deck. Over here on the right is the staircase to the basement, then the next door is the laundry room, and finally, the primary bedroom and bathroom are at the end of the hall. There's a small screened-in porch off the primary to the back that has the same view as the dining room."

The door to the primary bedroom was open, so Jennifer took a second to peek. It was every bit as neat as expected. The bed was made. The bedspread looked to be a homemade quilt created with bright and bold fabric. The flecked beige carpet had fresh vacuum marks, and the blinds were open wide to the daylight. Pictures graced the side tables on either side of the bed, more shots of Sam and Kara showing dazzling smiles. Jennifer couldn't imagine what it must be like to be all alone in this house with so many reminders that Sam's wife was never coming home.

"Back through the dining room, you can see the great room. Part of it was supposed to be the formal dining, but we used those walls for bookcases and added a small reading area to that side of the living room."

Jennifer stood at the edge of the dinner table and took in the open space. From where she stood, the living room had a bank of windows all along the right-hand side looking out to the deck and beyond. She had to pry her eyes away from the view to take in an L-shaped leather sofa and a matching overstuffed easy chair. Sam's laptop sat open on a side table next to it. *That must be where she sits when she works from home.* Now she'd have a mental picture of Sam reclined in the chair with her feet propped up when they were chatting on instant messenger, like they'd been doing on any given evening over the last few weeks. Not that she needed any help with imagery when it came to Sam. Minnesota was doing some crazy things to her imagination. She shook it off and focused on Sam's tour.

Directly ahead was an interior wall, likely the other side of the hallway leading to guest bedrooms. There was a woodstove on top of a stone hearth on the left. Orange embers glowed through the glass window. Centered on that same wall was a flat-screen TV and a bookcase to the right, balancing out the space. The living room was next-level coziness. The perfect place to curl up while blanketed by the warmth of the fire and get lost in a book.

"Does that stove heat this entire house?" Jennifer asked.

"Yeah, it can kick out some serious heat. When there's warmer temps, I spend most of my time outside, but this time of year, that thing keeps the damp chill at bay. I'll start another fire tonight when the temps drop. In the dead of winter, I feed it a ton of wood. There is a furnace in the basement just in case, but it rarely kicks on." Sam pointed to the left at the foyer. "That's the front door. It's rarely used. And back here are two guest bedrooms and the guest bathroom. There's a half bath back by the garage, just outside of the kitchen."

Jennifer loved the nine-foot ceilings. It gave the home even more of a spacious feel. While slightly bigger, it was laid out much like her old house. It was a functional space that she felt very comfortable in. She followed Sam up the hallway and peeked into the guest rooms and bathroom. The bed in the back bedroom was pushed close to the wall in a corner, making space for a sewing machine and fabric cutting table. Did Sam have a secret talent?

"Do you sew?" Jennifer asked.

"Nah." Sam pulled the door closed. "Kara does, did."

"Did she make that lovely bedspread in your room?"

"Yeah. She's made all sorts of stuff around here."

The sadness showed in her eyes. Jennifer felt horrible for asking the questions. It was the second time in the few minutes she'd been there that her words had instantly erased Sam's smile. She waited for more, but Sam offered nothing. She didn't want to pry and decided not to ask more questions. Instead, she followed Sam back through the living room and into the kitchen.

"Do you want a drink while we cook? I'm a kick-ass sous chef," Sam asked.

"Sounds great. How about some fun cooking music?" Hopefully, music would bring Sam's smiling expression back.

"What do you consider fun cooking music?"

"I like most everything, but the eighties and nineties are dear to my heart. You're letting me take over your kitchen, so pick whatever kind of music you like." The last three weeks had made it clear that Sam's musical tastes were very similar to her own.

Sam called out to the smart speaker, "Play upbeat eighties music."

"Don't Worry, Be Happy" by Bobby McFerrin poured out of the speakers scattered around the house. What made it better was the fact that Sam knew all of the words and sang along. Organizing the necessary items, Jennifer chimed in on the chorus while Sam whipped up a pitcher of frozen margaritas.

Sam handed her a glass of frozen delight. "A toast, to new friends and amazing food."

"I'll toast to that." Jennifer held up her glass. The scent of lime and tequila reminded Jennifer of her grandmother. Right up until the end, she'd loved her margaritas.

Sam tapped the rim of her glass to Jennifer's. She moved her free hand below the glasses in a failed attempt to catch any salt. She took a sip, set down her glass, and went in search of any items Jennifer requested. It was surprising how well they worked together in the kitchen. She hadn't experienced that with anyone besides her grandmother. Sharing Sam's kitchen was effortless; more than that, it was fun. Their movements were fluid, as if rehearsed. Sam was kind and thoughtful and funny and so enjoyable to be around. She was unlike anyone Jennifer had ever known. She was quickly becoming an important treasure.

"You weren't kidding when you said you could whip up a mean margarita. This is wonderful." Jennifer measured out a variety of spices into a bowl and set it off to the side.

Sam stood next to Jennifer and bent slightly over the bowl. "That smells amazing."

"It's my grandma's recipe. I hope you like it."

"If it tastes anything like it smells, I'll love it."

This was exactly the kind of afternoon that she'd needed. The food, the music, the cocktail, and especially, the company, were just what the doctor ordered. Jennifer sang along to a variety of songs while she prepared the sauce and fried the tortilla shells.

She set the large cookie sheet on the island and ladled sauce into the bottom. She drenched the gently fried corn shells in sauce and laid them flat in the pan. Next, she sprinkled some of the shredded chicken, green chilies, green onions, and cheese in each of the shells on the sheet and rolled them up before sliding them into a neat row. Sam was a quick study and helped with the next set. Jennifer bumped Sam's forearm with her hand and left behind sauce and a few pieces of shredded cheese.

"I'm sorry." She stifled a giggle.

"I'm not. Samples." Sam lifted her arm and licked the sauce from her skin. She moaned that same moan from at the bar. Jennifer laughed and hoped she was able to hide the surprising head to toe shiver she'd experienced after hearing the moan. What was going on with her? Sam ladled more sauce and spread out more shells. They repeated the stuffing process, laughing and crisscrossing hands like a game of enchilada Twister. Way too soon, all the ingredients were used. They'd shared such a confined space in the assembly efforts that Jennifer was disappointed when the sheet was full, and Sam stepped back. What she wouldn't give to have another tray to assemble. She ladled the last of the enchilada sauce over the top and topped it off with a generous helping of shredded cheese. "Now, thirty minutes in the oven and you get to enjoy my favorite dish."

"I can't wait." Sam wiped off her hands and opened the preheated oven. "Would you like another margarita?"

"Absolutely, but I'm cutting myself off after that. I still have to drive home at some point."

"There are clean sheets on the guest room beds if you change your mind." Sam refilled both glasses. "The sous chef does dishes. It's a rule of mine."

"Far be it for me to break the hostess's rules." While incredibly enjoyable, this was their first social evening together. She shouldn't consider sleeping over, but friends did that, didn't they? Friends crashed at each other's homes, especially if it was a long drive home. Did Sam consider her a friend? She sure hoped so because the thought gave her a warm and fuzzy feeling.

Jennifer carried the dirty dishes to the sink and then wiped down the island while Sam filled the dishwasher and washed the frying pan and pot. Once again, their time together was effortless, and before she knew it, everything was tidied up. Sam set the table with everything except the plates just as the oven timer sounded.

"That smells amazing." Sam stood at the island with a spatula in hand.

Jennifer laughed. "It's molten lava right now. Give it a moment to cool." She walked over to the refrigerator and grabbed the sour cream. "Here, take this to the table, and I'll be right behind you with plates."

She filled each plate with four enchiladas and carried them to the dining table. Sam sat at the end and had a place set for Jennifer ninety degrees to her right, which gave her a view of the property beyond the deck. It was already getting dark, and the landscape looked ominous, and yet, she'd not felt this comfortable in a long time. Sam had everything to do with that. Accepting this contract might just have been the best decision she could have made.

She heard the pop and crackle of wood burning. Her heart rate shot up. She spun in her chair to find flickering flames locked safely behind the glass of the woodstove. Relieved, she released her held breath. Sam was right, it warmed everything up very nicely.

"Thank you, for this. It was nice," Sam said and held up her glass.

Jennifer picked up her glass and gently tapped them. "Thank you. I agree. It was very nice."

Sam shoved a forkful of enchilada into her mouth, breathing in and out around the heat. After a moment, she chewed and swallowed the bite. "This is so, *so* good. You can use the kitchen anytime." She heaped another mound into her mouth.

Jennifer blew on her fork and took in her first bite. The taste exceeded her expectations and did indeed hit the spot. The preverbal cherry on top of a wonderful afternoon. Spending time with Sam was effortless. More than that, it was enjoyable. Jennifer had come across a lot of people in her consulting career, but there was something unique about Sam, which made the next few months something to really look forward to.

Chapter Seven

Sam bolted up in bed in a cold sweat. She looked over at the alarm clock. Two forty-three in the morning. Would this moment in time ever release its relentless hold on her psyche, or was this to be her curse for the rest of her life? She lay down, but her heart was beating wildly in her chest, and she was already too wide-awake to hope for any additional sleep. After a few minutes of staring into the void, she pulled on her sweats and a long-sleeved shirt and made her way to the kitchen. The coffee pot was ready to go. She turned off the timer and flipped the switch to the start position. It hissed and gurgled to life. While she waited for enough to brew that she could snag a cup, she walked to the living room, stirred up the coals in the woodstove, and added a few small kindling pieces. She then opened the flue for maximum air flow. It wasn't long before the aroma of coffee teased her nose and lured her back into the kitchen. She lifted the pause and pour carafe and started to fill her mug.

"What are you doing up? Are you all right?"

Startled, Sam spun and spilled coffee all over the counter. In her sleep-deprived haze, she'd forgotten that Jennifer had decided to sleep in the guest room instead of driving home. Maybe that second pitcher of margaritas hadn't been such a great idea. Although the light conversation and laughter that had carried on into the evening had sure been nice.

"Shit." Sam put the carafe back into the coffee maker and ran for the paper towel holder.

"Here, let me help." Jennifer pulled several paper towels and knelt next to Sam, dabbing at the coffee dripping down the front of the cabinet. "I didn't mean to startle you."

Sam had only ever seen her with her hair down, but now it was back in a messy ponytail. Her face looked different too, without the tasteful makeup, and while she looked beautiful with makeup, she was also quite beautiful without. She wore the long-sleeved shirt and rocket ship pajama pants Sam had given her the evening before. She looked adorable in an attractive, bashful, sexy kind of way.

Something stirred inside Sam. Something she hadn't felt for a long time. She shook her head to clear the cobwebs. Maybe she was still a little tipsy. Though that wasn't it at all, and she knew it. "I'm sorry if I woke you. You should go back to sleep. I'll be quiet. I promise."

"The coffee smells good. If there's enough left, can I talk you out of a cup?" Jennifer threw the paper towels away.

"There's plenty, but it's only three o'clock. Are you sure you don't want to go back to sleep?"

"Listen, if you want to be alone, I'll take my coffee back to the guest room, but I'd rather be in front of that woodstove, curled up on the couch in a blanket, watching the fire, and visiting with you." She leaned over and bumped her shoulder into Sam's arm. "I'll even let you tell me why you're awake at this ungodly hour."

Sam looked into Jennifer's kind and caring eyes. It occurred to her how short she was without her high heels on. She had to admit that it was nice to have her there. Even though she hadn't known Jennifer all that long, she was quickly becoming a dear friend. One who was getting to know her as she existed in this moment and didn't compare her current situation to a life long gone. "I'll grab us a couple of blankets from the hall closet."

"I'll meet you in the living room with the coffee."

When Sam returned, Jennifer was curled up in the corner seat of the couch with a steaming mug in her hands. She had her knees bent and her feet tucked up next to her. She looked relaxed and comfortable. Sam draped a blanket over her and walked across the room to add some larger wood pieces to the stove. It roared right to life. She closed the flue a bit to tame the dancing flames.

"When it's locked in a cast-iron box," Jennifer said, "the flames are so tranquil and beautiful, but when you have to drive through a raging inferno that's consuming both sides of the road and you can feel that searing heat through the car windows, it brings about an altogether different set of emotions."

Sam sat next to her, put her feet up on the ottoman and draped a small lap blanket over her legs. "Is your home close to that big fire burning in New Mexico?"

Jennifer nodded. "I shouldn't complain. I was one of the lucky ones. My house was saved when so many couldn't be. I'd been evacuated for a few weeks after my last job ended. I had no status on my house until we were finally allowed back into the area. I accepted this job the moment I realized that I wouldn't have to stay there and deal with insurance."

Being displaced by a forest fire had to have been an extremely stressful event, and on top of that, she'd taken a job far away from everything she knew, and yet she'd waltzed into Talley's when they'd first met as if she didn't have a care in the world. Just went to show that it wasn't always easy to know what a person was dealing with, especially when they were like Jennifer and handled it with grace. The more she got to know Jennifer, the more she wanted to know.

"Do you have family there?" Sam asked.

"My mom and dad live in Las Cruces, just north of the border with Mexico. Both of my brothers, Marcos and Alejandro, live close to my parents in the El Paso area with wives and kids. I'm the odd duck. The career-driven, divorced daughter who didn't want a house full of children."

Sam had never wanted children of her own either. It had nothing to do with her career. She just wasn't a kid person. Luckily, Kara hadn't wanted children either. "I don't think there's anything odd about wanting a career and not children. It isn't for everyone. Better to know before you have the child than to have regrets after. Do you like being an aunt?"

Jennifer shrugged. "I really don't see my brothers or their families all that much. My place is five hours north of my parents, almost due east of Santa Fe. I try to see them a couple of times a year, especially now that they are getting older. My brothers and I aren't all that close. I'm the oops baby, and there's a pretty big age gap between them and me. Both had moved out and started their own lives by the time I was in high school. My parents think the boys are perfect, and they've also been clear that I didn't live up to their expectations. How about you? Family?"

Sam couldn't imagine Jennifer not exceeding any and all expectations. She was amazing. Families were a fickle thing, and not everyone fit in. Her family was no different.

"My dad passed away a couple of years ago. My mom, one Mrs. Vivian, Vivvie to her friends, Phillips..." Jennifer tilted her head and raised her eyebrows. "Oh yeah, she's everything you're picturing, dyed red hair and all, retired to Florida. I have an older sister, Karen, who's married with two adult children. They live in North Carolina. I also have a younger sister, Becky. She's still finding her path. My sisters and I are so different. Honestly, if we weren't related, we wouldn't be friends." Enough about her goofy family. Sam wanted to know more about Jennifer. "Do you have anyone in the Santa Fe area that you're close to?"

Jennifer shook her head and shrugged. "No, not really. I'm a consultant. A three-month contract is my minimum, but most gigs are six months to nine months, give or take. If the contract was close enough, I'd go home on the weekends, and I typically spent a few weeks at home between gigs, but honestly, if I didn't like cooking so much, I could get rid of most everything and live out of my car. Pathetic, right?"

Sadness washed over Jennifer's face. Sam wanted to reach out and wrap her up in a hug, but so far, they hadn't been hugging friends. Besides, it was the middle of the night, and if it was unwelcome, she didn't want to make things awkward. Instead, she tried for a response that would welcome more sharing. "Only if you don't like your life."

Jennifer feigned a weak smile. "I've been traveling for more than twenty-five years now. The nomadic life is starting to wear on me. This job is the farthest from home I've been."

Sam couldn't imagine living a nomadic life. Starting from scratch in each new town. No lifelong friends. No favorite hangouts. No routine. No consistency. She didn't adjust to change all that well. A lot of people switched jobs every few years. Not her; she'd had three jobs in total since she'd graduated college. It likely would have been two, but the second employer moved the company out of state. She'd declined to relocate because her life was here.

"Do you get lonely? Or do you have friends scattered all over the country?"

"Lonely? Oh yeah, definitely. It's affecting me more as I get older. Always eating alone sucks, and weekends are the worst, so thank you for this." Jennifer waved around to encompass her space on the couch next to Sam. "I do have a few acquaintances scattered around the country, but I think I've found a friendship to treasure here in Minnesota."

Her warm smile could melt all of the ice in the artic. It certainly had an effect on Sam's heart. "Definitely a treasured friendship." Her response sounded lame, but she didn't know what else to say. It had been forever since she'd had a conversation with anyone like she was sharing with Jennifer. It was nice to hear what she was feeling and why. It was nice getting to know more about her than her excellent taste in clothing and incredible culinary talents. Bottom line, spending time with Jennifer was very nice indeed. "I, for one, am glad you expanded your contracting radius." Sam got up and added another log to the fire.

"Thank you, me too. Before the fire, I wouldn't have considered it, but the fire made me realize that things have shifted in the Southwest, and maybe it was time for a change. A big change. Although I never expected it to be so flippin' cold up here. I can tell you that much."

Sam returned to her spot on the couch and draped her lap blanket over her legs. "Midwest winters, and sometimes early spring, take some getting used to, but pretty soon, everything will leaf out, and you'll blink, and before you know it, the heat of summer is gone, and you're soaking in the brilliance of fall, and then you find yourself looking forward to the first big snowfall again. The changing of the seasons is nice. Each one offers something unique." Watching Jennifer take in the views from the bluff earlier had Sam thinking about what other Midwest experiences Jennifer would enjoy. She'd happily volunteer to be her guide.

"I don't know if I'll ever get used to the snow and bitter cold. I'm looking forward to summer. I'm especially looking forward to seeing everything green up. It's not the same kind of green in New Mexico like it is up here. At least, from what I saw in the pictures."

"The summer months are very nice. Do you think you'll go back, ya know, when your contract is up?" Sam held her breath waiting for an answer. She really wanted Jennifer to want to stay. She felt a connection with Jennifer that she couldn't describe quite yet but didn't want to lose, either.

"I'm not sure. I'm lucky enough to have options. I've hired a property management company to rent out my house while I'm here working. It keeps it from sitting empty and gives evacuees a place to live that isn't as expensive as a hotel. Hopefully, it helps in some small way while they rebuild. There are no words to describe the vastness of the destruction. It will be years before anything resembles normal in that area, especially if the drought continues. Seeing everything I saw, I'm not so sure I want to rush back."

The sadness in Jennifer's expression had Sam wanting to wrap her up in another hug. She wondered if Jennifer's experience in the hotel was like her experience at grief group, where she was not only dealing with her own emotions but also all those surrounding her. Everything about what Jennifer had been through with the effects of the fire sounded emotionally exhausting and stressful to the millionth degree.

"I can't imagine dealing with all of that." Sam sipped her coffee.

"Oh, I think you can. Maybe not the loss of a home but a loss much more significant than a pile of boards and nails." She twisted in her seat. "I've let you deflect long enough. Are you going to tell me why you're awake at three o'clock in the morning when we just went to sleep a couple of hours ago?"

For the bit of time that they'd talked, Sam had forgotten about the demon that woke her up every night. All of it came rushing back, and her chest tightened up beneath the weight of it all. "It was just a nightmare. No big deal."

Jennifer stretched out one of her legs and tapped Sam's thigh with a blanketed foot. "I have a feeling there's more to it than that. Do you have nightmares often?"

It felt good to be touched, one of the things she missed the most. "I don't want to dampen the—"

Jennifer cocked her head and raised her eyebrows. "Uh-uh. I answered your questions, and you answer mine. It's how this works." Her smile was so sincere. The expression around her eyes was soft and inviting.

Sam had an urge to curl up in her arms. She hadn't shared her reoccurring torment with anyone, but there was something about Jennifer that helped her feel comfortable doing so. She drew in a deep breath and let it out slowly. She stared at the dancing flames and hoped she could find the words. "Two forty-three. I never knew that three numbers could have such a hold on me. Truth is, they won't let go. It's like a curse. The flashing numbers from my alarm clock. Two forty-three. I wake up every single day at roughly two forty-three in the morning, often precisely. I thought it would stop at some point, and I would be able to sleep through the night again, but it's been more than a year, and I think it's now become a cruel habit I can't seem to break." She clenched her teeth, hoping to control the emotion behind her words. It'd been more than a year, and she still felt so raw inside.

"Is that when the car accident happened?"

Sam shook her head. "No. The accident was just before eleven o'clock, at least, that's what the paperwork said." Sam could feel her staring, waiting for more. She appreciated the time to formulate her words without coaxing and prodding. If only her family could learn that technique. "February ninth, the night of the accident, Kara was driving home from a weeklong work conference about three hours north in Minneapolis. She'd checked out of her hotel earlier in the day." Sam drew in a shaky breath and let it out slowly. "The last session ran long and didn't let out until well after eight in the evening. She called, saying she was going to grab a bite and hit the road. She was sick of hotels and wanted nothing more than a good night's sleep in her own bed." Sam could recall Kara's words, but it had been quite some time since she'd heard them in Kara's voice. She'd read that that was common and normal. It sure didn't feel common or normal. It felt like torture and made her question her sanity.

"Not long after we hung up, I went to bed, knowing she'd wake me up when she got home. Instead, I was jarred from a deep sleep by a pounding fist on the front door. I knocked all sorts of stuff off my side table while I tried to find the lamp. My alarm clock was upside down on the floor. The numbers displayed in bright red. Two forty-three. Kara wasn't home. She wasn't next to me in bed." Sam's chest tightened up more, as if that was possible. She tried to breathe through it. "Kara should have been home hours earlier. The persistent pounding wouldn't let up. I got dressed and peeked outside. There was a sheriff's cruiser. Deputy Jones stood at my front door with her cap in her hands. When I opened the door, she asked if she could come inside."

Sam was surprised by how well her words were flowing. She hadn't shared the details of that evening with anyone. Instead, they'd plagued her each night when she closed her eyes. The series of events were chiseled into her memory. She took a sip of coffee, hoping to swallow the lump in her throat. "Deputy Jones stood in my foyer and told me that she had some difficult news. There had been a single vehicle accident out on Route 13. Kara Richardson was pronounced dead at the scene. She went on to say that while they were still investigating, all indications were that she simply fell asleep at the wheel. There were no skid marks indicating she tried to avoid an obstacle. Her phone was in her purse, and her call to me, just before nine, had been her last communication. Jones said more, but I was spinning out, and her words sounded like Charlie Brown's teacher." She bit her cheek to control the emotion that threatened to spill over. Queasiness hit, along with the cold sweats that typically came with a bad case of the flu. It had become her new normal. It was how she felt when she woke up every single day at two forty-three in the morning.

She took a few deep, controlled breaths. "I didn't sleep much that first week. I was pretty much a zombie. There was so much to do, so much to power through, that it took a while before it really had a chance to sink in. The nightmares started that first night I was all alone, and now, I don't know how to make them stop. I've tried staying up late. I've tried sleeping pills. I've tried staying in bed and not getting up. Nothing helps."

"How about talking? Have you tried that?" Jennifer asked.

Sam shook her head. She was spent, and she hadn't even shared the actual nightmare yet. That urge to bolt hit hard. She wanted to run as hard as she could and escape the flood of feelings. She wanted to run until her lungs burned like they were on fire because then, she could focus on that and not how much her heart ached.

"Sometimes, talking through something takes away the power it has. I'd like to listen. What happens in the nightmares, Sam?"

Sam turned and stared at her. "She comes back."

"Who? Kara?"

Sam shook her head again. A fresh round of nausea and cold sweats hit, as if she'd just bolted up in bed. "Deputy Jones. She pulls that cruiser into the driveway and pounds relentlessly on the front door. Night after night. I can't ignore it, and I can't stop myself from opening the door. She stands in the foyer and describes every detail of the accident, but she doesn't stop there. The tone of her voice changes, and she's angry." Sam's heart felt like it was going to beat right out of her chest. "She peppers me with questions. Was my good night's sleep worth it? Why didn't I stay up and talk to Kara while she drove home? Night after night, I don't have an answer. I stand there, and I have no words because she's right. If I'd just stayed awake and chatted with Kara, she'd still be alive. Deputy Jones doesn't let up. She repeats the question, sometimes pounding on the wall or door or countertop until it's two forty-three in the morning, and I sit up in bed, soaked in sweat, and my heart racing wildly. She's relentless. She hasn't skipped a night." Sam was squeezing her coffee cup so tightly, she worried she'd shatter it in her grasp. She reached over to set it on the side table. It chattered on the coaster because her hand was shaking so badly.

"You blame yourself for her death." There was no judgment in Jennifer's voice. "Sam, it's not your fault. It was the very definition of an accident."

Sam looked at her, hands in her lap, and didn't say a word. Whether it was her fault or not, she was responsible because she did nothing to help Kara stay awake. She did the opposite by drifting off to sleep. How could she not blame herself?

"How often did Kara travel?" Jennifer sat up and leaned forward. She rested her hand on Sam's arm. Her touch was warm on Sam's cold, sweaty skin.

"At least once or twice a month. Sometimes, she flew, and other times, she drove." Sam was drained. Without consistent sleep, she always felt raw and like she was running on empty.

"For how many years?" Jennifer rubbed her thumb on Sam's forearm.

Sam picked at a thread on the hem of her shirt. "I don't know. She traveled to client sites for most of her career."

"Was your routine that night any different than any other time?" Jennifer asked.

It was a simple question. One she hadn't considered. She was still so raw with emotion from sharing that she couldn't concede. "Look, I see where you're going with this, but you don't understand. I knew she'd had a long day. I could hear it in her voice. Her phone was linked to the car. I could have asked her about the week. I could have told her about my week, but no. Instead, I curled up in bed and went to sleep." Sam focused on the flames dancing in the woodstove. "Truth is, I didn't even think to call her and see how she was doing."

"I'll ask you again. Was your routine that night any different than any other time she traveled?"

Sam's chin quivered, and tears welled in her eyes. "No, but in hindsight, it should have been different." Sam removed the blanket and stood. She walked into the kitchen and stood in front of the coffee maker with her hands spread on the counter, trying desperately to blink back the tears that were already spilling over. This time, she heard Jennifer walk up behind her. She was glad that Jennifer didn't try to turn her; instead, her hand rested on Sam's back. It was a grounding touch and felt soothing. After a few minutes, Sam gained some control over her emotions and shared the last of it.

"That night, after Deputy Jones told me about the accident, I came in here and made coffee. I had to do something besides stand in the foyer and listen to her tell me where the car was being towed and where they were transporting her body. I had to focus on something. I had to do anything that would help me hold it together. She followed me in here and stood over there by the island. I asked her a few specifics about the accident. When she answered, I got sick to my stomach and bolted for the bathroom. I don't know when she left." Sam swallowed that bitter taste in her throat. "Now, when I wake up and accept that there'll be no more sleep, I come out here and flip off the timer and switch the coffeemaker on, just like I did that night. I tell ya, sometimes, I turn around and fully expect to see Jones standing over there as if she's been here all this time."

Jennifer's hand moved to Sam's shoulder and tugged gently. Sam turned. She couldn't stop the tears from falling, and she was too tired to fight it any longer. Jennifer tugged on her hand. Sam followed her into the living room without another word. She had no more words to offer. Tears streamed down her cheeks. Jennifer sat in the corner of the couch and held her arms open.

Sam sat and stared at her. She'd just shared everything about her wife's death. Was it wrong to want nothing more than to be wrapped up in Jennifer's arms? If it was wrong, she'd deal with the guilt tomorrow. She leaned over into Jennifer's welcoming embrace. It felt so wonderful, so comforting, to simply be held. She lay there, consumed with all the emotion she'd kept bottled up since that fateful night. It was the best cry she'd never allowed herself to have. Eventually, the rhythm of Jennifer's breathing and her heartbeat lulled her into a deep, dreamless sleep.

CHAPTER EIGHT

Jennifer opened her sleep-heavy eyes and looked around the room. Sunlight streamed through the windows. It took her a moment to recognize her surroundings. She was in the living room at Sam's house. She must have drifted off to sleep. There was an unbelievable amount of pressure on her overly full bladder. She lifted her head slightly and looked to see what had her pinned to the sofa. Sam was sprawled across her body, sound asleep. She looked so peaceful. Given what she'd learned last night, Jennifer would hold it for as long as possible to let Sam get some decent sleep. She rested her head back into the corner of the sofa. Her heart ached for what Sam was going through. She had the urge to run her fingers through the soft curls of Sam's hair. She resisted, knowing it would likely wake her up.

Sam's arms were wrapped around her in the open space between the backrest of the couch and the seat cushions. Her hold tightened, as if giving Jennifer a great big bear hug, and then slowly released. She felt tender caresses on her back. The unexpected touch brought about a head-to-toe shiver and temporarily made her forget her full bladder. It had been years since she'd felt the warmth of another person's body draped across hers. It felt good. Sam's head shifted on her chest, and she drew in a deep breath. Her exhale was almost a purr. Slowly, Sam lifted her head slightly, looked around, and with squinting eyes, she finally looked at Jennifer. Her eyes grew wide, and she quickly pushed herself to a sitting position.

"Shit, I'm sorry. I apologize. I didn't mean to…I'm so sorry."

"Stop saying you're sorry. I'm glad you got some rest. I fell asleep too." Jennifer shivered. She already missed the warmth of Sam's body against her. She had the urge to pull Sam back into her arms.

"Wow, I crashed." Sam rubbed her eyes. "What time is it?"

"I'll look in a minute." Jennifer jumped up and ran for the guest bathroom. "I seriously have to pee."

When she finished, she washed her hands and looked into the mirror. Holy hell. She looked like a sleep-deprived rag doll. She picked up the new toothbrush and tiny tube of toothpaste that Sam had given her the night before. She took a moment to brush her teeth, comb her hair, and wash her face. Once she felt somewhat human, she returned to the guest room, stripped the sheets off the bed, and got dressed.

Sam was already dressed and standing in the kitchen making a fresh pot of coffee.

"Where should I put the dirty sheets and the jammies you loaned me?" Jennifer asked.

"I could have done that."

"That's not how I was raised. A guest isn't welcome back if she makes too much work for the hostess. PS, I'd like to be welcomed back." Jennifer winked and smiled. "So where should I set these?"

"You can toss them on the floor in front of the washer. I have laundry to do later."

Jennifer nodded. She dropped the bedding in a neat pile in front of the washer. When she walked out of the laundry room, sparkling rainbows of light caught her eye.

Sam's bedroom door was wide open. A small crystal hung from the latch on the window. The way the sunlight hit it shot tiny rainbows around the room. Jennifer wasn't surprised to see that the bed was already made. She stepped to the center of the room and stood inside Sam's space. She slowly took everything in. The bedroom was every bit, if not more so, a memorial as her desk was at work. Candid photographs of Kara adorned every available surface. Between the two dressers stood two poster boards covered in photographs of Sam and Kara, along with others she assumed to be family or friends. They must have been the memory boards from the funeral. Jennifer couldn't understand why Sam would want the constant reminders staring at her. How could she ever move forward when she spent all of her time staring at the past?

"Hey, did you get lost?" Sam called.

Jennifer retreated from her intrusion and returned to the kitchen. Her heart ached for Sam and all she'd been through. There had to be a way to break the nightmares that fed her guilt.

Sam held out a cup of coffee. "Would you like some breakfast? Eggs or an omelet or oats and yogurt? I make a mean breakfast."

"It's almost noon. I'd rather have enchiladas. Are you up for another plate of Mexican-inspired heaven?" Jennifer asked and accepted her cup of coffee.

"Oh, I'm all in for more enchiladas." Sam walked to the stove and pressed preheat on the oven. "Temp?"

"Three-fifty is fine." Jennifer loved that Sam was on board and walked to the fridge. She pulled out the tray of leftovers. Plenty for the two of them. Probably enough for two more meals. "We could heat this in the microwave too. If you'd prefer."

"Naw, the microwave will make them chewy. Oven warm-up all the way." Sam stood over the pan like she hadn't eaten in days. All that was missing was a string of drool.

Jennifer couldn't agree more. The oven was so much better than the microwave. And she had more admiration for Sam. She made herself at home and walked over to the cabinet that held cookie sheets. She grabbed a small one, dished out two servings, and returned the leftovers to the fridge. Sam had the smaller tray in the oven by the time she turned around.

"What do you think, ten minutes?" Sam asked.

"Sounds good to me."

Sam retrieved two plates, set them on the island, and grabbed the container of sour cream. "Coffee doesn't really go with enchiladas." She opened the fridge. "Hey, how about a beer?"

"Why not?" Jennifer accepted the bottle after Sam removed the cap. "It's the weekend, after all."

Sam held up her bottle. "Cheers."

"Cheers." Jennifer thought back to that first day they'd met. Looking back, everything made so much more sense. Sam wasn't withdrawn or sour, or maybe she was, but with undeniable reasons.

The timer sounded. They plated their food and sat at the island. "How do you feel this morning?" Jennifer asked between bites.

"Better than I have in a long time. I haven't slept like that since before the accident. I almost feel human again. I can't thank you enough." Her color was better than it had been since Jennifer had known her. She might as well have gone to a spa for the weekend given the difference.

She'd had no idea how important sleep was until knowing Sam. "It was my pleasure, although I'm not sure I did much aside from being your pillow for a few hours. I'm glad you were able to get some good sleep." She tapped her beer against Sam's bottle and took a sip.

"You were so much more than my pillow. Thanks for opening up about your life and for being here and listening. I mean it, thank you, for everything." Sam's expression said so much more than her words ever could. It was like she had this ability to share her heart and soul through her expressions. It was an endearing quality.

"You're welcome." Jennifer collected the empty plates. When cleanup was finished, she walked around the island and sat next to Sam. "Forgive me if I overstep with this next question, but I wonder, what do you feel when you look at the photographs of Kara? Does seeing the memories warm your heart or make you sad? Or do you feel something else completely?"

Sam stared at her beer. "It depends on the day, the minute, or even the second."

Jennifer rubbed the back of Sam's hand with her index finger. "What do you mean?"

"Sometimes, it feels like someone's ripping my heart right of out my chest. Sometimes, I'm furious, and I want to throw something or bust anything and everything I can get my hands on. Other times, I'm angry at her for leaving me, and I can't stand to look at her. But mostly, when I look at the pictures, I realize how sad and lonely and lost I am without her."

After Jennifer's grandmother had passed away, she'd felt a deep sadness when she'd looked at pictures of her or of the two of them together. So much so that she'd put the photos away until she could look at them and not feel that deep sense of grief. Her death was the only loss that had come remotely close to what Sam must be enduring. She wrapped her hand around Sam's. "If it causes you so much pain, why do you keep all of the photos out?"

Slowly, Sam raised her head. "Because it feels so wrong to…"

She waited for more. Instead, the muscles in Sam's jaw tightened, and a tear ran down her cheek. "It feels wrong to do what? Put them away?" Jennifer asked.

Sam nodded.

"What if it's for just a little while? It doesn't have to be forever." She let the words hang in the air. She wrapped an arm around Sam's shoulder and leaned her head over. She felt Sam's head lean against her own. "Have you changed anything about this house in the past year?"

Sam shook her head.

"Is there anything you'd like to change?" Jennifer asked.

"I don't know. I haven't thought about it."

Jennifer suspected as much. "I have an idea, if you're open to it."

"What's that?" Sam asked quietly.

"Is the dresser empty in the room I slept in?"

"I think so."

"The closet?"

"I'd have to look. I'm not sure."

Jennifer tugged on Sam's hand. "Come on, let's go check."

"Are you moving in?" Sam asked from behind her.

"You wish." Jennifer laughed.

"I do kinda like having you around," Sam said.

"I like being around." Jennifer shoulder bumped her. "I don't want you to get sick of me. I've already moved into your office at work without giving you much say in the matter."

"Trust me, I had a say," Sam said and opened the closet.

Her words warmed Jennifer's heart. She already cherished the friendship developing between them, and the more she got to know Sam, the more she cared for her.

"You can invite me over whenever you like. Next time, I'll know to bring an overnight bag." Jennifer walked to the dresser and opened the top drawer: empty, as was the case for the other four drawers. Perfect. She was worried they'd find some old photo albums or something that would change the course of her idea. She turned and looked over Sam's shoulder. The closet was empty except for a couple of extra blankets and pillows on the top shelf. She scanned the room. There was no artwork on the walls, and the bedspread was store-bought. She'd noticed the tag when she'd stripped the bed. The alarm clock on the side table had blue numbers instead of red. This might just work. Even if Sam's wife had picked out the decor, it was a fairly Kara-free zone. "Have you ever slept in this room?"

"No. It's the guest room."

"Good. Would you consider boxing up the photographs at work and in the living room for an experiment?"

Sam turned from the closet. "Why do I feel like there's more to it?"

"Because there is. I'd like you to move your clothes, shoes, and anything else you might need from your room into this bedroom. I'd also like you to use the guest bathroom too. The goal is to completely avoid going into your bedroom. And I mean, not for anything. Try it for a month. I'll help."

Sam looked at her as if she had two heads. "To what end?"

"How about for the sake of trying something new? Nothing will change if you can't figure out how to get some sleep, and a few extra hours one night isn't enough to offset the past year. This will offer a complete change of pace. Consider it a psyche shake-up." She reached for Sam's hand, sat on the edge of the bed, and pulled gently. Sam sighed and sat next to her. "You said it yourself last night. You've tried sleeping pills and staying up late and all sorts of things to get a full night's sleep. If none of those things worked, maybe it's time to try something completely different. After we talked, you were able to fall asleep. I don't know if it was the conversation or simply the location change, but you slept. Try this for me. Move into this bedroom where it's completely different, and the photographs and memories aren't constantly staring at you, and let's see if you can get some peaceful sleep. Bonus, Deputy Jones won't know where to find you."

"Humph." It wasn't a laugh, but it wasn't an objection either.

Jennifer would take it. "Are you game to try?"

Sam nodded. "One month?"

"One month."

Sam stood and walked out of the room. Jennifer jumped up and followed her across the house and into her bedroom. She walked over to the dresser, removed the top drawer, and set it on the bed. Jennifer looked at the contents. Sports bras had been laid flat in a tidy stack on the left side, and fitted boxers in every imaginable color lay flat on the right.

"You wear boxers? Sexy! I've never heard of TomboyX. I had no idea that was a thing." Jennifer tried to picture Sam in the fitted boxers. She'd seen women in sports bras and briefs with wider waist elastic at the gym. Maybe there was an athletic build beneath Sam's baggy clothes.

"Is this you helping?" Sam turned away from the dresser holding another drawer. Her cheeks were flushed. "Don't knock 'em. They're super comfortable."

"Well, if you're not going to show me, I guess I'll have to take your word for it." Jennifer winked and smiled. She picked up the drawer and carefully made her way to the guest room. It was probably best to let Sam put her underwear in the new dresser. Although, it seemed silly to return to Sam's room empty-handed. She opened the drawer, matched the placement, and carried the empty drawer back across the house, passing Sam in the living room.

"If you're still being helpful, there's another drawer on the bed," Sam said over her shoulder.

Jennifer returned to the primary suite after unloading the last drawer. It slid easily into the last slot in the dresser. The sound of hangers sliding on a rod came out of an open door about ten feet past the dresser. Jennifer turned the corner and froze. The gasp she felt on the inside must have sounded on the outside since Sam spun around.

"I'm sorry, and here I thought the kitchen was my favorite room in your house. This closet is a woman's wet dream, or maybe it's only me. Wait, that probably didn't come out right." The room was designed in an M concept. Closet rods ran along the left and right walls. Floor to ceiling shelves were on the either side of the door. Centered in the room stood a floor to ceiling peninsula. The endcap was covered in tilted shelves for shoes, as was the lower half of each side. Additional closet rods hung above the shoes. It was easily half of the size of the primary bedroom.

"When we had the house built, Kara said I went overboard on

the primary suite, but she managed to fill up ninety percent of the space in this room. This small section is all that I have, well, that and the bottom two rows of shoes by the door." Sam smiled that same sad smile.

"You still have her entire wardrobe." It was a statement. And then she spotted the large ceramic vase on the top shelf by the shoes. Deep inside, she knew it wasn't a vase. It was delicate and beautiful for an urn. No wonder Sam couldn't sleep. Out of the corner of her eye, she saw Sam turn to see what she was staring at.

"I don't know what to do with—" Sam's voice cracked. Tears welled in her eyes. "I had her in the living room, but it was too much, so I put her on top of her dresser, and that was too much. She made me swear not to bury her, but we never talked about anything beyond that."

"How about you worry about what to do later? Let's get your stuff to the guest room for now. Then we could put the photographs on an empty shelf in here. None of this has to be dealt with today. Would that be okay?" Jennifer asked.

Sam nodded and grabbed two handfuls of hanging clothes. She stood there, her weighted arms slowly lowering to her sides, staring at the urn.

"Would you like to take those to the guest room, and I'll bring the rest? You can organize the closet in there however it works for you."

Sam nodded. "Yeah, okay. I'll take the stuff on my shelves, but I don't need any of my suits. I've lost too much weight. They don't fit anymore."

That explained the baggy clothes. "How much weight have you lost?"

"Thirty pounds, give or take. I haven't had much of an appetite, and I haven't been back to the gym." She turned and walked out.

Jennifer lifted one of the suits off the rod. She slid her hand along the collar, admiring the fabric. Absolutely stunning. Sam certainly had great taste in clothing, or had it been Kara? Somehow, she felt like this was all Sam. She caught the whiff of cologne from the jacket. It was lovely. Earthy with a touch of masculinity that suited Sam's personality without being overpowering or macho. She held the suit closer and inhaled. She couldn't place the fragrance, but it was intoxicating. She returned the suit to its proper place, grabbed an armload of clothes off the shelf, and made her way to Sam's new space.

Walking across the house with the last of Sam's shoes, she hoped her idea worked, or at the very least, helped. When Sam went into the primary bath, Jennifer decided not to follow. She didn't need to fangirl over another room that Sam had designed for her late wife. Instead, she set about collecting framed pictures from the living room. It was quite the stack of memories. She'd been alone for so long that she felt a touch of envy for the relationship Sam and her wife had shared. She tried to remember the last time she'd even gone on a date. It must have been like six or seven years ago? She tried to picture what city she'd been in. It wasn't coming to her. There'd been so many jobs and locations between then and now that she'd lost track. It didn't matter because what she did remember was that he'd been extremely self-centered, and the date had been an abysmal failure.

Anymore, dating was the last thing on her mind. For now, she'd treasure this newfound friendship. While Sam was setting up her new temporary bathroom, she took the photographs to the walk-in closet and set them on an empty shelf. She collected the others from the various surfaces in Sam's bedroom and added those to the shelf. When she was done, she pulled the closet door shut and closed the primary bedroom door behind her. It was time to try something new.

Later that night, while setting out her clothes for the next day, Jennifer's phone chirped. She smiled when she saw that it was Sam: *The chair in front of my bedroom was a nice touch.*

Jennifer smiled. It had been a last-minute idea to take one of the spare dining chairs and place it directly in front of Sam's bedroom door. *A gentle reminder that you promised to try this for a month.*

Sam: *It helped. I walked to my room out of habit and stopped when I saw the chair. Is it weird that I wished you were here for the first night? I could clean out the other guest bedroom.*

A warmth washed over Jennifer. She'd hop into her car in a moment if Sam asked her to. *Let's see how tonight goes. If Deputy*

Jones comes back, call me, even if it's two forty-three, and I'll be there.

Sam: *Thanks. This weekend was nice. Good night.*

Jennifer smiled. Nice was an understatement. She enjoyed spending time with Sam. *It was very nice. Thank you. See you tomorrow at the office. Good night.*

Chapter Nine

The alarm clock woke Sam from a deep, dreamless sleep. She missed the radio feature of her own alarm clock, but the full night's sleep had been worth the effort it took to stream her favorite DJ on her phone.

It had only been a couple of weeks, but Jennifer's idea was proving to be a mildly bumpy success. Sam wasn't sure if it was due to being in a different room or sleeping on a different mattress. Maybe it was the blue color of the alarm clock numbers or the fact that she'd pulled the pillowcase that Jennifer had used from the laundry before she threw the white load in that Sunday. The scent of Jennifer's perfume had lulled her to sleep in the living room and was just as effective in the guest room. Something about any or all of it was working better and better each day.

She picked up her Jennifer-scented hugging pillow and placed it next to hers at the head of the bed. Hugging a pillow, hell, depending on a pillow like a security blanket that smelled like someone other than her wife seemed a bit like cheating. She justified the guilt with the fact that Jennifer's ideas were working. She was grateful for the sleep and because of Jennifer, Deputy Jones was, for the most part, leaving her alone.

She felt an extra little bounce in her step today. She'd spent the last few evenings after work clearing flower and weed remnants out of the four ten-foot-long raised garden beds. Instead of planting flowers this year, she wanted to try something new, something she'd always wanted to do, and planting tomatoes, cucumbers, and green beans were things she could enjoy all summer long.

Spring had finally sprung. The trees and shrubs had leafed out. The risk of frost was past, and today was a perfect day to take a road trip to buy some vegetable plants.

She took her steaming mug of coffee into the guest bathroom and looked into the mirror. Her long, unruly hair was starting to get on her nerves. It hung in her eyes and tickled her ears. Pat was right, she did look a little like Frodo Baggins. It was time to look like Sam again.

Kara had used scissors on the top and a variety of clipper attachments for the fade. It had always turned out perfectly. How difficult could it be? Sam dampened her hair and combed her bangs down. She picked up the scissors and cut a line just above her eyebrows on her forehead and discarded the loose hair into the trash. The length looked a little long, but it was a good starting point. She parted out the next section back, stretched it up, and cut again, matching the length of the first cut. The process continued until she could no longer see what she was cutting. She looked in the mirror and realized that she was rocking an eighties mullet. She'd hated the mullet back then and hated it even more right now. Ugh.

She opened the mirrored medicine cabinets on her left and right, but they couldn't help her see the back of her head. This was turning out to be harder than she thought. Shit. She couldn't go out in public like this. Then she remembered that there was a mirror hanging on the back of the door in the other guest room. Maybe that would help.

The hinges squeaked when she pushed the door open and stepped inside. The honeysuckle scent from Kara's favorite candle emanated from the closed-off room. She stood transported back in time. Pieces of Kara's last sewing project, a sundress for her and a matching button-up for Sam, sat pinned together on the sewing table, half-finished. Other pieces of fabric were cut to size on the table, and everything was just sitting as if patiently waiting for the seamstress to come back. Sam closed her eyes and pictured Kara sitting at the sewing table, the sounds of the machine weaving the needle in and out of the fabric. Kara humming along with the music playing in the background. The heartache was so powerful that her chest physically hurt. Profound loss crashed down on her like a tidal wave. She couldn't deal with this today. It was too much. Haircut forgotten, she pulled the door closed behind her, returned to the bathroom, and sought solace in a steaming hot shower.

Nothing helped ease the pain. Not the shower. Not the loud music that she blasted through the house. She thought about canceling her plans, but the thought of not seeing Jennifer all day made her feel worse. She had no interest in going back to long, lonely weekends cooped up in the house all alone. There was something about spending time with Jennifer that mended the broken pieces and helped her feel whole again.

Within an hour, she was in the heart of the town. The apartment that Jennifer rented faced the town square on the top floor of a low-rise, six-unit building. Sam pulled her truck up to the curb and shut off the engine. Her spirit lifted when she saw Jennifer's front door swing open. As usual, she wore the ordinary and made it look extraordinary. Her hair was down, cascading over her shoulders, a mane of thick, dark brown waves. Dark blue capris pants hugged her in all the right places, and the silky, white short-sleeved blouse matched her sandals. A sheer, dark blue scarf knotted around her neck gave her casual look, just the right amount of class. Sam hopped out of the truck and ran around to open the passenger door.

"Thanks for inviting me to tag along. It's too nice a day to stay inside." Jennifer wrapped her arms around Sam's neck for a hug, a hug she craved more and more as time went on. When Jennifer pulled away, she lifted Sam's chin and turned her head from side to side. "What are you hiding with the ball cap?"

Sam felt her cheeks flush. Slowly, she lifted the hat. "I thought I could cut it myself. Epic fail."

Jennifer covered her mouth in a failed attempt to stifle a laugh. "Oh dear. What look were you going for?"

"I couldn't see to cut anything in the back, and now, instead of looking like Frodo Baggins, I have Billy Ray Cyrus hair. I hate it." She put the cap back on. "Can you help me fix it? I have clippers in the car."

"Me? No, no, no. Trust me, you don't want me anywhere near those clippers. That is not a skill that I possess." Jennifer pulled her phone out of her purse. "Who cut it when you wore the fade?"

"Kara," Sam said quietly. "She cut hair to help pay for college. She's always cut my hair." That feeling of profound loss that she'd experienced earlier in the morning washed over her all over again. How could she miss Kara so much and simultaneously crave time with Jennifer? It was like she was living two different lives. One when she was alone, consumed with her grief, and one with Jennifer that made her feel alive. She shook the thought away.

"Ah, that explains so much. Now I understand." Jennifer's tone was sympathetic. The tenderness in her eyes assured Sam that she did indeed understand. "Well, it's Saturday. Certainly, we can find a barber around here that's open." She tapped on her phone. "How about a small detour on our way to the nursery?"

"Anything to not show up at work on Monday looking like this. Between Mike and Kelly, I'll never hear the end of it."

"Your secret is safe with me, Tiger King."

"Ha ha, very funny."

Jennifer hooked her arm into Sam's. "Come on, it looks like there's a salon just a few blocks up. Let's go see if they have an opening."

Sam locked her truck. The sun was shining above in a deep blue, cloudless sky. A perfect day for a walk through town with a beautiful woman on her arm. What could be better? The lighthearted feeling surprised her. It wasn't two minutes ago that she'd felt consumed by grief for Kara. She wasn't cut out for this emotional roller coaster. Would it ever get easier? Would the loss and the pain release its relentless grip on her heart?

Sam drew in a deep breath and let it out slowly. It was already getting easier. She was already recovering faster, and it had everything to do with the amazing woman who was walking by her side.

Jennifer stopped at the corner, waiting for the light to change. A team of landscapers halted the blades on their mower, waiting for them to walk by. "Ya know those quizzes that you take on Facebook? Where they ask questions about your favorite color and smell."

Sam nodded.

"Time and again, I'd see fresh-cut grass as a favorite smell option. I never understood that until this very moment. In New

Mexico, they landscape with rock. You don't have to water or trim rocks. So I never understood the addiction to this amazing fragrance of summer. Wow." She drew in a deep breath through her nose. "Now I get it. There's nothing quite like this scent. It smells crisp and fresh, just like I'd imagine the color green would smell like." She inhaled again. "It's addictive."

It was enjoyable to watch Jennifer experience something as simple as fresh-cut grass for the first time. Sam spotted a blooming lilac bush half a block away in the wrong direction, in the median between the sidewalk and the road. It was her favorite spring fragrance, and she wanted to share it. Hopefully, no one would mind if she stole a few blossoms. If Jennifer enjoyed the smell of fresh-cut grass, surely, she'd love the sweet scent of a spring lilac in full bloom.

"Let's go this way, a small detour from our detour." She led Jennifer down the sidewalk, pulled her small folding knife from her front jeans pocket, and cut a few of the tender branches from the tall bush. It was the deep purple variety, one of her favorites. She held it up to her nose and inhaled a fragrance unlike any other in the spring and way better than grass. She cut a couple more and made a small bouquet. "Grass has nothing on these. The blooms never last long enough for me." She handed the bundle of flowers to Jennifer. Memories of handing Kara a similar-sized bouquet of brightly colored spring tulips when they were first dating rushed to the forefront of Sam's mind. Sam shook off the guilt. This wasn't a date. She and Jennifer were amazing friends. She wasn't replacing Kara. The flowers didn't make it a date.

Jennifer held the small bouquet up to her nose and sniffed. Her eyes lit up. "Oh my, that's lovely. What are they called?"

"Lilacs. The bushes can grow quite tall. They only bloom in the early spring. Seeing you experience a Midwest spring for the first time reminds me why I love the area so much. When you've lived here for as long as I have, I guess you take things for granted." Same thing had happened in her marriage. Sam knew she'd grown complacent over the years. Looking back, she realized that they both had in some ways. Complacency didn't mean that they hadn't loved each other, just maybe forgot to say it often and show it more often. Sad part was, she hadn't realized it until Kara was gone, and it was too late to make changes. A fresh wave of guilt washed over her. When would this deluge of emotions relent?

"While the Southwest holds its own beauty, I don't think I fully understood how beautiful the Midwest would be. It's incredible."

And just like that, the switch flipped. The guilt subsided, and she felt alive again. Sam could have stood there all day watching her sniff the deep purple flowers. Jennifer plucked a bloom from the bouquet and tucked it above her ear. Sam held out her arm and enjoyed the warm fuzzy feelings when Jennifer tucked her arm into the bend of her elbow. She had to admit that this felt like a bit more than amazing friends. Jennifer had shared that she'd fought loneliness. Grief and loneliness plagued Sam too. Perhaps, this, whatever it was, was exactly the kind of friendship that they both needed right now. They made their way back up the street and returned to the original route to the hair salon.

The bell chimed when Sam pulled the glass door open. A young stylist with fuchsia pink streaks in her bobbed blond hair looked up from her magazine. "Hi, I'm Cassie, can I help you?"

Jennifer stepped forward and spoke. "Hi, Cassie, what haircut would you suggest for my friend here?"

"Come on over, let's see what you've got going on." She patted the back of the chair.

Sam took a seat in the barber's chair and removed her cap. Cassie ran her fingers through Sam's shorter, unruly waves. "Tried cutting it yourself, huh?" She chuckled. "I'm glad you left me enough to work with. You have very nice hair. What kind of style are you thinking of?" She caught Sam's eyes in the mirror before turning to Jennifer.

"I used to wear a short fade, but I'm not sure I want that anymore. What are some other options?" Sam asked. She didn't want to go home, stare into the mirror, and see herself as she had been in a life she'd never get back. Even the mullet would be better than that.

"Well, with your facial features, you could pull off a messy undercut or a taper cut or a full-on high and tight…"

Sam watched in the mirror for Jennifer's reaction to any of the suggestions.

Jennifer's eyes lit up. "What about a pompadour?"

"Oh, I like the way you're thinking." Cassie lifted the hair on the top of Sam's head. "There's enough left up here to pull off a pompadour. How tall?"

Jennifer tucked her fingers into Sam's hair. She lifted it at Sam's forehead. "I'm thinking more nineteen fifties Elvis when he had the soft, wavy pomp and less Johnny Bravo." She kept lifting Sam's hair.

Sam tried desperately to control the tingling shivers that ran down her spine. It was difficult to do while Jennifer kept combing her fingers through her hair. While her heart and spirit were sad and lonely, apparently, her body was starving for attention and affection. It responded to Jennifer's touch as if waking from a long, deep hibernation. Sam tried to breathe through it, hoping to keep the tingling flush feeling from creeping up her neck.

"Lucky for you, I love the old Elvis movies. I know exactly what you're saying. I can do that." Cassie walked over to the cabinet and picked up a nylon cape.

"What do you think?" Jennifer asked. She kept playing with Sam's hair, which made it difficult to think.

What did she think? Kara had cut her hair in that neat fade way back when she was in stylist school. Afterward, she'd told Sam how sexy she looked. She'd straddled her on the kitchen chair and leaned down for a passionate kiss. Sam had slid her fingers inside Kara's jeans, and then inside Kara. Their need had been insatiable back before their jobs and routine had taken over their lives.

She'd kept that same hairstyle all those years because after each cut, Kara would tell her that she was still just as sexy. She'd eaten the compliments up too. And then, Kara died. There was no one to feel sexy for. There was no one to dress up for. It didn't matter what she looked like because her heart had been shattered into a million tiny pieces. After that, worrying about her appearance hadn't been anything she'd wanted to deal with.

Until today.

For some reason, it was time. A pompadour would be a little longer than the fade. It would be different enough to not be looking back. If she didn't like it, she could just have it cut into what she was used to. Jennifer's fingers stopped moving in her hair, reminding her that she hadn't answered the question. Sam met her questioning eyes in the mirror. She wanted something new. It was time for a fresh start.

"I like the way Elvis wore his hair in the fifties. Let's do the pompadour."

Cassie wrapped the cape around Sam's neck and snapped it closed. Sam teared up when she shaved the hair from the back of her head. Part of the emotion felt like relief, but some of it felt like she was saying good-bye to the strands of hair last touched by her wife. Putting her emotions into words, even if in her mind, sounded ridiculous. It was hair, for God's sake. And yet, it was another task, event, or whatever she wanted to call it, where Kara was being replaced.

Before she knew it, Cassie was brushing the loose hair off her neck and removing the cape. "What do you think?"

She had to admit, it looked great. The sides and back were long enough to comb back but short enough that they didn't touch her collar or ears. Cassie put some gel in her hair and combed it up into the pompadour and messed it up slightly with her fingers.

"I like it. I like it a lot." She stood from the chair and turned to Jennifer. "What do you think?"

"I love it. Dare I say, I like it better on you than the fade, and that's saying something." She smiled back. "It suits you, Sam. It looks fantastic."

Sam nodded. It did suit her. Neat and trim with a touch of disheveled fun. She opened her wallet and gave Cassie enough for the cut and a nice tip. "Thank you for fitting me in."

"My pleasure." She handed her a business card. "Call me when you're ready for a trim."

"Will do." Whether she liked it or not, she now had a new hair stylist. Life was moving on without Kara.

When they were outside and halfway up the block, Jennifer spun and held up her hands, stopping Sam in her tracks. "You shut it down quickly, but I saw the emotion while you were in the chair. Did I push too hard? Did I overstep? Are you okay?"

The concern and the questions were exactly why Jennifer was becoming so important to Sam. She cared. She picked up on things that others wouldn't even notice. Sam shook her head. "No, you didn't push too hard. Not at all. You've been nothing but wonderful to me and for me."

A couple was walking up the sidewalk. Sam cupped Jennifer's elbow in her hand and guided her off to the side. "Yeah, there was emotion, another tiny good-bye, but because of you, I am recovering from it instead of it consuming me and taking me under. I'm good, really, I am. A little better each day, and you've been a big part of that. In fact, I think you're pretty great." Sam winked.

Jennifer's concerned expression turned into a sweet, caring smile. "You're pretty great too." Her eyes said so much more. "I can't get over how good that haircut looks on you. It's difficult to resist running my fingers through it. You're going to have to beat the ladies off with a stick!"

Sam easily recalled the feeling of Jennifer's fingers in her hair. It was a sensation that she'd remember for quite some time. Jennifer made her feel things besides sadness and feeling all of these new things felt good. "Come on, now that you can stand to be seen with me in public, how about we get to that greenhouse?"

Chapter Ten

Jennifer kept sneaking a peek at Sam. With the natural waviness to her hair, she had more of a James Dean vibe instead of early Elvis. Especially when she bent her neck down slightly and turned her head, which she did often because of their height difference. Holy sexy. Jennifer wasn't sure of what to make of these new feelings. She'd never found herself attracted to a woman before. The more time she spent with Sam, the more undeniable the attraction. Sam was sweet and thoughtful and smart and funny and so, so much more. The problem was, she had no idea what to do about it. It wasn't like she could ask Sam questions about all of these new feelings, or could she?

Before she knew it, they were standing in front of her apartment again. "Your chariot awaits." Sam unlocked the truck and opened the passenger door for her.

"Thank you." Jennifer climbed up into the seat and reached for her seat belt. Sam stood there for a moment as if there was something she wanted to say, but she simply smiled and closed the door before walking around to the driver's side.

Jennifer couldn't get enough of how sexy the new hairdo looked on her. "How far away is the greenhouse?"

"About fifty miles from here. It'll take just over an hour to get there." Sam pulled out of the parking spot. "Is that okay?"

"Absolutely. I'm yours for the day. I love a good road trip. I'm just surprised there isn't one closer." She'd have Sam's undivided attention for an hour each way. Now to figure out how to approach the topic of her attraction.

"There are several, in fact, but this one is special. You'll see." She had something up her sleeve, Jennifer was sure of it.

It wasn't long before they were outside of town on unfamiliar roads. The vast landscape of hills and valleys was breathtaking. Large swaths of farm fields that arched with the curve of the terrain were separated with patches of dense forest. It was the perfect thing to stare at while she figured out how to talk with Sam.

Her mind was completely blank. There were no words. How could she have no words? They talked all the time. They talked in the office each morning when they arrived at work. They ate lunch together every day and visited the entire time about anything and everything. They chatted on instant messenger if they were both online in the evenings. On the weekends, they typically spent both Saturday and Sunday together, talking almost nonstop. So why was she having such a difficult time with her words today?

She huffed and knew exactly why she was struggling with this conversation. It had been forever since she'd had someone like Sam in her life. Truth be told, she wasn't entirely sure she'd ever had a connection with anyone that came close to what she felt with Sam. What if Sam wasn't attracted to her? Was she willing to risk losing what they had by making things awkward, just because being around Sam made her all gooey inside? Besides, Sam was still very much in love with her late wife, and based on the emotions today, she wasn't ready for anything more than what they currently had. She'd have to continue to settle for her vivid imagination and self-gratification. My, oh my, what a vivid imagination she had when it came to what Sam would do to her naked body. Okay, this train of thought wasn't helping.

"Seems like you're a million miles away. Something on your mind?" Sam asked.

Jennifer twisted in her seat so she could see her better. There was a different way to go about this conversation. "When did you know you were attracted to women?"

"What? Seriously? That's what had you staring off into space?"

"Yes, seriously." Heat rushed to Jennifer's cheeks. Great, now she was blushing. *Ignore it and keep talking.* "I'm genuinely interested. Did you always know, or was it a discovery?"

Sam shot her a sideways look and a goofy grin. Jennifer was certain she saw right through her ruse. No doubt that Sam could read her like a book. "I can't remember the last time someone asked me that question."

"We don't have to talk about it if you don't want to. I guess I could ask someone else or check out a book from the library."

Sam laughed. Yep, she was on to Jennifer's little scheme of self-discovery. "No, no, I'll answer any questions you have. I'm prepared. Hit me."

"Same question: When did you know that you were attracted to women? Are you attracted to only women? Or do you find men attractive too? I mean, do you identify as a lesbian or…"

Sam held up her hand. "Whoa, easy there, one question at a time."

God, that haircut looked so good on her. Jennifer reined in her urge to run her fingers through it like she had in the salon. Good thing she was wearing her seat belt. It kept her on her side of the truck.

"Somewhere inside, I think I always knew, but I didn't consider myself a lesbian, and yes, that's how I identify. No, I do not find men attractive. That said, there are some knockdown gorgeous drag queens out there. I mean, wow."

"How'd you know? What was the deciding factor? I mean, what signs were there?"

Crap. There was that sideways look and goofy grin again. Busted. "Piper Ferguson."

"I'm sorry, did you say Piper?" Jennifer emphasized each P and laughed. "Seriously?"

"Do you want the scoop or not?" Sam's cheeks flushed. Embarrassed looked adorable on her.

Jennifer managed to contain most of her giggling. "Yes, please, continue your story about Miss Piper Ferguson."

"It was October. Homecoming. And I volunteered to help with the junior float. Piper's family let us use their pole shed and a hay wagon. We were about half finished. I showed up on a Saturday afternoon, and no one else was there to help. I was out there, all alone, cold, and annoyed, shoving differently colored Kleenex into molded chicken wire so it looked like carnation flowers that matched the diagram. I swear, I almost left, but Piper came through the door with two steaming mugs of hot apple cider."

Jennifer kicked off her sandals and twisted completely sideways. She leaned against the door and crossed her legs in front of her. The story had to be getting to the good part because Sam paused and licked her lips. "So Piper shows up with the cider?"

"She was way more"—Sam licked her lips again—"developed than any sixteen-year-old had the right to be. Every boy in school wanted to be her guy. I had an inkling that I wasn't like most of the girls because I too wanted to be Piper's guy. I dressed like the guys because that was how I felt comfortable. But that Saturday, Piper pulled me behind the float and planted a kiss on me that rocked my entire world."

She was so animated, Jennifer couldn't take her eyes off her. Her eyebrows shot up, and her chest rose and fell with each deep breath. Jennifer could picture it all in her mind. A young, rough-and-tumble, teenage Sam and a busty cheerleader type. Lip-locked, hands exploring all the curves. This was not helping her maintain self-control because at that moment, she wanted nothing more than to be Piper.

"We spent the next few hours on the hay bales behind that float. I explored, kissed, and touched every inch of Piper's body. She screamed out my name a couple times." Sam looked over and wiggled her eyebrows. "That experience was amazing, incredible, and so much more, that is, until Monday at school. She ignored me as if nothing had happened, and I'd never existed. She was all of my firsts, including my first heartbreak. Looking back, I get it. It was the eighties. No one was out. But after that Saturday, I knew, without a doubt, that I was a lesbian."

The effect that story had on Jennifer's body was real. Her attraction was amplified to the thousandth degree. She ached to share that kind of experience with Sam, and she wouldn't turn her away afterward. "I feel bad that she broke your heart."

"Ancient history." Sam threw up a dismissive wave. "I had a few more experiences the summer between high school and college that confirmed what I already knew. Then I met Kara. She was open and adventurous. I was hers for the taking after our first date."

Sun shadows flickering across the dashboard were reminiscent of the emotions that flickered across Sam's face with the mention of Kara's name. Tiny bits of happiness were replaced with deep, forlorn sadness.

Jennifer couldn't imagine what she was going through inside, still dealing with the loss of her wife. A sense of selfishness washed over her. It was too soon. The timing wasn't right. Today was not the day for this conversation.

"Any more questions about my sexuality?" Sam asked.

Jennifer shook her head. "No, I think you covered everything. Thanks for helping me understand." She tried to keep her voice light.

"I don't know who's more excited for the first release of your software changes on Monday: me, Mike and Kelly, or the clients."

Jennifer welcomed the change of topic. Maybe it would help her snap out of the desire to slide across the bench seat and ride shotgun with Sam's arm wrapped around her. She really had to get a grip. They were friends, and that friendship was one thing she was unwilling to risk. "I hope it helps with the stability and performance issues. I hate seeing you logged in all hours of the evening watching everything."

"If you see me logged in, then you're logged in too."

"Touché."

"The clients are already raving about the changes in the test environment. If they work half as good in the live environment, it will be a huge win. Thank you for seeing it through."

Jennifer nodded and stared out the window. "You know, I thought I'd miss the mountains when I came here. I assumed it would be flat farmland for miles. But this area isn't flat at all. With the tree's leafed out and the farm fields, it's so beautiful, especially with views like you have at your house for miles and miles."

"I can't imagine living anywhere else."

"I can see why." Jennifer reached over and touched her arm.

They came out of a valley and started climbing again. Jennifer looked out the side window and took in the breathtaking panoramic views. The headhunter had been right about the area being right out of a Lifetime special.

The truck slowed, and Jennifer turned to see why. "Is that a horse and buggy? Do they give rides?"

"Save your ticket money. This area is predominately Amish. They travel by literal horsepower. It's their way of life. I like to give them plenty of space so I don't spook the horses. There've been fatal crashes between the Amish and automobiles, and the Amish never win in those accidents."

Jennifer pulled out her phone to take a photo.

Sam reached across the truck and touched her arm. "No photos. They don't like their pictures taken. They believe that any painting or photograph promotes individualism. They're more focused on community and humility. Take a mental picture instead, okay? Today's about making new memories."

Jennifer turned and nodded. Sam was so thoughtful. She wasn't Amish, but she respected the culture enough to honor their values. Jennifer put her phone back in her purse and took in the mental image of the family in the buggy as they safely passed. They passed several more on the climb to the top of the bluff. All of it was such a new experience.

Sam flipped the blinker on and slowly followed an Amish family into a parking lot.

"So they park the horses and buggies right here with all of the cars?"

Sam laughed. "Yep. It's unsegregated. A parking lot for cars and buggies alike." She drove way out to a desolate area of the parking lot and backed the truck into a spot in the far corner of the very last row. Good thing it was a beautiful day for a walk. There wasn't a spot farther away from the entrance.

"Why'd you park way out here? There're a lot of open spaces."

"You'll see." Sam held out her arm and offered no additional information. Jennifer didn't mind. It was a beautiful day for a walk. She tucked her arm into Sam's, and they made their way toward the entrance.

A group of Amish people stood chatting just outside the gates. Jennifer couldn't get over the differences. She leaned in close. "Where do they buy their clothes?"

"They make them. It has something to do with modesty and their religion."

"So the Amish people live that differently and still interact with the modern people?"

"Money is money. I bet they take in enough in the spring, summer, and fall to sustain them all winter. You can't find healthier plants than at an Amish greenhouse. You can't find better baked goods than at an Amish bakery. I could go on and on. Cabinets, furniture, home construction. You name it. They are the best of the best and do it without modern conveniences like power tools and electricity."

"I had no idea." Jennifer felt like her head was on a swivel trying to take it all in. New Mexico offered Native American and Hispanic cultures which she'd been immersed in her entire life, but she'd never experienced anything like the Amish.

When Sam had invited her to go to a nursery, she'd pictured a single area full of plants. This was actually a series of several huge greenhouses linked by wide concrete paths. Perhaps living in a region with water created a vegetation demand that didn't exist in the Southwest. There were flowers everywhere. Some in baskets, some in pots, and others ready for planting. Jennifer loved bright, colorful flowering plants, especially if they offered a floral fragrance.

Jennifer tugged on her arm. "Can we look around in here for a moment?"

"Absolutely, anything you'd like."

"Do you think that these flowers would survive on my patio?" She picked up a brilliantly colored hanging basket.

"Not that one, the pot is too small. It will dry out too quickly. Over here." Sam tugged on her hand. "Impatiens will get root-bound in the smaller pots. These are deeper and hold much more soil, so they won't dry out as fast. You'll still have to water often since your patio gets sun for much of the day."

The scent of moist soil and flowers, so many flowers, teased her nose. Bright, bold, and beautiful colors. Based on what she read on the tag, her patio would be a perfect home for most anything she picked. She couldn't decide on which to choose and resisted the urge to get one of each. More and more, Minnesota was feeling like home. "There were always water restrictions at home, and besides, I wasn't there enough to take care of outside plants." She sorted through the larger hanging pots and found three.

"Wait here. I'll go get a cart."

Jennifer watched Sam try to make her way across the greenhouse to the nearest cart area. It reminded her of a game of Atari's *Frogger* from the early eighties. She stifled a giggle after a few close calls. When she was home free and on her way back, Jennifer added two pots of petunias to her three pots of impatiens.

"Is there anything else you'd like?" Sam asked. She'd come to the nursery so she could get some vegetable plants, and yet here she was, helping Jennifer shop. She was being the kind and thoughtful person who could capture Jennifer's heart.

"Do the potted tomatoes taste as good as the tomatoes on the vine in the store?"

Sam looked up from loading the last basket of flowers. "As good, no, more like a thousand times better. Come on, let's go get you a potted tomato plant." Sam got behind the cart and pushed it through the crowd.

Jennifer walked next to her with their arms hooked. It felt good to be connected in such a simple way. They walked side by side, up and down the vegetable aisles, pushing the cartful of flowers. Sam stopped for a few four-packs of tomato varieties to try in her raised beds, along with cucumber and pepper plants, and finally, a six-pack of bush beans. They browsed the other side of the greenhouse and found a five-gallon potted tomato plant for Jennifer's patio. It was going to be a jungle up there in the small space.

"I'm buying the plants. Ninety percent are mine, anyway." Jennifer pulled her card out of her purse. "You've been hosting all the weekends. Let me do this?"

"Okay, fine." Sam unloaded the cart. "It just means you'll have to come out and enjoy the fresh veggies with me."

"I won't turn that down." Jennifer wouldn't decline any invitation to spend time with Sam. The more time they spent together, the more she wanted.

"The bakery is on the other side of the parking lot. If you don't mind an extra trip to the truck, it would be easier to navigate without the plants. We can lock them up in the back seat while we browse the bakery."

"Sounds good. I don't mind the extra walk. It's beautiful up here." The truth was, Jennifer was enjoying the day and didn't want it to end. The bakery was much larger than anything she'd ever seen, and the smell, wow, the sweet scent of freshly baked bread and cinnamon was intoxicating.

Sam picked up a small arm basket and held it in her left hand. She held her right arm out for Jennifer. "So I don't lose you in the chaos."

Jennifer hooked their arms. "Can we go up and down each row?"

"Absolutely."

"Is there a limit?" Jennifer picked up a loaf of cinnamon raisin bread. "Oh, look, cherry pie."

"The only limit is to eat it before it goes bad. We can always come back. It's a beautiful drive and not that far from town." Sam picked up a tin of cinnamon rolls covered in cream cheese frosting and placed them in the basket beneath the cinnamon bread. "Although these are a must-have. Oh, and pumpkin bars. I don't care if it isn't fall. The pumpkin bars freeze well, so there's that."

Jennifer tried to add a loaf of freshly made sandwich bread to the basket and found that it wouldn't fit. She decided to carry it. "Okay, maybe this is enough for this trip. Remember, you said we can come back." Jennifer leaned into Sam.

Sam insisted on paying for their finds and carried the sack of treats in one arm and held her free arm out for Jennifer. *She must not mind being tethered.* Jennifer hooked their elbows and walked at her side all the way back to the truck, where she opened the passenger door to climb up inside.

"Oh, no. Not yet." Sam held up her hand to keep the door from opening.

What was she up to? She ushered Jennifer to the side and opened the rear passenger door, set down the bags, and pulled the cinnamon roll tin out and handed it over.

"Hold this, please."

Jennifer did as she was asked and watched to see what else Sam had up her sleeve. This must have been the "wait and see" part of the trip. Sam lifted the lid on a cooler and pulled out a small container of cream and then reached into a cardboard box on the floor in front of the back seat and pulled out a thermos, two plates, two forks, and two cups.

"Follow me." She walked to the back of the truck and lowered the tailgate. "Hop on up here." She held out her hand. Jennifer turned and planted both of her hands on the tailgate. One little bounce and she was seated, swinging her legs in the void.

"Is this something you and Kara used to do?" Jennifer regretted the question the second that the words escaped her lips. If it was something they'd shared, she wasn't sure she wanted to know. It would make this moment less special.

"Shopping for flowers in the spring? Yes, but we shopped at a different nursery, closer to town. One of her friends owns it." Sam set down the two cups, filled each with coffee, and added cream to one. "There's this small shop in town that sells treats from this specific Amish bakery but only in the fall. I look forward to them all year long. I was searching for a different nursery and found this place high up on the bluff. I had no idea that my actual favorite bakery was so close, and they're open year-round. Win-win. My favorite Amish treats and plants all in one. We both got to enjoy a new experience today."

Jennifer felt bathed in warmth, and it had nothing to do with the sun. Definitely a day of making new memories. She'd never felt more special.

Sam dished out a serving of gooey heaven onto each plate. She hopped up on the tailgate next to Jennifer and handed her a plate. The view was unbelievable. Rolling hills went on for miles. Horses and cattle grazed in lush green pastures. Now she understood why Sam parked way out here. It was perfect. More than that, it was sweet and romantic.

"Thanks for joining me today, Jennifer." Sam held up her cup of steaming coffee.

"Now I get why you parked way out here. Well played. I should be the one thanking you." She tapped the rim of her coffee cup to Sam's, took a sip, and set it down. "I'm dying to try this cinnamon roll. It looks decadent." She stuck her fork into the gooeyness and lifted a bite to her mouth. A moan erupted from deep in her throat. "Dare I say, this is so much better than savoring a Lonely Blonde."

Sam laughed. She took a bite. "I think it might be a tie. There's something to be said for savoring an ice-cold Lonely Blonde." She rested her plate in her lap. "Can I ask you something?"

"Always."

"Have you found happiness in being single?"

The question was surprising. Probably just as surprising as Jennifer asking Sam about her attraction to women. If she had asked that same question a couple of months ago, Jennifer would have been all in on having found happiness in being single. Being single meant that she could do whatever she wanted, whenever she wanted, without worrying about or considering someone else's feelings. More and more lately, that was no longer the case. Not that she felt like she had to consider someone else. It was quite the opposite, actually. Now she wanted to consider someone else. A very specific someone else.

She found it very difficult to get her off her mind. When she thought about doing something, she wondered if Sam would enjoy it too. She couldn't remember feeling quite like this with anyone else before. The connection, or attraction, was so much more powerful than anything else she'd experienced before. There was so much about her feelings that she still didn't understand. The honest answer to that question would have to wait until she had a better handle on her emotions.

"Wow, that's a good one." Jennifer took a bite and tried to figure out how to answer honestly without confessing her soul.

"You don't have to answer. I was just curious."

"No, it's a good question." Jennifer sipped her coffee. She looked off in the distance, still unsure how to answer. "Why do you ask? Are you finding happiness in being single?"

"I don't know if I'd call it happiness. Your friendship has made being single, being alone, much less daunting. I guess I'm learning to live with it." Sam ate the cinnamon roll piece off her fork.

Her response was worded perfectly. Jennifer could work with that. "All I can say is that the time I spend with you makes being single less daunting for me too."

Sam set down her coffee and plate. She wrapped her arms around Jennifer's shoulder and pulled her in for a sideways hug. The answer couldn't have been more accurate. For now, making single less daunting was enough.

CHAPTER ELEVEN

Two quick raps on Sam's office door interrupted her thoughts. Kelly popped her head through the opening. "Hey, hey, it's FriYay! God, I just can't get over how good that haircut looks. It's like a whole new you."

"Thanks. It feels pretty good too." More and more, she was feeling whole and new.

"Should we save you a seat at Talley's after work?"

"We'll find a seat if we swing by," Sam said and returned her focus to her screens.

The door latch clicked. That was odd. Kelly was usually much chattier. It was for the best. Sam had to focus on the final step linking the newly created cloud servers to the VPN tunnel that was already connected to the new client's fire wall. The link would allow the client to have an up-to-date local copy of some of the tables from the Walsh software database, which in turn would enable them to create their own custom reports without risking live data integrity. One wrong click and she'd have to start all over.

"We? Did you get married again and not tell me?"

Sam bolted out of her seat. Her heart hammered wildly in her chest. "Jesus, warn a person. I thought you'd left."

"I had a feeling you were getting in too deep. I'm worried about you, Sam." Kelly sat in Jennifer's empty office chair and rolled to the side of Sam's desk, essentially blocking her in.

Sam pasted the twenty-one-digit encryption key into the proper field and clicked connect. Fingers crossed it was all configured correctly. The link indicator turned green. Phew. Now all she had to do was to set up the database replication across the new tunnel. "What, exactly, worries you?"

"The *we* that you're referring to is you and Jennifer?"

Sam leaned back in her chair and didn't bother to hide her annoyance. "Yeah. *We* hang out on the weekends and sometimes after work."

"You're falling for her, aren't you? Not that I blame you. She's awesome, classy, and totally your type. One tiny issue, though, she has an ex-husband, not an ex-wife. I don't know that much about being a lesbian, but I'm pretty sure nothing good happens when you fall for a straight woman. That is, unless she swings both ways?"

Sam could hear Pat whispering in her ear: *Straight women are much like spaghetti. They're only straight until they get a little hot and wet.* At the moment, that was probably not the best response. The best response was honesty, not snarky sarcasm. "We're friends."

"Uh-huh. Keep telling yourself that. I see the way you look at her. It's much the same way you used to look at Kara. You adore her."

Sam did adore Jennifer. No doubt. Still, she couldn't imagine looking at anyone like she'd looked at Kara. Kara was her once-in-a-lifetime soulmate. "You don't know what you're talking about."

"Oh, I think I do."

"We're friends." As far as Sam was concerned, the line between friendship and something more had become quite blurry. Little things that Jennifer did had her wondering if she wasn't feeling the same way. Either way, it was something that she and Jennifer needed to figure out. It wasn't Kelly's business.

"So if I set you up on a blind date, with someone else who is totally your type, you'd go? Heather's been asking about you."

"The snowplow gal?" Sam rolled her eyes. Apparently, Kelly didn't know her well at all. Heather was definitely not her type. She was more accurate on her first guess. Jennifer was totally her type.

"Yes, the snowplow gal, who also landscapes in the summer. You'd know that if you ever went outside. She's cute, and she's a lesbian. So would you go out with Heather?"

"No, because I'm not dating. I never claimed to be dating. Besides, being lesbian doesn't make her my type. You are so out of touch. If Mike was dead, would you go out with Brent? He's a guy who's into women, he must be your type."

"Fair enough, I hear you, but be honest with me. It's no because you're already falling for Jennifer."

Whether or not that was the truth, Kelly was not the person who would learn about it first. "For the last time, we're friends. We hang out. What's the problem?" Why couldn't everyone back off and leave her alone? "First, you tell me that I'm too withdrawn and need to be more social. Now I'm being more social. I'm actually having some fun, and you're still not happy. What do you want from me?"

"It's not about what I want from you. It's about what I want for you. There's a difference." She leaned forward and rested a hand on Sam's arm. "The problem, Sam, is that Jennifer's a consultant who lives in New Mexico. She'll only be around for a few more months, then she'll be off to the next job. I'm afraid that you'll end up devastated all over again when she's gone. I don't think you're strong enough to survive another loss like that yet."

"It sounds like my problem, not yours." She didn't even want to consider the notion of Jennifer going back to New Mexico. Not yet. She couldn't imagine not having her in her life.

The office door burst open. "Sam, great news! The clients love my changes so far." Jennifer froze in the doorway. "Oh, I'm so sorry for interrupting. I'll give you two some privacy." She disappeared before Sam could say anything.

Given the choice, Sam would much prefer that Kelly had been the one to leave.

"You're glaring at me."

Kara had always said she'd never make a good poker player. Aggravation and defensiveness flared on the inside. Who did Kelly think she was? They'd always been friendly, maybe even work friends, but it wasn't like they were friends outside the office, other than FriYay happy hours and a few games of pool. She was the boss's wife. No more, no less. Jennifer already knew Sam way better than Kelly, and she'd known Kelly for the past twelve years.

Sam tried to soften her features. The look on Kelly's face said she'd failed miserably. "Kelly, this job kept me going after the accident. It gave me a reason to get up in the morning and push through the day when all I wanted to do was curl up into a ball and surrender. I appreciate everything that you and Mike have done for me. I appreciate the fact that you let me cancel my retirement date last summer. I appreciate that you two put up with me this past year. I'm sure I wasn't easy to be around. That said, my life is just that, my life. You don't get to decide who I spend time with outside of the office."

"Understood. I'll let you get back to work. Have a great weekend." Kelly stood, pushed Jennifer's chair back to its proper place at her desk and walked out. The door closed hard enough to rattle the glass.

Sam stared at her notes for setting up the database replication. Her ability to focus on something that important was long gone. It could wait until Monday. She typed up an out-of-office for her email account, picked up her coffee, and decided to call it a day.

Kelly's words stung, mostly because deep down, Sam knew there was some truth to them. What she felt for Jennifer had probably, okay, most likely, already crossed beyond the friendship zone. Why did everything have to have a label? She and Jennifer weren't hurting anyone. They were both living lonely lives. What was so wrong with enjoying each other's company? Even if she looked at Jennifer like she used to look at Kara, it didn't mean she was replacing Kara with Jennifer. Kara had been her wife for thirty-four years. Jennifer was an amazing new breath of air who expressed her feelings with gentle touches and who liked to walk arm in arm. The closeness felt incredible, and Jennifer had helped her with her grief more than anyone else.

Before she knew it, she was walking into Talley's. The bar was quiet. The lunch crowd had already left, and she had a couple of hours before FriYay happy hour started. Sam sat at the same corner seat at the bar as when she'd first met Jennifer not so long ago. She felt a tinge of guilt. Not because she'd left the office early but because she'd left without telling Jennifer that she was going or why she'd walked out.

"Hey, Sam, late lunch?"

Good, Steve was bartending today. "Hey, Steve. No food today. How about a shot of Jack and a Lonely Blonde on tap?"

"Coming right up." Steve set the shot glass in front of her and filled it to the brim with good ol' number seven. The next thing she knew, a frosty mug slid down the bar. Perfection.

"Excuse me, Sam, is it? Don't I know you?"

An older gentleman sat on a barstool close to the seats she used to sit in with Kara. He did look familiar, but she couldn't place it.

"The haircut threw me off, but your eyes give you away. Piercing blue, just like my sweet Cathy." The gentleman pushed his empty plate to the back edge of the bar and tucked a few bills beneath it. He stood and walked down next to Sam. He had creases in his jeans as if they'd been ironed. She'd seen that recently but still couldn't place it. "I'm Bill, from the grief group at the community center. If you're who I think you are, you left before you had a chance to share."

Aha. "Grief group wasn't really my thing. I didn't need more sadness."

"Fair enough. Indulge an old man. Would you tell me what brought you by that day?" He pulled the stool out next to her and sat. So much for some solitude.

"I think it was George who summed it up nicely. Probably because someone died."

"Ah, yes, good ol' George. He's had a rough go of it."

"Haven't we all?" Sam asked. "It was a grief group." Why, of all the days, did Bill have to be here, sitting at the bar? She could do without another opinion about how awful she was handling things.

"Indeed. Indeed. George lost his only child to leukemia, and shortly after, his marriage fell apart, his business folded, and he did a stretch living out of his car. Loss is tough enough, but losing a child, well, that creates a special kind of living hell for the parents."

"I can't begin to imagine," she said.

"You never told me what brought you in that day."

If nothing else, he was persistent. The kindness in his eyes reminded her of how Jennifer saw her, without judgment. What the hell, she might as well tell him. "My wife was killed in a car accident fifteen months ago. A friend told me that I was stuck and suggested I give grief group a try."

"Is that what has you sitting at a bar at two o'clock in the afternoon with a shot and beer?"

Sam thought about the question and was surprised by the answer. "Honestly? No."

"Not much of one for words, are ya?"

She'd never been much of one for words. She'd only ever found the ability to share anything and everything with two people: Kara and Jennifer. Sam twisted her stool slightly. "Okay, Bill, here's a question for you. Did you live here, in this town, with your wife Cathy?"

"Yes. We settled here shortly after we were married. We raised our boys here. This area's been home for more than fifty years. Why do you ask?"

"After you lost your wife, how did you deal with everyone expecting you to be the same person you were when your wife was alive and an everyday part of your life?"

He scratched the stubbly beard on his chin. "I'm not quite sure I follow."

"Did you have colleagues, friends, or couple friends that you and your wife spent time with? Dinners or game night or anything like that?"

"Yeah, sure we did."

"After your wife died, did you still hang out with the people who knew you with your wife, or did you make some new friends who know you as you are now, without the shared memories?"

"A bit of both, I suppose. I'm still not following. How about you just tell me what you're struggling with, and I'll see if I can't share some words of wisdom?"

She nodded and played with the napkin beneath her full beer mug. "My wife and I…our entire world existed in this area. We met in college, U.W. over in La Crosse. After college, we moved back here and shared an apartment for a short time with another couple, one of whom was my wife's best friend." She was surprised that her words weren't weighed down with grief. Sharing memories about Kara was getting easier. "We met a few other couples on softball teams and such over the years. Eventually, there were six to eight of us who got together almost weekly. Barbecues, holidays, game nights, stuff like that. They were all there at the funeral too, many of them spoke." Sam drew in a deep breath and waited for the heaviness of the memory. It didn't hit with the force she'd grown used to. "It was an entire day and evening of remember this or remember that until I couldn't take one more story about a time in my life that I'd never get back. After the funeral, I sort of pushed them away. I ignored the texts and calls until they stopped trying. I'd bump into them here and there shortly after the funeral, and it was more of the same. It was like we had nothing else to talk about, nothing in common, without my wife around. Did you have anything like that?" The ability to put all of that into words with someone she didn't know was as surprising as the fact that she wasn't sinking. Maybe she was too upset with Kelly to be consumed by grief.

"I think I know what you're saying. I take it you don't spend much time with that group of friends anymore?"

She shook her head. "Not really since the funeral. I bumped into Pat, part of that couple from college, at the grocery store a couple of months ago. She's the one who told me I was stuck and to try grief group or therapy or something."

"Sounds like she still cares about you. Did you try therapy when grief group wasn't a good fit?"

Again, she shook her head. "No. That day, after I walked out of grief group, I came here, to Talley's, and oddly enough, met a new friend. One who only knows me as I exist right now. There're no 'remember when' conversations or talking about how much she misses Kara. She's really helped me work through some stuff. We get along great."

"Then why are you sitting here all alone at two in the afternoon with a shot and a beer?"

Sam sighed. "Because as much as people keep telling me that they want to see me heal and move forward, I'm not so sure that's the case." She picked up the mug and drew in a mouthful.

"Well, now, let's pretend that I'm a dense old man and that I'm once again not following."

"I've worked for the same two people at the same small company for more than twelve years. My wife and I attended their children's weddings and went to each and every company outing and picnic. Small-world moment, the new friend that I met on the day of failed grief group is a consultant who accepted a contract at that very same small company. Actually, we share an office, my office." Another one of Jennifer's great ideas. It had been an adjustment at first, but now she couldn't imagine coming into work and not seeing her sitting in the desk right next to hers. "Today, one of the owners said she was worried about me. She thinks I'm falling in love with my new friend and thinks I'm making a huge mistake because I'll be all upside down again when her contract ends in a few months, and she leaves the state."

"I see."

"I bet you're sorry you asked. You could have just left me alone with my shot and my beer." Secretly, she was already glad he'd struck up a conversation. More and more, it felt good to talk things through. Another thing that Jennifer had helped her with.

"Well, the question begs to be answered. Are you falling in love with her?"

Well now, that was the million-dollar question, wasn't it? Hence, the desire to sit and ponder the entire conversation. There was no denying that she had feelings for Jennifer, but were the feelings that of a friendship unlike any other, or was there more to it? "Maybe yes, maybe no, hell, I'm not sure I can honestly answer. She's becoming very special to me. I know that I love spending time with her, and for the first time in over a year, I am feeling again. Feeling again feels really good. Is that so wrong?" It felt good to admit that truth.

"After a loss, feeling again is a wonderful thing. Does she have feelings for you?"

"Beyond friendship, I have no idea." Sam thought about the touches and the way Jennifer liked to "fix" her hair when it was messed up. The way her eyes lit up when Sam showed up unexpectedly or the way Jennifer leaned into her when they walked arm and arm. Then again, Jennifer had never talked about attraction, and they talked about everything. Sam sighed. "I know she cares about me and notices things no one else would, especially when a wave of sadness hits. We're getting to know each other. We're both alone, and it's nice not to be alone, especially when you really enjoy the person you're spending time with. We have fun together. We talk. We enjoy each other's company. Even if it's short term, isn't that enough?"

"What would you do if she left at the end of the contract?" he asked.

"I wouldn't stop caring about her. It's not like there aren't ways to communicate." Once again, she didn't want to think about it.

"Would you stay here or maybe see where the wind blows you?"

"I haven't thought about that. Sometimes, I do think of packing up and moving. A fresh start, ya know, somewhere where I'm not constantly reminded of how much my life has changed."

"What stops you from leaving? For that matter, what keeps you here?"

He was asking some doozies. What was stopping her from packing up and starting over somewhere else? Was it the house? No doubt, she loved her home. She'd been the one to design it. Was it the area? She loved that too: the lakes, the bluffs, the depth to the landscape and the changing of the seasons. She was enjoying them now more than ever because she was experiencing them for the first time all over again with Jennifer. This was home. Maybe she just needed more time to heal, and the old memories wouldn't feel so suffocating.

"Are you dating?" she asked Bill.

"Do you always answer a question with a question?" He chuckled. "Actually, I've been seeing a lady friend from church. I guess you could call it dating. She's a widow too."

"Did your buddies give you shit for spending time with your new lady friend?"

"No, actually, my best bud, Mark, sort of set us up. One day, after church, he invited me out for coffee and pie. His wife invited Maddie. That was our first double date. I walked her home afterward."

"Do you love her?"

He scratched the stubble on his chin again. He looked on, staring at everything and yet at nothing. "I care for her very much. Yes, I love her."

"Is it the same love you felt for Cathy?" She'd considered this question well before Kelly had burst into her office. Could she love another like she loved Kara? Or was everyone limited to one true love?

"Cathy and I shared a lifetime of memories. We were married for almost fifty-four years. We had children together. We shared some big wins and some big losses and somehow survived. I don't know that any love will be the same as what Cathy and I shared. That said, my love for Maddie isn't less, either, just a love all its own. I'll always love Cathy, just like Maddie will always love her late husband, Walter. I don't expect to replace him. Maddie has no intention of replacing Cathy. Neither one of us is trying to erase our pasts or each other's pasts, for that matter, but that doesn't mean we can't enjoy our future."

Profound relief washed over Sam. That made sense in an odd way, the notion of honoring the past and enjoying the future was comforting. It gave her hope. For the first time, she didn't feel like the rest of her life had to be sad and lonely. "How long after you lost your wife was it before you were able to enjoy a future?"

"Grief isn't a switch. You can't just turn it off. Think of it more like a dimmer light, the kind that's far too sensitive, and the slightest touch either blinds you or engulfs you in total darkness. At first, you spend much of your time battling the two extremes. Then you figure out the feel of the switch and can pinch it just right to adjust the light without the huge swings. To me, it sounds like that's where you are right now. Do you find that you're recovering just a little bit quicker these days?"

"Yeah, I do. Especially these last few months." There was a flicker of hope that she was coming out the other side.

"Since meeting that new friend?"

"Yeah." She smiled. "Since meeting that new friend. She's helped more than I could ever explain."

"Seems to me that she's exactly the kind of friend you need right now in your life. Your other friends just don't want to see you hurt, if that should happen. They're all protective of you. It just means that they care."

"Do you think I'll end up hurt?"

"What am I, a fortune teller?" He laughed. "Everything is a risk. Isolation certainly isn't the answer. I think a strong friendship is a great foundation and can withstand most anything."

"Ya know, for being a dense old man, you're pretty awesome when it comes to advice. Thank you for taking the time to help a confused soul. Can I buy you a drink?"

"Thank you. You're kind. I'll take a rain check on the drink.

Maddie is probably done with her ladies' luncheon, and I promised to be outside waiting."

"Please know that I appreciate your insight. I wish you and Maddie nothing but happiness."

He nodded and smiled. "You know where to find me on any given Sunday if you need an ear."

She nodded. Indeed, she did, but for some reason, she doubted she'd need him again. For the first time in a long time, she had hope. She didn't have to spend the rest of her life grieving and alone. It was okay to feel happiness again with someone special. She pushed the full shot glass and the mostly full beer to the back edge of the bar, tossed down a ten and a few ones. She wanted to get back to the office. Maybe she could clear the air with Kelly.

She didn't need to worry about that while enjoying the weekend with Jennifer. She still wasn't sure what Jennifer had up her sleeve. It was all very secretive. Whatever it was, they were certain to have fun.

CHAPTER TWELVE

If everything worked out as planned, this would prove to be a birthday weekend Sam wouldn't soon forget. Hopefully, in a good way. It was a miracle that everything had come together in the few days Jennifer had to pull it off. She hadn't even known that Sam's birthday was coming up until a card had been passed around the office for signatures.

For the past few months, Sam had gone out of her way to introduce Jennifer to the Midwest by way of so many amazing experiences and, in doing so, had created so many new memories that she'd cherish forever.

Her doorbell rang. Jennifer took a deep breath and opened it. Now was the moment of truth to see if she really knew Sam well enough to give her a fantastic birthday weekend full of new-to-her firsts. If nothing else, she wanted Sam to feel special because she certainly was special to Jennifer.

"Hey, you. Happy birthday." Jennifer greeted her with a hug. She caught a whiff of that same sexy scent from her suit jacket. What she wouldn't give to know what fragrance that was. "Did you get new jeans? Wow, they fit nice, very nice. You look great." Sam was wearing a cream, short-sleeved, collared button-down tucked into a pair of dark blue Levi's that showed off how tall and fit she was. Completing the outfit was a sharp-looking pair of western boots that Jennifer remembered admiring when she'd helped Sam switch bedrooms. To top it off, her leather belt matched the boots perfectly.

She looked hot. Jennifer was still confused by her attraction and found it more and more difficult to resist urges she'd never felt for another woman.

"Thank you." Sam pulled her out of her thoughts. "As always, you look absolutely amazing. I like your hair in a French braid. It's the first time I've seen it back like that, outside of your messy ponytails when you sleep over."

Jennifer enjoyed the compliments. She'd found herself taking extra time planning her own outfits to see Sam's response. Today's choice of a light cotton sundress with thin shoulder straps and modest matching pumps was every bit the simple winner she'd hoped it would be. "Thank you. Where's your stuff?"

"Everything I need fits in here." Sam turned to the side and showed off a black backpack slung over her shoulder.

"My, how differently we travel, my friend. Are you ready to go?"

"Sure, where're your bags? I'll help carry them down."

Ever since enchiladas night, Jennifer always came to Sam's house with all of the essentials; that meant two carry-ons, covering any need, always in the car. "They're already loaded." She picked up her purse, locked the front door, and tucked her arm into Sam's at the elbow. It was a simple touch that she looked forward to during the off-hours more and more.

"Do I get a hint as to where we're going?" Sam asked.

"Patience, dear friend. One birthday surprise at a time." When they got to the bottom of the steps, Jennifer pulled them to a stop. "Close your eyes for a few seconds. Please? For me?"

"You're not going to scare me, are you?"

"No." Jennifer tugged on her arm. "Come on, close them."

"Fine, they're closed."

She led Sam down the sidewalk a ways before guiding her to the street. "Slight step down...now." She tucked the key fob into Sam's hand. "Okay, open your eyes."

Jennifer held her breath with nervous anticipation as Sam scanned the area. She glanced at Jennifer with that adorable goofy grin and held up the key fob. She pressed the unlock button, and the dark purple four-door Jeep Wrangler Rubicon chirped.

Jennifer let out a sigh of relief when Sam's eyes lit up. "It's ours until tomorrow afternoon. I thought maybe you'd like to drive?" She was certain she already knew the answer.

Sam looked like a kid who'd woken up on Christmas morning to find every gift on her list beneath the tree. Her eyes sparkled with smiles. "Holy shit, are you serious? I've always wanted one of these. Oh, it has the convertible soft-top. Really, it's okay that I drive?"

Jennifer couldn't recall a time that she'd ever seen Sam so animated. "You're on the rental papers as an approved driver. I was so happy that they had one with the convertible. It's all you've talked about since they came out with that remote feature."

Sam ran around to the passenger side and opened the door for Jennifer. The smallest acts like that made her feel like an adored princess. She climbed up in and pulled her seat belt across her lap.

Sam skipped around to the driver's side. Surprise number one was definitely a winner. The deep purple color, one of her personal favorites, was icing on the cake. She released the soft-top clip above her sun visor, and Sam did the same. If Jennifer decided to stay in the Midwest, she'd seriously consider trading her car in on one of these, just so Sam would want to drive all the time.

She silently laughed at herself. *If she stayed.* Who was she kidding. She already knew she'd stay as long as she had Sam in her life.

"You'll let me know if it's too much wind, right?" Sam asked while pressing the button to fully open the top. It tucked nicely on top of the cargo space in front of the tailgate and spare tire.

"I'm prepared for the wind." Jennifer patted her braid.

"Aren't you clever?" Sam started the Jeep. "Where to?"

"It's already programmed into the navigation. Just follow the instructions." Jennifer pressed the go button on the map screen. "I also have my phone connected for an epic birthday playlist."

"You've thought of everything, haven't you?" Sam put the Jeep into gear, and they were on their way. "This is fantastic, thank you." She reached over and squeezed Jennifer's hand.

She squeezed back and didn't want to let go. After their conversation on the way to the nursery, she'd spent a fair amount of time online, trying to better understand sexual identity and sexual orientation and everything she could find about women loving women. None of which had ever been a topic of discussion when she was growing up. At fifty years old, she felt silly for not figuring this out sooner. Although it wasn't until she was fifty that a certain someone walked into her world and tilted it off its axis.

Now she was after all the information she could find to help her understand her undeniable attraction. It was as if she'd discovered a whole new world, and photos of masculine women helped her identify the type of women she was most attracted to. Sam was the sexiest woman she'd ever laid eyes on, and imagining her beneath the sheets had a profound effect on her body. Jennifer drew in a deep breath and let it out slowly. Now was not the time to entertain those thoughts.

The wind tousled Sam's hair, which turned her into the sexiest woman alive. She tapped the steering wheel to the beat of the obnoxiously loud music and sang along, Jennifer sang right along with her. Every single thing with Sam was so much fun. They fit together perfectly, and the time they shared felt effortless.

One thing kept Jennifer from confessing everything she felt: fear that there wasn't room in Sam's heart for her. The stories and the photographs had made it very clear that Sam's world still revolved around Kara. As much as she wanted to be loved and adored, she had no idea how to compete with a ghost for Sam's heart. The thought alone was almost more guilt than she could bear. Unless Sam opened the conversation or took that next step, she'd contain her urges and treasure what they had for as long as they had it.

Before she knew it, an hour and a half had passed, and they were pulling into a little town called Turtle Cove, Wisconsin. The signs on the side of the road were starting to give away the second phase of the surprise birthday weekend.

Sam followed the instructions into the hotel parking lot, driving slowly because people were walking all around them with large glasses of draft beer. Sam turned with a smirky smile and a raised eyebrow. "What is this?" she asked while spinning every which way in her seat to look around.

Jennifer beamed with pride. Sam's expression said it all: Her idea was a winner. "From what I understand, it's just a good ol'-fashioned Wisconsin beer festival. Happy birthday, Sam."

"Shut up! Are you serious? I've never been to a beer festival.

I mean, we had block parties in college, but not a real, sanctioned community booze festival. This is awesome!"

"It'll definitely be a first for me too. I like that we get to share new things together." More memories to treasure. She took a picture of Sam behind the steering wheel and filed it under favorites. That was a keeper.

"Me too. You couldn't have picked a better birthday activity." Her smile was ear to ear. Winner.

With two clicks, they secured the top back in place. Despite it being her birthday, Sam insisted on carrying her backpack and Jennifer's two small suitcases. Yup, she was spoiled rotten.

The hotel had her reservation on file, but they'd oversold and only had one room with two queen beds instead of the adjoining rooms she'd reserved. Sam shrugged it off and joked that it wouldn't be the first time they'd slept together.

Jennifer, on the other hand, was a jumble of emotions. She forced herself to get a grip. It was Sam's birthday, and there were two beds. Not a problem. Within minutes, they had a keycard and a map of the festival activities. They dropped the luggage, and Jennifer swapped her heels for a pair of sandals. It was time to head out in search of lunch and an ice-cold beer.

"What made you think of this?" Sam asked on their way out of the parking lot.

"On the first day we met at Talley's, Steve said that some Wisconsin town imported Fulton Lonely Blonde for their annual beer festival?"

Sam tilted her head down with that seductive, James Dean smile. "You kept that tucked away all this time?"

"Don't give me that much credit. I remembered we had some conversation that seemed to really interest you that day, and it had something to do with the lovely Lonely Blonde that made you moan. I had to hunt Steve down to get the specifics. Then I did some mad googling." She tucked her arm into Sam's at the elbow and leaned in close. "I take it you approve?"

"Oh, I more than approve. This is amazing." Sam leaned her head against Jennifer's.

There were those butterflies again. She drew in a deep breath. She did not want to risk ruining what they had. She cared too much about Sam to push her into something she might not be ready for. Even if this was all they'd ever have. It was wonderful and more than enough.

"Oh, Sam, look, fry bread. Have you ever had it? It's one of my favorites."

Sam laughed. "I wasn't born under a rock. I bet it goes perfectly with an ice-cold beer."

They each ordered a Navajo taco with beef instead of the traditional mutton but with all the fun taco fixings. After a bite, Sam studied the festival map. "Okay, it looks like we can find a Lonely Blonde just a few carts up, and later, we have to get a brat. It's a Wisconsin thing."

"Deal. Let's go find the beer and a spot in the park to sit and eat."

Once beverages were secured, they found an empty picnic table. Sam sat next to Jennifer instead of across from her. Her heart did the pitter-patter of a teenager. Off in the distance, she heard the various bands warming up.

"Thank you for this. You've made my birthday so very special. Already quite memorable." Sam leaned over and bumped Jennifer's shoulder. At some point, that had become their little sign of affection, like a sideways bump hug.

"I'm glad you like it so far. You've done so much for me, more than you know. I wanted to say thank you for being who you are. I treasure you and what we have." She raised her red Solo cup. "Happy birthday, Sam."

Sam tapped her cup. When they finished eating, they made their way around the square, arm in arm, checking out the bands while sampling different beers and various treats. The first band was a bit too indie for them. The second, on the next corner stage, was much more fun, performing covers of upbeat country songs. There was a large swath of grass roped off in front for dancing. At least thirty people were already moving to the music and laughing. Jennifer hadn't danced in forever. It looked like so much fun.

"Do you want to go up there and dance?" Sam asked.

For some reason, the question surprised her. "Could we?"

Sam grabbed her hand and led her out to the dance floor. The next song was a Darius Rucker, "For the First Time" from the album *When Was the Last Time*. It couldn't have been more appropriate. Everything about her time with Sam was full of firsts.

Sam pulled her in close. "Do you two-step?"

"I don't think I ever have." Jennifer laughed. "I'm willing to try."

"Follow my lead." Sam placed her right hand behind Jennifer's left shoulder. "Put your left hand up on my bicep. Consider it a guide." Sam took her right hand and held it about shoulder height, a little off to the side. "I'll step forward with my left foot, and you go back with your right. Do the same with the other foot. Two fast steps and two slow steps. Ready?"

Jennifer smiled and nodded. She was not at all ready, but she wasn't about to admit it. As it turned out, Sam was the perfect partner and guided her with a soft, leading touch. Holy hell, resistance to her feelings was futile. The more time she spent with Sam, the harder she was falling for her. If what they had was enough, then why, oh why, did it keep getting better and better?

"Ready for a spin?" Sam asked. She spun her out and pulled her back in close.

Jennifer stayed in closer. She could hear Sam singing along, especially the chorus. She could take a lifetime of firsts with Sam. She wanted so much to lift up on her tiptoes and whisper her secrets into Sam's ear. Confess everything. Her wants, her desires, her love. Holy hell was right. For once, Sam seemed to be having fun and not grieving for her wife. There was no way Jennifer could hit her with all those new feelings. Not today. Not this weekend. She had to keep it together and get a grip. She stayed in the moment and danced, savoring their first.

Way too soon, the song ended, and a few notes of a slow ballad started to play. "Let Me Down Easy" by Billy Currington. It was perfectly romantic. She knew the words by heart. It was everything she'd been feeling and everything she wanted to say. Everything. She didn't want to leave the dance floor. She looked up into Sam's eyes and lifted her arms around Sam's neck. Without a word, Sam pulled her in close, and they swayed to the opening beats. It was magical.

Jennifer lifted onto her toes and cupped the back of Sam's neck. She held on and sang the entire first verse and chorus into her ear. Then, to her surprise, Sam leaned down, wrapped her arms around Jennifer's back, and sang the entire second verse and chorus to her.

If she didn't know better, Jennifer could have sworn she was in the dreamiest, most romantic moment of a Lifetime special. It was everything. Their bodies touching almost head to toe, she sang the last seven lines to Sam and heard Sam singing the same lines to her in a slightly deeper voice. Pitch-perfect. Amazingly wonderful and over way too soon.

The song ended, and a fast beat song had people filtering off the dance floor around them. Disappointment washed over Jennifer. What she wouldn't give for another meaningful ballad.

"I don't know the steps to this one," Sam said when people migrated into position for a line dance.

Jennifer wanted to release the pent-up feelings she'd been holding inside. She wanted to confess her deepest desires, especially in light of the fact that Sam knew all the words to the song Jennifer played on repeat when she was daydreaming and pining…for Sam. Then she reminded herself, today was Sam's day. She'd planned this entire weekend *for* her. She drew in a deep breath and savored the memory of the most romantic slow dance ever.

But the night was still young, and Sam had sung the song to her too. Maybe, just maybe, she'd be the one to take that next step.

"Me either. I'm thirsty. How about a refill?" Jennifer tucked their arms together. It was becoming their thing, and she loved it. For right now, it had to be enough.

"Deal. We can check out the other bands and see what they're playing."

"I like it." She needed to catch her breath because all she wanted was to know what a kiss from Sam would feel like. All she knew was that it felt like she was falling head over heels for Sam and had no idea what to do about it besides wait.

With two fresh beers, they made their way to the next corner. This band was more of an old-fashioned rock band covering seventies hits. They stood off to the side and listened to a couple. It was okay, but nothing they could dance to in the way Jennifer wanted. "How about one more beer?" She turned her empty cup upside down.

"Sounds good. Would you like to see what the last band is playing?"

She nodded. She'd stay out here all night if she could enjoy a stroll to the last stage, the park, or wherever else. To her surprise, the last stage was home to an eighties cover band. She tossed back the rest of her beer and waited for Sam to do the same, then pulled her onto the dance floor. The band was really good, with male and female singers covering all her favorite songs.

Sam didn't seem to mind. She was smiling and dancing and singing along too. They danced fast, and every so often, they had the chance to dance slow again. Something about the look in Sam's eyes when they danced close gave Jennifer hope that she was struggling with her feelings too. Maybe it wouldn't be so long before Sam was ready to experience another first, a first kiss, with her.

Way too soon, the band called it a night. The beer festival was over. Disappointment washed over Jennifer. Their chance for another head to toe, full-body slow dance had been dashed.

Sam held her arm out, and Jennifer accepted the needed contact. "Other than the country band, that was the best of all," Sam said on their way back to the hotel.

"That Billy Currington song is my new all-time favorite." Jennifer leaned in close. It was her favorite because it was everything she'd been wanting.

"Mine too." Sam wrapped an arm around her shoulders. It was surprising how wonderful it felt to be snuggled up against her. She wrapped an arm around Sam's waist and savored the walk back to the hotel. How on earth was she going to control herself in the same room with Sam? She'd simply have to. She'd already decided that tonight wasn't the night for a love confession.

She ran out to find ice while Sam jumped in the shower. She didn't dare stay in the room. She'd had a little too much to drink and didn't trust herself to not join Sam beneath the steaming hot water. When she returned, Sam was sprawled on one of the two beds in dark purple—of all colors—fitted boxers and a white tank top.

Oh, holy hell yet again. How was she supposed to resist that?

It was the first time she'd seen her in such form-fitting clothes. Sexy was an understatement. Jennifer set down the ice and went into the bathroom for an ice-cold shower. Something had to help.

Feeling refreshed and a bit more in control, she walked out with her damp hair combed out, wearing a silky top and matching shorts. There was still a part of her that hoped maybe, just maybe, she'd be irresistible. The whiskey bottle she'd set out as a nightcap gift was on the dresser, still full.

"That's my favorite, thank you. I thought about opening it, but I've already had too much to drink. Ice water?" Sam asked. She held one out for Jennifer.

That was probably best. She'd also had a fair amount to drink, and while she didn't feel the buzz anymore, she didn't need more liquid courage urging her to cross a line that couldn't be uncrossed. But my, oh my, how she was tempted to straddle Sam and take a leap of faith.

"Thank you, Jen, for making this an amazing birthday," Sam said, still lounging on the queen-size bed, her back against pillows propped up on the wall. She looked sleepy and sexy.

Jennifer tapped her glass to Sam's. "It was sincerely my pleasure." The understatement of the year. She'd savor each of the memories made on this night forever. She took a drink.

Sam did the same and set the cup on the side table. She adjusted her pillows and slid into the covers. Jennifer looked at the empty bed that was still made. She'd held back her confessions because Sam deserved a day without grief and stress, but that didn't mean she couldn't snuggle with the birthday girl. Right? No pressure there.

She threw caution to the wind and crawled into the queen bed next to Sam. "I know I have my own, but if you don't mind, I'd like to sleep here with you tonight."

"I don't mind at all." Sam rolled over on her back and extended her arms. Wow, more than she'd hoped for. Jennifer snuggled in close, her head on Sam's shoulder and her hand on Sam's chest, just below her neck. Sam reached over and turned off the light. In the darkness, Jennifer felt Sam's arms wrap around her and hold her. Dreamy. "Good night, Jen. Thanks again, for an amazing day."

"Good night, Sam."

Jennifer tried to muster up the courage to confess a tiny bit of truth. She'd rehearsed it in her head the entire time she was showering. *Sam, the words in that Billy Currington song, I feel each of those lyrics deeply, about you, and I don't know what to do with that.* If nothing else, it would open up the conversation, but was she ready to let that cat out of the bag? Maybe, after an entire day of drinking, she should wait. Sam's breathing changed, and in that moment, the decision was made for her.

But how could she just fall asleep like that? Maybe Jennifer had misread things, and the dance didn't mean that much to her. Or was she still so in love with her wife that all they'd ever be was friends? The thought created a knot in her stomach. She twisted a bit to roll over and go to the other bed, but Sam tightened her arms. If this one night was all that she'd get, then so be it, she'd take it. Jennifer snuggled in closer and drifted off to sleep, wrapped up in Sam's arms.

Chapter Thirteen

It had been two days, and yet, Sam kept replaying the morning after her birthday over and over in her head. She'd really screwed up. When she'd woken up that morning, Jennifer had her hand up along the side of Sam's neck. It had felt wonderful.

Until Sam had realized that her hands were in some very inappropriate places. The arm that Jennifer was curled up in was wrapped so Sam's hand lay beneath that silky top, cupping Jennifer's breast. She'd felt the edge of her nipple rub against her palm with each breath. Sam's other arm crossed Jennifer's leg—that was draped across her body—and her hand was beneath Jennifer's silky shorts, cupping her bare ass. It had started as the best dream in a long time. At least until she'd woken up, and then, she was mortified.

She had held her breath while carefully extracting her hands, desperately hoping beyond all hope that she wouldn't wake Jennifer. Once her hands were in a more appropriate location, she'd carefully pulled her arm out from beneath Jennifer's neck and head and had gotten out of bed. That wasn't something a person should have done to a dear friend, even if it had been in her sleep.

Sam had gotten dressed and went down to the lobby for a cup of coffee. When she'd returned, Jennifer was already up and dressed. They'd left a few minutes later. The excuse was that Jennifer had wanted to get the Jeep back to the rental agency before the one o'clock deadline. The drive back had been awkward and quiet. Sam was certain she'd really fucked up.

Part of her thought she should avoid Jennifer this week, and part of her couldn't possibly imagine a week or even a day without seeing her. That second part was winning by leaps and bounds. The night of her birthday, that dance, and later, sleeping with Jennifer curled up in her arms had made one thing very clear. Sam wanted more than just friendship and definitely more than simple companionship. The big question was, what did Jennifer want? Replaying that slow dance in her mind, how Jennifer had sung to her, had her hoping that maybe she wanted more too. They needed to talk. Not doing so was making it impossible to concentrate on work or anything else, for that matter. Ten hours in the office already today and she'd accomplished much of nothing, except sneaking a peek across the room at a certain someone every few seconds. Waiting until next weekend wouldn't work. It was only Tuesday. The weekend was too far away.

Jennifer let out a frustrated growl. "This claims module is kicking my ass. The code's all over the place. It's calling objects that I can't even find. Who wrote this shit?"

Sam walked around the desk and stood next to her. She swallowed against the nervous energy and tried desperately to find her normal voice. "Walk away from it for the night. If you don't have any plans, maybe you'd like to come out to the house? I could pick up a pizza."

Jennifer slowly spun her chair. She looked tired, as if she hadn't been sleeping well. "I'd like that."

"I could follow you to your apartment, and we could take my truck if you'd rather not drive."

Jennifer was quiet for a moment. The look on her face had Sam worried she was changing her mind. "I don't mind driving." She closed the lid on her laptop.

"Perfect. If you're up for a short walk, swap the suit and heels for casual with sneakers. There's something I'd really like to show you." Sam slid her laptop into her briefcase, grabbed her coffee cup, and they walked out together.

She was super excited to see Jennifer's reaction to her surprise. The fireflies were finally out. She'd noticed them last night while sitting on the dock at the edge of the pond contemplating what to do. Jennifer had mentioned that she'd never seen them. Sam had been shocked. She couldn't imagine having never experienced a warm summer evening without the brightly lit beetles. Knowing that it would be another new experience, Sam wanted to be there when she saw them for the very first time. She couldn't wait to see her reaction.

The sun was quickly dropping in the sky when Jennifer finally pulled in. Sam thought for a moment that she'd changed her mind and wouldn't show up at all. The pizza boxes sat on the counter, probably cold. Sam didn't care about the food. She had a hunch that Jennifer knew exactly where her hands had been at the hotel, and she needed to apologize. Maybe seeing the fireflies would help ease into that extremely awkward conversation.

Sam walked out through the garage. Jennifer was just sitting there in her car. She walked up to the driver's window and tapped on the glass. Jennifer opened the door and put one sneaker-clad foot on the driveway.

"Hey, you." Sam held out her hand. "If you're not starving, maybe we could go on a short walk first?"

Jennifer nodded. "I don't know why, but I'm nervous."

"Me too." Sam led her around to the back side of the house. The sun was dropping quickly, and she really wanted to be by the pond when the landscape lit up. "I know that I owe you an apology and an explanation."

"You don't owe me anything, Sam. It was entirely my fault, not yours. I'm the one who owes you an apology. I don't blame you for being upset and wanting to take off in the morning. Maybe I drank too much, I don't know. What I do know is that I had no business climbing in bed with you Saturday night. I didn't mean to make things awkward or uncomfortable."

"What? No." Sam stopped just shy of the pond. "You didn't make me feel uncomfortable. Everything about Saturday and Saturday night was perfect. I was the one who crossed the line. Even if I was sound asleep when I did it, you deserve better from me."

"What are you talking about? What did you do in your sleep?"

Sam squeezed her eyes shut. Shit, now she'd gone and done it. She'd confessed to something Jennifer had slept through. She wasn't about to lie about it now. "Jennifer, I overstepped. Sunday morning, when I woke up, my hands were beneath your clothing."

She drew in a deep breath and let it out slowly before admitting the worst part. "Cupping certain parts of you. That's why I left the room. It had nothing to do with you crawling in bed with me. I was embarrassed. I'm so sorry. Please forgive me. It was wrong and completely inappropriate." Sam stared at Jennifer, trying to read her reaction.

Jennifer stared at her for a moment too. "And I missed it? God, I wish I'd been awake for that."

Sam's heart skipped a beat. Judging by Jennifer's expression, she was disappointed, not upset. Sam breathed out a sigh of relief. "I thought you were awake. I thought you were upset, and that's why you barely spoke to me that morning. I thought that was why things have been awkward between us."

"No. I had no idea. I've been a little distant because I felt horrible for crawling in bed next to you. I shouldn't have pushed myself on you like that. These feelings that I have for you are all so new to me. What I feel for you keeps growing deeper and deeper, and that song, that goddamned amazing song. I sang it to you, and you sang it to me, and I lost all self-control. I know you're still grieving. I know you need time. That said, I'm not sure how to rein in my feelings for you, Sam. I feel every single word of those lyrics on such a deep level, and I don't know what to do about it. I haven't felt like this before about anyone."

"What? Really?" Had she just heard what she thought she'd heard? Jennifer had feelings for her? There was hope for something more amazing than the friendship they already had?

"Yes, really." Jennifer blushed and buried her face in her hands. "I wanted to tell you that night, but you were having so much fun, and it was your birthday. I didn't want to do anything that would cause you stress or bring up a wave of sadness. I planned the weekend so you could cut loose and have some fun. The last thing I wanted to do was add pressure or make you feel uncomfortable."

Sam was speechless. How had she missed the signs? She wished, oh how she wished, that Jennifer had confessed everything on that dance floor. She would have skipped the rest of the night to know how Jennifer felt. "And here I've been telling myself that our friendship had to be enough. That's not to say that I don't have feelings for you because I do. Every single word of those lyrics resonates deep in my soul, but I never imagined you would feel the same way. All this time, I thought you were into guys. You never said anything."

"I thought I was too until I met you, Sam. I catch myself daydreaming about you more often than I care to admit. I've wondered what it would feel like to kiss a woman...not just any woman. You. I've wonder about your touch and what it would feel like to touch you. I'm a fifty-year-old woman, and I feel like a teenager experiencing that terrifying, spine-tingling excitement for the very first time. I've never felt like this before. Never, ever, like this."

"What if you don't like how it feels? My kiss, my touch?" It was one of a thousand questions swirling around in her head. "I don't want to lose you."

Jennifer looked up. "What if I do? Kara was your world. Is there room in your heart for me?"

Sam stepped forward, cupped Jennifer's face, and leaned in close. Jennifer tilted her head and wrapped her arms around Sam's neck. Her lips were warm and velvety soft. She parted them, and their tongues touched for the first time. Jennifer moaned, and fireworks erupted everywhere in Sam's body. She bent slightly and lifted Jennifer into her arms.

Jennifer's legs wrapped around her waist. Sam supported her with one arm and caressed her back with the other. A tender, emotional kiss became heated and passionate, as if she was expressing everything she'd been feeling in that one first meaningful, memorable kiss. Sam lost herself in it, lost all track of time and had no idea how long she'd been standing there with Jennifer in her arms. When she lifted her head slightly and broke the kiss, her legs were shaking from excitement, not the fatigue of supporting their melded bodies. Her heart was beating wildly. She was breathless; they both were.

Slowly, Jennifer released her legs. Sam stooped until her feet were once again on the ground. She was glad it happened like that, and she didn't have time to overthink or worry about guilt and comparisons. Kissing Jennifer had been beautiful and completely unique.

Jennifer touched her lips. "Wow."

"Wow, indeed." Sam leaned down and touched their foreheads together.

"It might sound silly, but I've missed you. For the last two and a half days, I've missed you so much." Jennifer stepped in close and held her.

"I missed you too. From here on out, let's agree to talk right away. I don't want things to be awkward like that ever again."

"Agreed. But, Sam, the mosquitos are eating me alive. Can we go back up to the house?"

Sam looked out across the field and smiled. Good, they hadn't missed it. "Before we do, would you turn around for me?"

"What?" Jennifer released her and spun in Sam's arms. She gasped. "Wow, that's beautiful. What is it?"

"A field full of fireflies. They emerged in droves last night. Glowing while dancing around the pond. It's the biggest turnout I'd ever seen. I think it's all for you." The entire field was covered in a brilliantly sparkling dance, like fairy dust falling from the sky. "That's how I feel inside when I'm with you. Pops of electricity anywhere and everywhere. I wanted to be with you when you saw them for the very first time."

"It's every bit as magical as you described. Like something right out of a fairy tale." She leaned back in Sam's arms. "How long will they be here?"

"For the summer, mostly at dusk."

"So any evening at sunset, we could walk out here and watch them dance for us?"

Already, the spectacular show was starting to spread out and fade. "Any evening, every evening, whatever you'd like."

"What makes them glow?"

"The desire to find a mate."

Jennifer stood still, wrapped in Sam's arms for a few more minutes. Sam wished she could see her face, but holding her like this worked too. It was almost completely dark when she twisted around. "Even if you can't see it, you should probably know that I'm glowing…hoping to lure you in with my light."

Without saying a word, Sam scooped her up. Jennifer's squeal made it all the more fun to carry her to the house. Having Jennifer's arms around her neck and her head nuzzled close was an added bonus. She set her on the driveway, collected the two suitcases from the car, and followed her into the house, pausing only to close the garage door. Once inside, Sam set the two suitcases down and kicked off her shoes, placing them next to Jennifer's sneakers. The house was dark except for the dim light above the stove.

"I'm a jumble of jitters again," Jennifer said. "Excited, happy, and surprisingly nervous." She stepped into Sam's arms. "I swear, I'm not a tease."

"That thought never crossed my mind. Hey, whatever happens next happens at our own pace, okay? We set the rules, no one else." Sam held her for a few minutes. "Would you like to have dinner with me?"

"What, like a date, tonight?"

"A real date can happen another night, dress clothes and all. Tonight, let's keep it simple. I have pizza and beer." Sam held her close and hoped she wanted to stay.

"Now you're speaking my love language."

Sam walked over to the fridge and grabbed a couple of beers. She tucked a bottle opener in her back pocket, wetted a dish cloth, and rung it out. Finally, they picked up the two boxes of pizza. "Follow me."

Kara had never been in love with the screened-in deck off the primary bedroom. In her opinion, it was too small for entertaining, a useless space. Sam liked to work out there in the evenings when the weather was nice, or she'd sit and enjoy the view. Eventually, she'd adopted the space as her own, which made this idea feel even more right.

She went out through the dining room and in through the door from the deck. She used her elbow to flip on the light next to a dimmer switch and thought briefly about her conversation with Bill. Recently, especially the last month, she'd felt like she'd reclaimed a bit of control instead of having grief dominating her existence. She set the pizza on a chair and wiped the dust off the tabletop. She walked over to the porch swing, wiped the dust from it as well, and wiped and fluffed up the comfy pillows tied in place on the seat and backrest. After a quick check for spiders, she turned back. "How about we enjoy dinner with a view? There's a meat-lovers and a supreme. And look, there are still a few fireflies out by the pond dancing for us. Bonus, no mosquitos."

Jennifer's smile said it all. "I've never seen this space. I love it. This couldn't be more perfect."

Sam opened the beers, and they each grabbed a slice. Once Jennifer was seated in the swing, Sam dimmed the light and sat next to her.

"Do I get to snuggle with you in bed tonight?" Jennifer asked around a mouthful.

"I'd like that very much. I'll try to behave."

Jennifer laughed. "If you don't, at least wake me up so I can enjoy it." She slid to the center of the swing and leaned against Sam.

Without saying a word, Sam tapped the neck of Jennifer's beer with her own and took a sip. The ice was broken. Truths were spoken. And nothing more was needed to make the evening perfect.

Chapter Fourteen

The subtle squeak of the chains supporting the porch swing was every bit as soothing as the gentle, swaying motion. Jennifer nuzzled in Sam's arms, replaying every moment of that amazing first kiss. Her lips still tingled, and her body buzzed for more. She tried to remember what she'd felt like when she'd been with her husband for the first time. Had she been this nervous with wonder and anticipation? Even though he'd been her first, she didn't remember feeling anything like this. Gender aside, Sam was someone entirely different. Already there was an emotional connection that she'd never had with anyone else. A connection that seemed to amplify every touch with an undercurrent of electricity.

"Did you get enough to eat?" Sam asked.

"I did. Thank you."

"Are you ready to go inside?" Sam's breath tickled her ear.

Jennifer nodded and stood from her cozy spot. Nervous butterflies fluttered deep in her belly. She picked up the pizza boxes and waited for Sam to get the door and lights. Once they were inside, the light above the stove illuminated a dim path into the kitchen. Sam set the empty bottles on the counter and tossed the dish cloth into the sink. She took the pizza and found room for it in the fridge. After she closed the door, she turned and held out her hand.

The moment Jennifer rested her hand in Sam's, her body buzzed as if she'd been plugged into a wall socket. Sam stepped in closer. Jennifer wrapped both arms around her neck. Consumed with emotion and desire, she yearned to feel Sam's touch everywhere on her body. It was as if a dam had burst wide open, and the floodgates of desire could no longer be controlled.

Sam kissed her with a passion that set her on fire from head to toe. She lifted her onto the island counter. Jennifer pulled her in close with her legs. She needed the pressure of Sam's body against her own and tilted her hips back slightly for better contact. Sam responded by cupping her ass with strong hands and holding her in just the right place. It felt incredible.

Jennifer's gasp broke their fiery kiss. Sam nibbled a trail to her collarbone. It was as if she had a magical map guiding her to Jennifer's favorite places to be kissed and touched. She leaned back and cupped Sam's head. Everywhere she touched created a sensation better than the last, a sensation she was certain couldn't be topped, at least until she felt the next touch, kiss, or nibble. If they didn't move off the counter, Jennifer would beg to be taken right there.

"Can I take you to bed?" Sam asked in a breathless voice. She must have read her mind.

Jennifer nodded and released her.

"No. Please, don't let go."

Sam lifted and carried her across the living room, into the bedroom that she'd moved into almost two months ago. Jennifer was glad that their first time would be in a neutral space all their own.

The room was faintly lit by the tiny nightlight in the hallway. Sam put a knee on the bed and, in a fluid motion, rolled so that she was on her back and Jennifer was on top. Jennifer tucked her knees alongside Sam's hips. She enjoyed being on top, as if Sam had put her in control of what would happen, all without saying a word. Sam slid her hands up Jennifer's legs, up her arms and shoulders until they met at the top button of her shirt. She gazed into Jennifer's eyes, her expression requesting permission. Jennifer smiled and tilted her head back.

Sam surprised her by sitting up and kissing her neck while releasing the top button of her blouse, then the next. She took her time. It was every bit the kind of seduction Jennifer had read about in countless romance novels and had dreamt of for herself.

Sam released another button, and Jennifer lifted slightly, offering better access. She was rewarded with hot breath and warm lips teasing that delicate spot between her breasts. With the last few buttons freed, her shirt slid down her arms. She closed her eyes and savored the touches and tender kisses along her collarbone. Her lacy bra unclasped, and the straps slid forward on her arms and disappeared. She kept her eyes closed and immersed herself in the sensations. More warm breath on her skin as the tip of Sam's tongue teased the hollow of her neck and trailed down between her breasts. Air caught in her lungs in anticipation of Sam touching her breasts. With her eyes still closed, she leaned forward, seeking contact. Her breath caught again when she felt Sam's breath on her left nipple. She leaned forward a bit more, hoping Sam would grant her silent request.

"You're beautiful," Sam whispered.

Jennifer opened her eyes as Sam brushed the delicate skin of her breasts with her fingertips. She buried her fingers in Sam's hair and tilted her own head back. She felt the warm, wet swirling pressure from Sam's tongue on one nipple and, moments later, the other. Cool air teased her wet skin. Jennifer inhaled a sharp, short breath as Sam caressed the sides of each breast, then trailed touches down along her stomach. Seductive teasing at its finest. As much as she wanted to take the time to enjoy every breath and touch, she also wanted Sam to finish undressing her and grant her some relief.

All in good time, she told herself, because while she wanted to rock herself to an orgasm, she also wanted to experience Sam's affection for her, and deep inside, she knew that was exactly what they were sharing in this amazing moment. An accumulation of their feelings for each other, their desire to please one another and the patience to savor the moment.

Heat surrounded her nipple again. Pressure from Sam's tongue teased and flicked her stimulated skin. She cupped the back of Sam's head and held her against her breast. She felt Sam's fingers at the waistline of her shorts. *Yes, please touch me.* Her legs quivered. The button released, and she heard the zipper slowly fall. Sam's hands rested on her hips before sliding around her ass. She lowered herself onto Sam's lap and pushed into her. Sam's moan into the side of her neck was the perfect reward. If there was ever a night where she could achieve multiple orgasms, tonight would certainly be that night. She was already so close.

Sam leaned back against the mattress and gently pulled her down. Each kiss ignited a fresh wave of passion. Sam held her close and rolled her onto her back. Jennifer took advantage of the new position to tug Sam's shirt free from her jeans and pull it over her head, breaking the magical kiss to fling the shirt to the floor. Sam slid down a bit and rose onto her knees. Her eyes seemed to drink up everything she saw. Jennifer had never before felt so adored, so craved, and so wanted. Sam playfully tugged on her shorts. Without hesitation, Jennifer lifted her hips and welcomed the removal of the last barrier to her body. Sam moved to the side and helped guide one leg and then the other from the final barrier.

"I want to feel all of you too."

Sam removed her sports bra and tossed it to the side. Jennifer reached for the belt on her jeans and unbuckled it. She teased the skin on Sam's stomach before unbuttoning and unzipping her Levi's. Sam looked so sexy kneeling with her jeans hanging open, showing off the band from her fitted boxers.

Jennifer rose to her knees. She stared into Sam's eyes and watched her reaction while she explored the newly exposed skin with her fingertips. Goose bumps erupted everywhere, and her nipples tightened beneath the touches. Jennifer teased the outline of her breasts similar to the way Sam had touched her. Hers were much smaller, perfect handfuls of heaven. She covered one and slid her palm across the nipple. Sam tilted her head back and closed her eyes. Jennifer bent and kissed that space between her breasts. She worked her way across the soft flesh with kisses until she could wrap her lips around the firm nipple. Sam buried her fingers in her hair. Jennifer took that as a sign of approval.

Never in her wildest dreams would she have imagined how erotic it would be to explore a woman's body. She used all her senses. Watching Sam lick her lips, tilt her head back, or draw in a quick breath of air was tantalizing in the dim light. Touching and teasing her delicate skin was like running fine silk through her fingers. She couldn't get enough. She leaned in closer and inhaled the amazing scent of Sam's cologne. She nuzzled in and left a trail of kisses down the side of Sam's neck, savoring the slightly salty taste. The sound of her deep moan created an instant pulsating need between Jennifer's thighs. She was immersed in the moment, and it was incredible.

Sam still had way too many clothes on. Jennifer slid her hands down Sam's waist and pushed on her jeans and boxers until they were around her thighs. She guided Sam down and pulled the jeans and underwear off one leg at a time. Finally, she tugged on Sam's socks and tossed them to the floor. Jennifer sat for a moment at the foot of the bed and admired Sam's long, lean body. She was sexy and handsome and so beautiful.

Jennifer held out a hand and pulled her back to her knees. She stared up into Sam's eyes. "May I touch you?"

Sam held her gaze. "Yes. Anywhere you'd like."

Jennifer placed her hands on Sam's collarbones and slowly and thoroughly explored the front of her body. When she got to Sam's waist, she shifted slightly to the side and slid one hand down her hip and around to her inner thigh, all the while staring into Sam's smoldering eyes. She explored the soft, curly hair with her fingertips. Sam touched her bare hip too, slowly sliding toward her inner thigh. Touching her while being touched added to the excitement. Jennifer slid a hand between Sam's legs. She was soft and warm and so wet. It was such an erotic experience to explore her in a way she'd only ever pleased herself, lately while fantasizing about Sam. Reality far exceeded anything she could have imagined. Sam bent and slid a hand between her legs. She tried to stay still and let Sam explore, but all she wanted to do was thrust on Sam's fingers until they were deep inside as she wondered what it would feel like to be inside Sam.

"Is inside okay?" Jennifer asked. She barely recognized her own voice.

Sam spread her legs and pushed onto Jennifer's hand when her fingers were in just the right spot. It was incredible to feel her tighten inside as her fingers slid inside Jennifer too. She tried to go slow and savor the moment, but the need for fulfillment was too great. She buried her face in Sam's neck and pressed her pelvis against Sam's thigh, pushing her fingers deeper. She needed to feel that pressure everywhere. She thrust her hips, trying desperately not to forget about Sam's pleasure. It was difficult to focus on both.

Sam moaned and tilted her head back. She began to quiver inside, and Jennifer couldn't believe how amazing it felt to experience that through her fingers.

Sam's eyes fluttered close, and she drew in quick breath. "Jen, please, don't stop."

She couldn't if she wanted to. She was so close to exploding herself. She felt Sam tighten around her fingers and pulse against the heel of her hand. That sensation of Sam coming for her tipped her over the edge. She held her hips tightly against Sam's leg, pinning her fingers inside. She shuddered and shook with orgasm over and over while tiny aftershocks coursed through her. Sam's skin was damp with sweat, mixing with that amazing fragrance she wore, flat-out sexy.

"Wow." Jennifer could barely breathe, and her legs were shaking.

"Wow, indeed." Sam held her close with her free arm.

Everything felt right. Everything felt amazing. Jennifer didn't want to move, but her legs were starting to cramp. She slowly pulled her hand from between Sam's legs, instantly missing the way it felt. Sam did the same, collapsed on the bed, and pulled Jennifer into her arms. Their naked bodies melded together perfectly. Sam kissed her with such passion that her body responded all over again before it even had a chance to recover. Everywhere Sam kissed or touched was pure sensory overload.

She couldn't recall craving anyone like this. Any nervousness or trepidation she'd had about whether or not she'd enjoy being with a woman was long gone. Now she couldn't imagine an experience quite so intense with anyone else. Being with Sam was so much more than sexual gratification. What they shared was emotional and sensual. Next-level incredible. Her body responded as if making up for a lifetime of missed moments. Without inhibition, she enjoyed an orgasmic evening unlike any other.

CHAPTER FIFTEEN

Loud beeping from the alarm clock pulled Sam from a deep blissful sleep. Jennifer's naked body stirred in her arms, and she was grateful it hadn't simply been another lovely dream. She was really here. Last night had really happened.

"Good morning." She kissed the top of Jennifer's head.

Jennifer burrowed deeper in the covers and snuggled close. "No. Not yet. I need sleep."

"We could take the day off and spend it right here in bed." Sam tickled her back with her fingertips.

"Hmm, that sounds nice." Jennifer lifted her head and looked at her. "We'll really be the talk of the office."

"I couldn't care less. Let 'em talk."

Sam let her eyes close and let the sound of Jennifer's breathing lull her asleep.

Boom, boom, boom.

Sam's eyes popped open. No. Nothing good happened when someone pounded on her front door in the dark, early morning hours. She froze and held her breath.

"What in the hell is that?" Jennifer sat up.

Boom, boom, boom. "FBI, we have a search warrant."

"FBI?" Sam looked at Jennifer, who was looking back at her with the same confused expression.

Sam flipped on the light and dressed as quickly as she could find her clothes. Jennifer did the same, swapping Sam's shirt for her shorts.

Boom, boom, boom. "FBI, open up, or we will enter with force." "Jesus, what the fuck?" Sam fastened her belt and ran for the front door. She peeked out the side window. "Show me some identification."

There had to be six or more agents on her front stoop. Each flashed a badge. What on earth was going on? Certainly, they had to have the wrong house.

"We have a warrant to search the property." An agent held up a legal document in the side window.

The font was so small, but she was still able to make out her full name and address on the top. Shit, they had the right house, but why? What was going on? She released the dead bolt and opened the door.

"Samantha Phillips?"

"Yes." It was like déjà vu. She looked around for Deputy Jones. This guy better not ask her if she was married to Kara Richardson. She wouldn't survive that question again. Her heart pounded in her chest.

"I'm Special Agent Anthony Foster. Is there anyone else on the premises?"

"Yes. Me. I'm Jennifer Delgado." Jennifer walked up behind her.

"Anyone else?" Agent Foster asked.

"No, just us. What's going on?" Sam's mouth was dry. Her words wobbled and cracked.

"Samantha Phillips, we have a warrant for your arrest. We also have a warrant to search your property. Where can I find your ID?" Agent Foster handed her the papers.

Sam had to think quickly. Her ID. Where on earth was her ID? "I think my wallet is in my briefcase. In the living room by the recliner." She glanced at the warrant. "Arrest? I don't understand. What are the charges?"

"Ms. Delgado, please step outside. We need you to wait with an agent by our vehicles. We'd like to take you in for questioning."

Sam didn't understand what was going on. Arrested? She was ushered outside in her socks. "Wait, shoes. Can I get our shoes? Jennifer has bare feet, and the concrete is cold."

"Where are your shoes? I'll get them," a female agent asked.

"In the kitchen, by the back door going into the garage. A pair of sneakers and a pair of brown loafers."

The agent disappeared into the house. She returned a moment later with the two pairs of shoes. Jennifer held Sam's arm while she slid her feet into the sneakers. Sam stuffed her feet into her loafers and was led farther outside by the female agent.

"Is there anything sharp in your pockets?"

"My pockets? I don't know. I barely had time to find pants."

"Please empty them on to the hood of the vehicle and pull them inside out."

Sam dug her hands into her pockets. They were empty. She pulled them inside out.

"I'm going to remove your belt."

Sam stood still while the agent unbuckled her belt and slid it free of the loops. She set it on the hood of the car.

"Spread your arms and legs. I'm going to pat you down."

Her heart thumped wildly in her chest. Sam lifted her arms and held them out. She stepped out to the side and spread her legs. This couldn't be happening. It had to be a mistake. The agent untucked her shirt and felt inside the waistband of her underwear and jeans. She patted Sam down like the police on TV did. There wasn't a place she didn't touch. She even lifted her pant legs and checked her socks and inspected each shoe.

"Put your hands behind your back."

Sam's mouth was as dry as if she'd stuffed it full of cotton balls. Her mind was racing and blank at the exact same time. The agent handcuffed her wrists and read her rights, just like on TV. Certainly, she was having an out of body experience. There was no way this was happening.

"Stand here and keep your back against the side of the vehicle." She turned to Jennifer. "Same questions, anything sharp in your pockets?"

A wave of protectiveness flared inside Sam. Search her, cuff her, fine, but they needed to leave Jennifer alone. She hadn't done anything wrong. Neither of them had done anything to warrant this.

"No. I don't believe I have pockets." Jennifer spread her arms and legs. She was dressed in shorts and a thin blouse. There wasn't anywhere for her to hide anything. When the agent finished searching her, Jennifer picked up the warrant from where Sam had set it on the hood. "It has to do with work. The warrant is for anything connected to Walsh Software. What in the hell is going on?"

"I wish I knew." Sam's head was spinning. She'd never been handcuffed before, not even for fun. She'd never been arrested. Hell, she'd never been in trouble beyond sassy teenager stuff.

The female agent stepped between them. "Ms. Delgado, we need you in a separate vehicle. You two can't be talking."

"Why not? I don't understand."

"A search warrant is being executed for your home too. I need you to step over there with Agent Rhaske. At this point, you're not under arrest, but we do need you to come in for questioning. Ms. Phillips, you'll ride with me in this car."

No, don't go. Having Jennifer close was her one thread connecting her to reality because the rest of this was surreal. This had to be a nightmare. *Wake up, wake up, wake up!* She squeezed her eyes shut and then opened them, hoping to be staring at the bedroom ceiling. It didn't work. She watched as Jennifer was led to a different SUV. At least she wasn't in handcuffs.

"Sam, I—"

"Quiet." Agent Rhaske overpowered the rest of her sentence.

What she wouldn't give to know what Jennifer was going to say. Her imagination gave her plenty of ideas. "Sam, I'll be right behind you," or, "Sam, I know it will all work out." "Sam, I enjoyed last night." "Sam, I love you." Any or all would be welcome, especially the last one. Finding a good finish to her sentence was much better than focusing on the mess she found herself in.

"Come on, let's go." The female agent tugged on her arm.

"I need my stuff. Wallet, phone, keys. Jennifer needs her purse and phone. Can I grab our stuff?"

"No, you are under arrest. I have your wallet." She held the back door open.

"I don't understand." Sam was on the edge of full-blown panic. Her heart rate rocketed to the stratosphere, and she couldn't get any air into her lungs. The agent helped her climb into the back of the SUV. She climbed in next to her and fastened her seat belt. There was a driver already in the front seat. The vehicle started and backed up by Jennifer's car, turned, and drove up the driveway. Sam twisted around. She'd never been so scared. Fear squeezed her insides. She swallowed the huge lump in her throat. "What's going on? Can you tell me anything?"

"No, I'm sorry, I can't. My instructions are simply to bring you in. Please sit back and be quiet."

She stared out the window. What could have possibly happened at work? Walsh Software Design was Mike's brainchild. Was there a flaw in the initial design? If there had been a flaw, they would have given proper notice. Mike would have known and corrected any issues in the past twelve years.

Within thirty minutes, she spotted the office from the main road that led into town. The parking lot was full of black SUVs like the one she was sitting in. What in the hell had caused all this? She'd studied the regulations inside and out. She used to joke with Mike that as the IT mastermind, her job was to keep him out of striped pajamas. Had she missed something? Was all of this due to something she'd done wrong? Somehow, it had to be her fault because she was the one under arrest. The driver continued through town and merged on the interstate heading north. She twisted in her seat, hoping to see Jennifer, but the other SUV wasn't behind them.

"Where are you taking me?" Sam asked.

"The field office in Minneapolis."

Holy hell, this was really happening. She was really under arrest. It had to be a misunderstanding. Her mind raced, trying to figure out what act had warranted this reaction, what she might have missed, or what she'd done wrong. "That's, like, two and a half hours away. Why couldn't you ask me what you wanted at my house? I'm sure there's a logical explanation for all of this." Logical, ha. Nothing about this seemed logical. Had someone breached her network security? Had she configured something wrong? She must have missed something, done something. Mike and Kelly must be furious.

"That's not how it works. Not when it's a federal felony case."

Shit, this was so much more serious than she thought. Felony? She knew enough to know that no one was charged with a felony for missing a simple step. She didn't miss steps. She was focused and methodical. She was why they'd passed the electronic health record certification. There had to be a mistake. "A felony? What is going on?"

The agent ignored her. She stared out the window. She hadn't brushed her teeth or her hair. Hell, she hadn't even had a cup of coffee. She was wearing yesterday's clothes. Within eight hours, she'd enjoyed a blissfully new highest high and now a new lowest low. Well, almost the lowest. She tried not to worry, but that was impossible.

Two hours and sixteen minutes later, the driver turned into a parking lot and parked by a back door. The agent sitting next to Sam unbuckled her seat belt, opened the car door, and got out. "Come with me, please."

She said it as if Sam had a choice. Still in complete disbelief, Sam slid across the seat and, with the agent's help, stepped onto the blacktop. The parking lot was more than half-full of black SUVs. She was led to a door. Once she went in, how long would it be before she saw daylight again?

The agent scanned her badge. There was a buzz, and the lock released. The agent pulled it open and led Sam inside. The door clicked closed behind them. Sam kept walking because the strong hand on her arm insisted she do so. The floor was polished gray concrete. The cement block walls were painted glossy white. There was a drop ceiling with fluorescent lighting every other tile and closed doors lining the hall. Stark and sterile. Scary as shit.

"Up ahead on your left. Three, two, one, stop here." The agent scanned her badge. The door clicked, and she pushed it open. "Go inside and take a seat on the bench."

Sam did as instructed. Her heart was in her throat. The room was a concrete cube and lacked any windows.

"Hey, Charlie. I've got one for booking. Are you ready now, or should I hook her to the bench?"

"It's been a crazy morning. Hook her to the bench. I'll take her back in a bit."

"Roger that." The agent removed the handcuffs and replaced them with a new, very cold pair secured around each wrist behind her back once she was seated. Her shoulders already ached from the unusual position. "Charlie, I'm going to grab a cup of coffee. You want one?"

"Sure. Thanks."

What Sam wouldn't give for a cup. Did she dare ask? She was too scared to open her mouth. Better question, how could she drink with her hands cuffed behind her back?

"Black?"

Black coffee would be perfect, thanks. If only she could get the words out. Maybe the agent would find her comment funny and lighten up.

"Yup," Charlie said.

"Got it. I'll be right back with the booking info."

Sam closed her eyes. She'd never been booked before. What did that entail? What crime could she possibly have committed? Nothing made sense. She'd read somewhere that profanity released endorphins or some calming chemical in the brain. *Holy shit. Holy fuck. Holy hell. Holy motherfucking, asshole, son of a bitch.* It didn't work. She was not calmer. Maybe she was supposed to scream it. Yeah, no. That wouldn't get her any answers or a cup of coffee.

The agent exited. The sound of the door latch echoed in the room. Not only was Sam chained, but she was also locked inside. She sat there in shock; her heart continued to thump wildly in her chest. Two and a half hours in and she still had no clue what was going on. Why would they bring her so far from her home? Where was Jennifer? Was anyone else from the office here? Or were they just accusing her?

The only sound was the clock behind her on the wall. The persistent *tick, tock, tick* of the second hand was unnerving and relentless. It seemed like hours before the female agent returned with two cups of coffee. Sam inhaled the dark roast aroma. Not having a cup of her own was every bit the torture of listening to that damned clock.

"Okay, your turn." Charlie walked around the bench and released the holds on her wrists. "Follow me."

Sam followed him into a small room with the ruler on the wall that she'd seen in mugshots on TV. Fuck. This was really happening. He motioned for her to sit in a chair on the side of a desk. She did.

Anything to not be cuffed again. She spent the next few minutes confirming who she was and where she lived. Charlie scanned her fingerprints into the system using technology she recognized from a convention she'd attended, and then he took her photo as if she was at the DMV, except this experience wasn't a simple annoyance. It was utterly terrifying.

"That's it. Head back out to the bench." He had that same firm, guiding grip on her arm.

Sam froze as if cemented in place. She was missing one crucial piece of information. "I still don't know why I'm being arrested."

"Neither do I," He tugged on her arm. "My job ends once you're booked into the system."

The female agent was waiting by the bench. "Hands behind your back."

Apparently, she'd finished her coffee. The cup was nowhere in sight. Sam turned and put her hands behind her back. The cuffs that she'd worn earlier were no longer warm. Ice-cold metal secured her wrists.

"This way." The still unnamed female agent led her with a steering hand on her right tricep into the bleak hallway. Sam still held out hope that this was a very detailed nightmare. *Please, please be a nightmare.* If only she'd wake up and have the chance to walk into the kitchen and flip the coffee maker from timer to start. Never before had she wished for that, and now, wouldn't it be so very nice? Any moment. *Please wake up. Please.*

CHAPTER SIXTEEN

The tiny room where Jennifer had been asked to wait in was absolutely freezing, so cold her teeth were chattering. What she wouldn't give for a pair of Sam's rocket ship pajama pants and one of her cozy flannels. At this point, she couldn't care less about fashion.

She paced, trying to stay warm. She had no idea how long she'd been left to wait. There wasn't a clock in the room, certainly an intentional act. In all of her years consulting, this was a first. Never had she been dragged out of bed by the FBI. She was confused and angry with the cloak-and-dagger tactics. It had been so much worse for Sam. Watching her being handcuffed had been torture. She'd never felt more helpless. She couldn't imagine Sam doing anything illegal. It had to be a misunderstanding. None of this made any sense.

The door buzzed and opened. A stocky, round woman, not much taller than Jennifer, walked in with a laptop and a very full file folder under her arm. Behind her was a tall man in a poorly made suit. It was too big in the shoulders and too tight across his well-fed belly. The door closed behind them and clicked, locking her in like a caged animal.

"I understand that you're Jennifer Delgado?" The agents each pulled out a chair and sat.

"Yes, that's correct."

"Please take a seat."

"Could you turn on some heat? That metal chair is as cold as ice, and they wouldn't let me change this morning. Trust me, these shorts and blouse aren't offering much in the way of warmth."

"Give me a moment," one said. They stood, collected their things, and scanned out of the room.

Frustrated, annoyed, and totally freaked out, Jennifer kept pacing. The wait was much shorter than expected. The female agent handed Jennifer two blankets on her return. Each was folded and sealed in a plastic baggie.

"Warming blankets. I turned off the AC too. You should be more comfortable soon."

Jennifer ripped the plastic open and wrapped a blanket around her shoulders and another around her waist like a long skirt. She felt better already.

"Now, would you please take a seat?"

Jennifer nodded and sat in the chair.

"I'm Special Agent Cassidy. I'm a technical expert in the fraud division, and this is Special Agent Palmer, he's the lead on the case." Palmer didn't say a word. He stared at her like he was performing a Jedi mind trick. Agent Cassidy opened her folder and set a legal pad off to the side. "How long have you been employed by Walsh Software Design?"

"I'm not an employee. I'm a consultant. I've been working there for two and a half months."

"What does Walsh Software Design do?" Agent Palmer asked.

"The company designs software packages. Their primary package is an EHR for medical insurance companies that offer supplements for Medicare with a TPA module option for claims processing."

Agent Palmer picked up his pen. "EHR stands for what?"

"Electronic health record."

"Could you clarify?"

If he was the lead on the case, he should know all this already. "The software creates the digital version of patient charting folders at a doctor's office or hospital. Same thing is needed for the insurance companies that offer Medicare supplements. Each person insured needs a chart, and TPA is third party administrator."

"What does the TPA module offer to your clients?"

"Digital claims entry for provider payments."

Agent Palmer tapped his pencil on the pad of paper. "Layman's terms?"

"Walsh's clients are insurance companies that cover what Medicare might not cover. If an insured person goes to the doctor, the doctor's office submits a claim to the insurance company, i.e., Walsh's client, for payment. As a third-party administrator, employees at Walsh Software Design scan or import those claims and attach that claim to the insured person's file. The software figures out the proper amount to pay and electronically sends payment to the provider."

"Thank you." Agent Palmer scribbled something on his notepad.

"Are you a programmer?" Agent Cassidy asked.

"Yes."

"What languages do you write in?"

"The list is long. My current contract involves a lot of .NET and SQL."

Agent Cassidy nodded. She opened up the laptop. A flatscreen monitor on the wall flickered to life. "Our records indicate that you were the last person to access this file yesterday. Is that correct?"

What was that, like, eight-point font? Did everything have to be so difficult? "May I get closer to the monitor?" Jennifer asked.

"Yes."

She stood and stepped closer. It was the claims module. "Yes. I was in this file yesterday."

"Was it at the request of your office mate, Samantha Phillips?"

"Sam? No. Well, other than the fact that she's eager to see the stability issues resolved. She was part of the reason I was hired in the first place. She's been after Mike to get someone on staff to figure out what was wrong with the software."

So the FBI was investigating something about the claims module. Jennifer's amateur sleuth mind went into overdrive, trying to recall anything questionable in the code. That was laughable because there was an unbelievable volume of questionable tactics used in the code, but were any of them illegal?

Agent Cassidy pulled Jennifer out of her own head. "Is Ms. Phillips ever in the code?"

"Seriously? No. She has to use Google just to write a basic PowerShell script. She's more a hardware, operating system, and networking wizard."

Agent Cassidy scribbled down some notes. "What changes did you make yesterday, specifically, to the file displayed on the screen?"

Did she have a copy of the source code at home? Maybe on a thumb drive or something? Then she remembered that the agents were searching her house too. Even if she had a copy, it likely wouldn't be there when she got home. "I haven't made any changes yet, other than to add comments as I stepped through what the section of code was doing, referencing, and calling. It's a mishmash mess. Stuff that should be active has been marked as inactive, and it calls other sections of code that I can't find. Multiple programmers with vastly different approaches and styles have worked on this software, worked on this specific module. Some of the code is quite elegant, while other parts are abrupt and crude. There were sections that called on objects that I couldn't find. If you'll scroll down...a bit more...stop. See, like this section right here. I spent an hour looking for that object, and it wasn't where I expected it to be in the software package."

She'd no sooner given up on finding it than Sam had invited her out to her house. Fireflies had been the visual fairy dust sprinkled on an incredibly magical evening. Hopefully, they could get to the bottom of this quickly. What she wouldn't give for a do-over without the rude awakening.

"Did you ever find that specific object?" Agent Cassidy asked.

"No. I called it a day at six o'clock last night. I closed my laptop and left the office. I didn't even take the laptop home with me. I needed a break from it." And the break had been lovely, but she didn't add that part.

"Did Ms. Phillips have access to your laptop after you left?"

"No, she walked out with me."

"She could have returned later, correct?"

"Yes, but if she'd badged in, wouldn't it show up on the door access logs?" More cloak-and-dagger games. She wished Agent Cassidy would just get to the point.

"She has remote access to the network, correct?"

"Sure, but trust me when I tell you that she wasn't accessing work last night."

"How can you be sure?"

"Because I was with her." Now this was getting ridiculous.

"All evening?"

"Not every moment but most of it. She stopped for pizza before I got out to her place."

"So she had time to remote into the network?"

"I guess so, but it would show up in the logs." Jennifer tried to keep her frustration from showing, but she doubted she was successful.

Agent Cassidy jotted down another note. "Does Ms. Phillips know your password?"

"No. I don't make a habit of sharing my passwords." Good thing too because her current password was about her feelings for Sam.

"Do you always use the same password?"

"No, I rotate through several and add new passwords to the mix quite often." Hence, her new password about Sam.

"How many digits are your typical passwords?"

"I take security seriously. My passwords vary between sixteen and twenty-five digits. Capital letters, numbers, spaces, special characters, you name it. I've had my passwords tested. It would take years to crack them with today's tools."

"While at Walsh Software Design, have you ever come in to find your password reset or not working and found that you had to reset it?"

"No. Never." They must think that Sam had altered some code under her credentials. That made no sense. Sam wasn't a programmer, and she'd never set Jennifer up to take any kind of fall. No, that couldn't be it. But Sam was the one under arrest, not her. Nothing added up to explain why they'd been yanked out of the house.

Agent Cassidy set down her pencil. "Our team found the object you were looking for. It was on an administrative server, in the cloud environment, in a hidden share. It's only called when the instance name includes the capital letters, PROD."

Jennifer turned away from the monitor. "Production. The version of the software that the clients use for day-to-day operations. Sam mentioned that the stability issues only occurred in the production environment. She couldn't replicate the performance issues in other versions of the software that were used for testing and training. May I see the code of the object?" If she could see the code, maybe she could figure out who wrote it, and maybe then, she could help figure out who was setting Sam up.

"I'm sorry, but I can't allow that. It's evidence in an ongoing investigation," Agent Palmer said.

"Please? I'm not asking to be at the keyboard. I'll stay right here. I've spent the last three months immersed in the code for this software package. Maybe I can help."

"Other than the owner, she is our greatest resource," Agent Cassidy said to Agent Palmer.

He sighed and nodded. Jennifer did a small fist pump of success. Agent Cassidy clicked on another file and displayed the source code.

Jennifer stepped through the code of that object. She recognized the programmer's style and saw exactly why they were at the FBI headquarters. It felt as if the blood drained out of her body. It was much more serious than she ever could have imagined.

The code transposed the amount due on a claim and then skimmed the difference into a bank account. The provider was paid the accurate amount, and the insurance company had no way of knowing they'd been overcharged without a line by line claims audit. If this was what Sam was being accused of, she could go away for a long, long, long time. There was no telling how many laws that section of programming was breaking, but one thing was for certain: It was far too intricate for Sam to write. No way this was her work.

Jennifer had to convince Agent Cassidy to keep digging. "No way did Sam write that. She's not capable, and she's far too ethical. She doesn't have the programming skills. She couldn't do this. She wouldn't do this."

"The bank accounts in that object are in her name."

Jennifer stared at the routing and account number highlighted on the screen. No way. There had to be an explanation. "Isn't it much more plausible that her identity was stolen?" The more Jennifer reviewed the programming, the more the gravity of the situation sank in. If convicted of what that code was doing, Sam faced decades in prison, if not life. "Agent Cassidy, do you program?"

"Yes."

"Would you agree that developers have their own cadence? What we do is, in essence, an art form, and each artist has a unique stroke. Much like a novelist has a unique voice, or a musician has style, a programmer has a distinct method of coding that creates a specific signature, as it were."

"Yes, I would agree with that statement."

Jennifer felt the slightest glimmer of hope. "Do you have all of the source code from the office?"

"Yes."

"Would you open the module for attaching a claim to an insured member's file from a production instance?" Jennifer felt alert and alive now. There might be a way to prove that Sam was being set up, and it was all in the code.

It took a few minutes for agent Cassidy to find the file. Finally, it flashed up on the screen.

"Down toward the middle, where it matches the insured member to the claim and validates eligibility. Yes, stop, right there. This section of code. Does it look familiar?"

Agent Cassidy leaned forward, her finger moving along on her laptop screen as if tracing the logic of the code.

"Now, if you go into the database side and pull up the corresponding database object code..." Jennifer said. Her mind was working faster than she could formulate words. She kept talking while the software loaded. "Like I said, I've spent the last three months mapping out this software package. There are at least five distinct programming styles throughout, but they didn't work in collaboration, more of a succession. It became evident that each one thought they knew better than the last just how to solve the problem, but they only tackled that one problem at a time, and the solution often created several other problems because they weren't looking at the big picture."

Finally, Agent Cassidy opened the requested query window.

"Do you see where it's calling to see if the member has paid their premiums and is in good standing? I commented out the code and rewrote it, but I kept the original for reference. The way this programmer overutilized an inefficient way of verification made this section of code extremely hard on the server resources for what they were trying to accomplish. This was the very reason I was brought into Walsh Software Design, to fix code that put too much demand on the servers. This inefficient style is sprinkled throughout the software. I can show you hundreds of examples. It's everywhere. Believe me, it's been a mess to clean up, and it matches the style in that illegal object. Has your team pulled time stamps or logs to see which programmer created which code?"

"They're working on the deep dive now. The investigation will move quickly now that we have access to everything."

"I really hope so because you have the wrong person in custody. She can't even cheat at a game of darts. There's no way she's capable of this. Not ethically, not morally, and not to mention, she doesn't have the skill set."

"If you're right, she'll be exonerated. If not, she'll be going away for a good long time."

"Is there anything I can do to help prove her innocence? I can show you countless examples of that programmer's work. Sam's wife died last year. Maybe the programmer worked to set her up while she was away. That could help, couldn't it?" Jennifer hoped and prayed the agent said yes. She'd never wanted to help with something more in all of her life.

Agent Palmer stood. "You've answered all of the questions we have for you. I'll have an agent take you home."

"Wait. I'm happy to stay and help. Certainly, you have more questions?"

"That's all for now. Thank you," Agent Palmer said. Agent Cassidy offered a half-smile but closed her laptop and disrupted the signal to the monitor. The interview was over.

"But my car is at Sam's. I don't have my purse or my keys."

"The agent who will take you home has your purse, personal electronics, and keys. She can take you to Ms. Phillips's home, where you can retrieve your car. The office for Walsh Software Design is closed pending the outcome of the investigation. Even if you have access from a personal laptop, do not attempt to remote in and modify anything. You're free to go to your apartment. It was cleared and is no longer part of our investigation. Please stay in town and available in case we have additional questions."

Jennifer flopped in the chair. Her head was spinning. Somehow, she felt like she'd failed Sam. No matter how clear it was to her that Sam was innocent of this unbelievable scheme, she'd have to remain in custody.

It was another hour before anyone showed up to take Jennifer home. Her stuff was in a large, sealed plastic bag. When she followed the new agent out of the small interrogation room, she looked at the many doors up and down the long hallway and wondered which one, if any, Sam was trapped behind. She wanted to scream. She wanted to assure Sam that it would all be okay, but the truth was, she had no way of knowing how this investigation would turn out. The one thing she believed in was Sam's innocence.

Three and a half hours later, Jennifer finally made it to her apartment door. There was a thirty-day eviction notice taped front and center from her landlord. Apparently, he didn't appreciate having the FBI crawling all over the complex. Jennifer hadn't appreciated the FBI all that much, either. She ripped the notice off the door and unlocked the dead bolt.

Her small apartment was unrecognizable. If she hadn't known any better, she'd swear she'd been burglarized. Stuff had been tossed everywhere. Every cabinet door in the kitchen was open, and most had been emptied on the countertop, along with the majority of the drawers. The living room had been tossed. The couch cushions were on the floor, and the contents in the end tables had been emptied on the coffee table. The bathroom was just as bad, if not worse. Items from the vanity were in the sink, and all of the linens and towels were in a messy heap on the floor.

Her bedroom, however, was the worst off. Her beautiful, expensive, professional clothes were strewn all over the bed. Any available pocket had been turned inside out. Her shoes had been tossed about as if they were dime-store flip-flops. Every dresser drawer was open and had been effectively rifled. She wanted all of it laundered before putting any of it on her body. The box containing the sexy lingerie she'd wanted to wear for Sam someday was unwrapped and tossed on the floor. Even though the culprits were law enforcement officers instead of criminals, it didn't make her feel any less violated.

She returned to the living room and tipped a chair until the stuff in the seat slid to the floor. No longer caring about neatness, she swiped her arm across the top of the small dining table. It was mildly gratifying when everything crashed to the linoleum. *What's a bit more mess to clean up?* She ripped open the large plastic bag and pulled out her personal laptop. Learning what she had at the FBI office, one thing was certain, Sam needed an attorney.

She opened a browser window, searched for defense attorneys in Minneapolis, and sorted them by ratings and reviews. One firm stood above the rest. She pulled her cell phone from the bag and dialed. Luckily, it was just before four o'clock in the afternoon. Within an hour, she'd briefly explained what was going on and had an attorney with experience on federal cases on retainer for herself and, more importantly, for Sam. Chase Craden, part of Craden, Stevens, and Pose, Attorneys at Law, promised to head to the FBI building and represent Sam from that point forward.

Finally feeling like she'd helped in some small way, Jennifer went into the kitchen and opened the liquor cabinet. She poured herself a whiskey neat, tossed it back, and poured another. She felt numb and angry and still quite helpless. There wasn't anything more she could do at this point for Sam. She hoped beyond hope that Agent Cassidy would look at the code and see the nuances she'd tried to convey. She knew the answers were in the code. She knew the identity of the offender would be revealed in the log files, given who was logged in and working when the code had been modified. It was all so crystal clear to her, but then, this was her world, and she was damned good at what she did.

She took her glass into the bedroom and began the daunting task of cleaning everything up. It might as well look neat for the thirty days that she had left to live there. Less than twenty-four hours ago, she'd opened her eyes to the possibility of something more, possibly a future, with Sam. Any fantasy she'd conjured in the last couple of months paled in comparison to what she'd experienced last night. Now, instead of a day snuggled up in bed, she sat there worrying if the FBI would keep looking, or if they were satisfied with what they perceived to be the evidence against Sam.

What a difference a day made. One thing was for certain, she believed in Sam. She'd shared as much with the FBI, and now, all she could do was hope that Sam would be exonerated.

Chapter Seventeen

Sam sat in what the agent called a holding cell. It was really just another small concrete room, but at least she had a chair, a cot, a toilet, a small sink to wash her hands, and a paper cup for water. Bonus, she wasn't with anyone else. There wasn't a clock to be found. She had no idea what time it was or if it was day or night. Someone had delivered a tray of cafeteria-style food. A bland, and very dry, ham and cheese sandwich and a banana that had been on the shelf a little too long. She wondered if this was what prison would be like. Deep down, she had a feeling that this was much better than prison. She ate her food and was glad she was still wearing her own clothes.

Hours later—or it could have been days; time seemed irrelevant in this place—the door buzzed, and an agent asked her to step outside. She was nervous to do so. She had no idea what to expect next. Would she ever find out why she was even here? She did exactly as she was asked because it was what she was supposed to do. She was led up a hallway that looked like the one she'd been in earlier, or yesterday, who knew when? Same polished gray concrete floor, same glossy white block walls, same fluorescent lighting, and the same gray doors every five strides.

She heard footsteps approaching. She'd never been so excited to hear footsteps. She saw someone being led by an agent in the same manner as her and recognized him instantly. "Mike!" She felt the tiniest bit of relief at seeing a familiar face.

"No talking." The agent squeezed her arm.

Mike didn't look happy to see her. He was led into one of the rooms behind yet another gray door. Was he being booked too, or was he like Jennifer and only there for questioning?

"Stop here," the agent said to Sam and scanned his badge to open a different door. "You'll wait here. Someone will be with you in a bit."

He didn't even step into the room. The moment she stepped inside, he pulled the door closed, and it clicked. She sat for what felt like hours, her mind spinning in circles. Finally, the door buzzed open.

A tall, broad-shouldered man in a badly made suit walked in with a thick folder in his hands. "Samantha Phillips?"

Sam drew in a deep breath and nodded. He looked at her expectantly. She stood. "Yes. I'm Samantha Phillips."

He nodded and sat.

She looked at him and sat again in the cold metal chair. "And you are?"

"Special Agent Palmer. How long have you worked for Walsh Software Design?"

"Twelve years, but you probably already know that." She sat back in her chair. "Should I have a lawyer present?"

"Do you need a lawyer?" he asked.

"I don't know. This is my first time in a situation like this."

"We're just talking. You haven't been charged with a crime yet."

"That doesn't make me feel better. Am I free to go?"

"No. You're still arrested and booked. We can hold you for seventy-two hours without officially charging you with a crime."

"Can you at least tell me what I was arrested for?"

"We'll get to that." His face lacked any emotion or expression. That wasn't helpful. "Are you a programmer?"

"No."

"What is your position with Walsh Software Design?"

"IT Administrator."

"What do you do for the company?"

"IT stuff. I design, configure, and create new servers for our in-house programming environment and create other, cloud-based servers for our clients to run production versions of our software. I create secure data tunnels between our cloud servers and the client's local servers for any data in transit and configure database replication so clients can have a reporting environment. Stuff like that."

"Do you write any code in the process of those duties?"

"No."

"Not at all?" He gave her a hard stare.

"Look, I can write some very basic PowerShell scripts. Rolling reboots for the servers and user imports for account creation and the like, but no, I don't code in the way that the programmers do who create the software at work."

He nodded and jotted down a note. "Who was responsible for the majority of the programming for the past five years?"

Sam leaned forward. Five years? They'd had quite a bit of turnover in the last five years. Shit, that was before her world had turned upside down. How on earth would she remember who all was on staff for the past five years? "You'd have to look at employment files. I don't remember who all has rotated through that office."

He nodded and referred to his notes again. Nervousness and fear were being replaced with annoyance. If he had all of the answers, why was she here? "Does Michael Walsh contribute to the programming source code?"

"What? I don't think he's written any code for years. He wrote the original source, but now he says that the language has evolved, and he became a CEO."

Agent Palmer leafed through the papers in his folder. "Who is Jennifer Delgado?"

"She's the consultant that Mike hired a few months ago to help with some stability issues we've been experiencing."

He nodded. "Curt Fountain?"

"He worked at the office in the programmer's group. He was in charge of the group. I wish he would have stuck around. He was good. Things ran smoother when he was around."

"When was that?"

"It's been years, but I couldn't tell you exactly when he started or when he left."

"Brent Olsen?"

"He took over when Curt left. I have nothing good to say about Brent. Everything went downhill while he was on staff. We were all glad to see him go."

Agent Palmer nodded and wrote something on a legal pad. "In what way would you say things went downhill?"

"We started having client complaints about stability issues. The server resources started being consumed and wouldn't release without a reboot. We lost a few clients because of it. We lost some good, experienced staff while he was there too."

"I understand that it was you who identified the module causing the issues."

Sam stared at him. How on earth could he know that? "I believe so, yes, but again, I'm not a programmer."

"How is it that you isolated the module?"

"How do you know that I'm the one who isolated anything?"

Agent Palmer pulled some papers out of the folder and spread them on the table. "Did you author these documents?"

Sam picked up one. It was a printout of an email from her to Mike about the server issues and what the clients were doing when the issue occurred. Embedded in the email was her root cause analysis for him to share with the client. She remembered sending this shortly after they'd lost the Eastman account. It was what had brought Jennifer into her life. "Yes, I authored this document."

"How is it that you isolated the module?"

"I work closely with our client's IT people. I listen to them and ask questions. They only noticed the issues when they paid the provider claims. They only paid claims on certain days of the month. After that process, the resources on the servers ramped up but never released."

"It's also possible that you identified the module because you wrote the code that caused the issue?"

"What? I told you. I don't write code."

"We found your accounts. It's hard to believe you can accumulate millions when skimming change."

"What accounts? I don't have millions." The dollar amount sunk in. "Millions?"

"Pretty crafty, really. A provider claim is entered for one hundred and sixty-eight dollars, and your software actually leads your client to believe it was for one hundred and eighty-six dollars. It doesn't happen with every claim. Just often enough to call it a glitch or a data entry typo. You pay the provider the proper amount, and the software deposits the difference into your account. Multiply that times thousands of claims submitted each month. It adds up quickly. We caught you because of a random audit."

"What do you mean caught me? I didn't do anything. I don't write code. I don't even think like that. I don't have any accounts with millions. You can check all my accounts. Can't you check surveillance or something to see who opened the bank accounts that you think are mine? I swear that I don't know anything about an account with millions. Holy shit. That's illegal as hell."

"You've got that right. A whole lot of illegal. Years in prison kind of illegal. Life in prison kind of illegal. It would be best if you came clean now."

Sam heard his words; the gravity of the situation sank in. Who could have done something like this, and why would they set her up? "Please, Agent Palmer, keep digging. It wasn't me. I didn't create the issues. I fought to get the issues fixed. We brought Jennifer on to help figure it out. Talk to her. I'm sure she can shed some light. She's really good."

"Oh, you mean the Jennifer who you share an office with? The same Jennifer who was with you, in your home, at five o'clock in the morning?"

The memory of five o'clock in the morning warmed her. It felt so right to hold Jennifer in her arms. Just the mere mention of her name reminded Sam how much she missed her. They hadn't had enough time. "Yes! She can help you figure out who's behind this. She's already fixed all sorts of stuff."

"We're already looking into her."

"No, she hasn't done anything wrong. I'm saying that she can help you figure out who might be behind this."

"We already know who's behind this. We have the money from the account in your name."

Sam's heart stopped beating for a moment. They weren't going to investigate any more than they already had because in their eyes, she was guilty. Hopelessness washed over her. "For the last time, I don't know what you're talking about. Please, don't stop digging. There's been a mistake. You're going to keep looking, aren't you?"

"It's an ongoing investigation."

"Listen, man, I'm sure you hear this all the time, but you have the wrong person. I didn't do this. I don't code. There's got to be a way to trace IP addresses or some forensic computer shit that you can do to prove who did this."

A knock on the metal door startled her. She heard the already familiar buzz and click. The door pushed open. A short, stocky woman with brown hair pulled back into a ponytail poked her head into the room. "Counsel for Samantha Phillips is here and insisting this interview stop until she can talk to her client."

Agent Palmer looked at Sam. "I thought you didn't have an attorney."

Sam just sat there. She wasn't sure what to say because as far as she knew, she didn't have an attorney. The door opened farther, and a very tall version of Jennifer, wearing Jennifer's favorite designers, stepped into the room. The click of her high heels on the concrete was somehow comforting while also reminding her how much she missed the real Jennifer.

"Chase Craden, I represent Samantha Phillips." She handed Agent Palmer a business card. "I'd like some time alone to talk with my client."

Agent Palmer took the card, collected his things, and walked out. The little red light on the camera up in the corner of the room went dark. Sam remained seated. She'd watched enough TV to know that this could be a trick. Maybe an FBI agent was pretending to be her attorney.

"Sam, you can call me Chase."

"Are you really an attorney, or are you with the FBI?" Sam asked, as if an FBI agent would be required to tell the truth.

"I'm really an attorney. I was hired by Jennifer Delgado, and in the spirit of full disclosure, our firm is also representing Michael and Kelly Walsh."

"So you're their attorney too?"

"Not me specifically. I'm focused on your case, but another attorney in our firm is working on their behalf. Jennifer said you might be skeptical. I'm supposed to tell you that cinnamon rolls taste best when shared on the tailgate of a pickup truck overlooking a valley, and if you still have doubts, I'm to tell you that fireflies make the first kiss quite magical. You are very special to her."

"She's very special to me too." It had been a long time since

Sam had felt as happy and content and whole as she had that morning while waking up with Jennifer in her arms. Knowing that Jennifer believed in her gave her the strength to hold out hope. Jennifer was in her corner. Jennifer was out there pushing to find the truth. Unexpectedly, Sam was overcome with emotion. Her chin quivered. Her eyes welled up, and everything blurred beyond the tears. Jennifer had hired her an attorney. Now if only the FBI could figure out who was really to blame. Chase handed her a tissue.

"Can you get me out of here?" Sam asked.

"I'm working on that. What have they asked you so far?"

Sam shared what she could remember of the questions from Agent Palmer and her answers.

Chase nodded and typed furiously into her laptop. "I have a chat screen open with my team at the office, so I can get up to speed in real time. They are doing a quick deep dive while I talk with you. The investigation pointed at you when they found the bank account. What can you tell me about it?" Chase asked.

"Nothing. Until a few minutes ago, I didn't know it existed."

"It appears to have been opened in mid-February, a little over a year ago."

"There has to be a mistake. Mid-February, a little over a year ago, I had just lost my wife in a car accident. I wasn't anywhere to open a bank account. I barely left the house."

"It wasn't opened in person. It's an online bank. They have a copy of your driver's license and Social Security card from when the account was opened. Mail was sent to the office at first, and the address changed to a box at the post office in the town you live in."

Sam felt like she was losing her mind. She didn't have a post office box. She hadn't opened an account online. None of this made any sense. "How would someone get my driver's license and Social Security card?" And then she thought about the hassles she'd had opening a brokerage account with Kara a few years ago. They needed all sorts of stuff, like an existing account to draw the initial funds from. "Do they have any way to see who has access to the account? Where did the initial deposit come from? Certainly, there's a routing number and an account. How are they withdrawing the money? Any cameras? I mean, where is the money going because I don't have it."

"I have investigators researching all of that. Have you had to replace a missing driver's license and Social Security card in the last two years?"

"No, nothing like that." Sam thought back. "Wait. There was something at work. You'll need to talk to Kelly for specifics. She does all of the payroll and HR office stuff. She found her office open, and the employee filing cabinet was open. It's been a while, maybe before Kara's accident. Mike and Kelly always felt like I was a worrywart when I'd nag her about security. She used to toss her filing cabinet keys into an unlocked drawer in her desk. After she found her office open like that, she finally started carrying the keys with her, and I put an autolocking system on her office door, just like we have on the exterior office doors. Kelly hated having to scan in and out of her own office, but at least everyone's files were secure. But if a photocopy of my license and Social Security card were used from when I was hired, wouldn't the license show as expired? I've had to renew it a few times since my hire date."

"We'll check that out." Chase typed on the laptop keyboard. "Are there cameras at the office?"

"Yes, and we added more after the incident with Kelly's office. Each hallway, the two entrances, and the server room." All was not hopeless. It seemed that Chase also believed in her. Mike had often picked on her for being overzealous with security. Now, perhaps it would pay off.

"How long are recordings kept?"

"Short answer, forever. I was part of the team that helped the company get EHR certified. Part of that certification is to keep iterations of the code and to keep strong security records. All key swipes are time-stamped and backed up too. Same with all video. It's automated using special software."

Chase kept asking questions, all the while typing. "Does anyone else know where or how the backups are kept?"

The more specific Chase's questions were, the more hopeful Sam felt. Her insistence on doing things based on best practice might just be what could prove her innocence. Sam had set up the cloud storage. Mike had never seemed interested and told her to do what she thought was best. "I don't know. I've just always taken care of it. I'm not even sure Mike knows. It's documented, but I've never seen his credentials in the access logs on the documentation software."

Chase nodded and typed.

Sam thought about all the crime shows she'd ever watched. They always caught the bad guys, even when they'd tried to mislead the investigation. If all of this occurred while she was on leave after Kara's accident, one suspect stuck out in her mind: Brent Olsen. "Ms. Craden, there have to be cameras at the post office or something that can help figure out who's actually responsible for all of this."

"We'll do everything we can to get to the truth. In the meantime, do not talk with anyone without me present. Absolutely no one. I'm sure it's terrifying, and you want to clear this up, but you can quickly dig yourself into a hole and not know it. I mean it, Sam, talk to no one without me present. I can't stress that enough."

Sam nodded. "I understand."

"Unless they charge you, you'll be held here in a detention room. They can only hold you for seventy-two hours without charges. I will do everything in my power to get this cleared up before that time is up. Hang in there, okay?"

"Can you tell me one more thing?" Sam looked across the table. "How long have I been here? What time is it?"

"It's seven o'clock in the evening. You've been here for fourteen hours. Have you eaten?"

"Someone delivered a tray of food, but I wasn't sure if that was breakfast or lunch or—"

"I'll try to get you something a little better for dinner. Keep your chin up, Sam." Chase closed her laptop and stood from the table. She knocked on the gray door. The buzz sounded, and an agent opened it. "Are there any other questions for Sam while I'm here?"

"No, not at this time," Agent Palmer said.

"She is not to be interviewed again without representation from my firm."

The agent nodded. "Please stand. We'll take you back to the holding cell."

Sam looked from Chase to Agent Palmer. She stood. Tears started to well up again. She couldn't figure out who would do this to her. Why set her up at a time in her life when everything was upside down? Maybe that was precisely why and when they'd done it.

"Chase, please find out who set me up."

She nodded and walked out of the room. Sam listened as the click of her heels faded down the hallway. She'd never felt more alone.

CHAPTER EIGHTEEN

Sleep was impossible. Jennifer had never felt more helpless. It was six o'clock in the morning, and the car had been packed for a couple of hours already. She stood in front of the mirror applying the final touches to her makeup. She was decked out in her favorite designers. Sam would say that she was head to toe expensive Italian excellence. Today was a good day to wear the designers that made her feel invincible. She had a few outfits that instilled in her a commanding confidence and made her a force to be reckoned with.

She couldn't just sit idly by while Sam was locked up in a holding cell. It was time to head back up to Minneapolis and remain there until she could bring Sam home. She knew in her heart that Sam would do the same for her. That was what made them an incredible pair. If her timing was accurate, she should arrive shortly after the law offices of Craden, Stevens, and Pose opened for business. Sometimes, a phone call just wouldn't do.

The drive up was uneventful, even with the small detour to buy Sam some new clothing. She imagined that after more than two full days in the same outfit, she'd be ready for something clean. She'd even found a store that sold fitted boxers similar to what Sam wore. Jennifer wondered if Sam had been permitted to shower or if she was still catching whiffs of their night of lovemaking like Jennifer had the day before. For her, it had been a pleasant distraction from the insanity of the day, but she wasn't so sure that anything would help distract Sam from the fact that she'd been arrested.

Jennifer weaved in and out of traffic, lost in her thoughts. Sam had walked into her life when she was questioning what might be next. Who knew the answer would sweep her off her feet? The amazing friendship they'd developed, their time together, and the trust they'd shared seemed to be exactly what Sam had needed too. Everything about being with her felt right. Jennifer only hoped that Sam felt the same way. Deep down, in her heart, she knew there were no regrets. Sam's suggestion that they spend the day snuggled up in bed together had offered Jennifer all the assurance she'd needed. It was too bad that they'd been woken up and whisked away before they'd ever had a chance to talk.

What was it like for Sam? Was she in a jail cell, or was she being held in a freezing cold room like the one Jennifer had been in yesterday? Given her arrest, was she even permitted to wear her clothes from Tuesday, or was she in an orange jumpsuit with the word INMATE stenciled across the back?

Jennifer had far too many questions and not enough answers. Aside from TV shows, she didn't have a clue about the inner workings of the FBI. She hoped they could get through this and never have a reason to figure it out.

Finally, she pulled into the parking garage and parked. She checked her makeup in the rearview mirror and grabbed her black Jimmy Choo Varenne tote. Once out of the car, she smoothed out any creases in her skirt and lifted her matching Dolce & Gabbana double-breasted virgin wool blazer from the wooden hanger in the back seat. When the blazer was buttoned, she grabbed the shopping bag with a change of clothes for Sam. She'd gone a little overboard shopping, but Sam could have the other items when she was free. She locked the car and made her way to the eighth floor. It was time to channel her most confidant inner diva. More than that, it was time for answers. It was time to bring Sam home, no ifs, ands, or buts.

The words Craden, Stevens, and Pose, Attorneys at Law graced the wall behind the receptionist's desk. Typically, the first name listed in a law firm partnership was the most prominent and powerful of the organization. The founder was the one who set the tone for how cases were handled. It didn't matter the cost. She wanted the most powerful of the firm representing Sam.

She enjoyed how her shoes sounded on the marble floor as she walked up to the receptionist and waited for him to finish a phone call. He was young, clean cut, and looked cute in his suit jacket, white shirt, and plaid bow tie. "Welcome to Craden, Stevens, and Pose. How may I help you?"

"Hello. I'm Jennifer Delgado. I wonder if Chase Craden has a moment to speak with me." She squared her shoulders and smiled her best smile.

"I'll see if she's available." He typed on the keyboard, read the screen, and typed some more. Finally, he looked up. "I can take you back now."

It appeared that the law firm filled the entire eighth floor. The design was clean, crisp, and elegant. All interior walls were frosted glass, allowing the natural light to fill the spaces while also ensuring privacy. Photographs of Chase Craden being interviewed in her home gave Jennifer the impression that she had also been the one to design the interior. If she were as astute with the law as she was with interior design, then Jennifer had made a solid hire. She followed the receptionist up a hallway to a corner office. Chase Craden was etched into the glass at eye level, just to the right of the door.

He tapped his knuckles twice on the glass and pushed the frosted door open. "Ms. Craden, Jennifer Delgado to see you."

"Thank you, Eric."

Once Jennifer was inside, Eric disappeared. The crystal-clear view out across the skyline was amazing. Chase Craden stood from behind her desk and walked into the center of the room. Jennifer felt instant admiration. She was absolutely stunning with her long, wavy brown hair and bright green eyes. She was wearing one of Jennifer's favorite designers. She recognized the DG symbol embossed on each button of the merlot-colored double-breasted shantung Turlington blazer and matching slacks. She'd debated that purchase. One hundred percent silk at its finest, and now that she could see it in person, there was no doubt she needed to add it to her collection.

She'd spent much of last night researching Chase Craden. Her case success rate was not only the top in the state, but her firm was recognized far and wide. On top of that, she had amazing fashion taste to boot. Now it seemed that Sam had two determined women in her corner, both wearing power suits. A kindred spirit, that was for sure.

"Jennifer, so nice to meet you in person. I must say that your suit is absolutely gorgeous. What brings you up to Minneapolis?" Chase stepped forward and shook her hand.

"I am in awe of your taste as well. Head to toe excellence." Jennifer touched her hand to her chest in appreciation. If their similar taste in designers encouraged Chase to fight harder to free Sam, Jennifer would take full advantage of it. "I apologize for showing up without an appointment. I'm not very good at sitting on my hands and waiting. How's Sam? Have you seen her? I brought some clean clothes. And I have some notes that may be useful. Some nuances I've found in the code. It may help identify the developer behind the crime." She knew she was rambling, but she couldn't stop herself.

"How about we sit and talk?" Chase motioned to a glass table surrounded by four white leather chairs. Chase Craden gave the impression of first class all the way. No doubt she carried that confidence and grace into interviews and the courtroom. Another observation that made Jennifer feel good about her choice of attorneys.

Jennifer nodded. She set her tote and the bag with Sam's clothes on the marble floor and took a seat. Chase walked to her desk and retrieved her laptop, then returned and sat next to her.

"To answer your first question, yes, I've seen Sam. I spent time with her last night after you and I talked on the phone. She's as you'd expect for someone who's been arrested and is in custody. She's scared and eager to clear her name." Chase stopped messing with her laptop and turned to face Jennifer. "I can tell you that knowing you hired an attorney to represent her lifted her spirits but not anywhere near as much as your words to assure her that it was actually you who sent me. The look in her eyes when I mentioned the cinnamon rolls and first kiss fireflies, well, admiration and adoration like nothing I've seen."

Jennifer thought about the photographs on Sam's desk and how Sam had looked at Kara. Chase had no idea how much emotion Sam could convey with a simple expression. The closer they became, the more Sam's expressions could make her melt. She was certain that she'd only scratched the surface. There was no way she would ever gain the depth of affection that Kara had enjoyed for more than thirty years. If only she could be so lucky.

"She's very special to me too. More than you know," Jennifer admitted.

"I have no doubt. You've only known her for a few months, and yet you sought out the best of the best to represent her. You believe in her innocence. That says something."

"I do my research, yes. Now please, don't disappoint me." Jennifer sat up, once again channeling her inner diva. "I want Sam to come home sooner than later and with the honor of her name intact."

"I have no intention of disappointing you. As far as the case goes, Sam waived privilege where you're concerned." Chase opened the laptop again. "Based on what you told me yesterday and what I learned from Sam last night, the most damning evidence that the FBI has is a bank account where the skimmed money was deposited. It's in Sam's name. Her driver's license and Social Security number were used to open the account."

"There's no way she's responsible for that. She doesn't have it in her to steal."

"I don't disagree. Our saving grace is that none of her personal accounts were used to initially fund the account in question. The person responsible was foolish enough to use his own account to fund the minimum requirements to open the account under investigation. He certainly made life uncomfortable for Sam, but he wasn't the genius mastermind that he thought he was. We've uncovered quite a bit of incriminating evidence, and my team has bumped into the FBI a couple of times, so at least they're still investigating too."

Jennifer sat back and breathed a sigh of relief. "If they have another suspect, when will Sam be able to come home?"

"They're not going to release her until they have a solid case and charges have been filed against someone. We won't give up hope, and neither should you."

"Is she in a jail cell with criminals?"

"No, right now she's in a private holding cell, and that's where she'll stay unless she's charged."

"Is there any way I can see her?"

"No. Not at this time. I'm sorry." Chase reached across the table and patted the back of her hand.

"I have a change of clothes for her." Jennifer bent and picked up the bag. "Would you take them to her?"

"Sure, I'll make sure she gets these," Chase said. "I'll call when I learn more. Are you staying in town or heading back down to Houghton?"

"I'm staying until I bring Sam home. I can't sit on my hands in my tiny apartment and do absolutely nothing. The office is locked up. Sam's house is too. I'm sure hers looks as ransacked as mine did after the search, if not worse, but I can't get in to clean. My next stop is to see Agent Cassidy and find out what she can tell me." Jennifer stood and smoothed her skirt. She had to stay strong for Sam.

"Jennifer, I know you're worried about Sam, but bugging the agents isn't helpful. My team is already pushing their buttons. I'd like you to reconsider. Go home. Or back to a hotel. I'll call you when I know more."

Easier said than done. Jennifer had never been comfortable waiting in the wings. She picked up her tote. "I'll let you get back to it. Thank you very much for all you're doing."

Chase led her to the door. "I'll walk you to the elevators."

A few minutes later, Jennifer stepped out into the parking garage and almost crashed into several people waiting just outside the elevator doors. Her breath caught when she came face-to-face with Kelly Walsh. She looked frazzled, as if she hadn't slept in days, with dark circles beneath her eyes. She wasn't wearing her trademark makeup, her hair was disheveled, and her clothes were wrinkled. She was almost unrecognizable compared to her normal attire. Jennifer hadn't seen her or Mike since the day before the FBI had showed up at Sam's.

"Kelly? How are you? How's Mike?"

"Jennifer? What are you doing here?"

"Excuse me, I'd like to get on the elevator," a tall man said while trying to step around them.

"I'm sorry." Jennifer gently pulled Kelly to the side. "Do you have a second to talk? How are you holding up?"

"Honestly, I have no idea. This whole thing is so completely fucked-up. I swear, I'll totally lose my shit if I sit and think about it all. The last fifteen years of our lives, our reputation, the business.

You think you know people. You think you can trust them." She ran her fingers through her hair and shook her head.

Jennifer tried to tamp down her anger and protectiveness. "You don't honestly think Sam's responsible, do you?"

"I'd like to think she isn't, but they have all this evidence. Whoever is responsible needs to rot in prison. Mike's been with the FBI since yesterday morning. I hope he can sort this crazy mess out. My phone has been blowing up with calls because clients can't use the software or get to their data. Reporters are camped out at the office and in front of our home. Clients are threatening us with lawsuits. This twisted scheme will destroy us."

How could she have known Sam for so long and have any notion that she was behind this scheme? Sam had done nothing but go out of her way to protect them, not steal from them. Jennifer had only known Sam a few months and already knew enough to trust in that. It was like Kelly didn't know her at all.

"I'm telling you, it's not Sam. I've seen the code. It's one of the programmers. Hell, maybe it was your husband."

Kelly recoiled, but the more Jennifer considered the nuances of the code, the more she considered that it might just be Mike. Whoever it was, they'd copied Brent Olsen's bad practices but hadn't quite pulled it off.

"Yeah, you heard me," Jennifer said. "For your sake I hope it wasn't him, but that's how ridiculous it is to think it was Sam."

Fire flickered in Kelly's eyes, and then her shoulders dropped, and she stared at the floor. "I'm sorry. I'm sure you're right. Sam's been with us since the beginning. Maybe I'm spinning out. I really should get upstairs. I made a mad dash up here. Apparently, I need to sign some papers." She turned and pressed the button for the elevator.

Jennifer had expected the flash of defensiveness but not the submission that followed. Kelly knew more than she was sharing.

She couldn't worry about that right now. Her focus was solely on Sam. "I wish you both the best." With that, she turned and walked toward her car.

What a whirlwind of a day, and it wasn't even lunchtime yet. She sat in her car, trying to figure out what to do. She could get a hotel room and stick around until she had a sense of what was happening. The other option was to drive the two and a half hours back to her apartment and wait there. Either option left her feeling useless. Her phone rang before she had a chance to make a decision. Craden, Stevens, and Pose displayed on the screen.

"Hello?"

"Jennifer, it's Chase. Are you close by?"

"I'm still in the parking garage. What's going on?"

"I know I told you to go home, but don't leave town yet. There have been some developments. I'm packing up now to head over to the FBI field office."

"Is Sam being released?"

"I can't say for sure. They want to talk with her again, and they're waiting on me. I just wanted to catch you before you drove two hours home. Stay close to the phone. I'll be in touch."

What Jennifer wouldn't give to be in that interview room. She opened the map app on her phone and looked for a coffee shop or a restaurant close to the FBI office. She found one directly across the street from the entrance. She'd sit there all day if there was a chance Sam would be released. She wanted to be the first person Sam saw when she stepped out of that building. She never would have believed that she could miss someone so much, and the chance of a future with Sam suddenly looked so much brighter.

CHAPTER NINETEEN

The room felt even colder than it had yesterday, if that was possible. Sam sat in the metal chair, shivering despite having the blanket from her cot wrapped around her shoulders. The air-conditioner vent was blowing like a 747 engine. It had to be part of the process, a means to break her spirit. It might just be working. She hadn't slept a wink and was now on day two without a cup of coffee. Her head thumped out the warnings of caffeine withdrawal. Feeling so powerless drove her crazy.

The one thing she seemed to have an abundance of was time. Hours and hours of uninterrupted time to think and feel and ponder and reflect. What she wouldn't give to be back in bed, at home, with Jennifer wrapped in her arms. Jennifer: without a doubt, her heart's desire.

Was she betraying Kara's memory by finding a love that felt so right? It no longer felt like that. What she'd shared with Kara for all those years had been different than what she had with Jennifer. The love she felt for Jennifer wasn't less than. It was, well, just different in a pleasant, amazing, new way.

There were parts of her that Jennifer knew better than anyone ever had. Likely because she was a different person now. More experienced in life than the young woman Kara had known and fallen in love with. Different than the woman Kara had aged with and planned to retire with. Since she'd met Jennifer, she'd learned to be more open with her thoughts and feelings. She was different than she'd been a year ago when the accident had happened. She was stronger, with a better sense of identity.

Time with Jennifer helped her recognize and learn from some mistakes she'd made with Kara. She'd do everything in her power to not grow complacent. Take each day or road trip or walk through town as an opportunity to make a new memory. She wanted to wake up knowing that each day was a gift and not to be taken for granted. Watching Jennifer experience everything about Minnesota for the first time had helped her see that.

Jennifer. Always on her mind and in her heart. What she felt made her dizzy and giddy and alive. She only hoped that at some point, she'd see the light of day again and could share all this with Jennifer in person.

The unknowns were the worst part. Not since the time right after Kara's accident had she felt such a profound loss of control over her life. She had no idea what Chase was working on or if the FBI had any new leads. The only thing she was permitted to do was to sit in this tiny room and think and wait. Jennifer believed in her, and that made all the difference in her ability to persist through this craziness. With any luck, the seventy-two-hour window would expire without charges, or they'd find out who was really responsible and set her free.

The door buzzed and clicked. She remained seated. Maybe it was time for breakfast or lunch or dinner. Who knew how long she'd been there? There was no sense of time without windows.

The door pushed open, and a new agent stepped in. She hadn't seen him before. What was he, like, twelve? Maybe it was his first day. His jacket was buttoned, and his tie was knotted perfectly. He was clean-cut and had such a baby face that Sam was sure he could go a week without shaving and still have softer skin than her.

"Please stand without the blanket."

She sighed. She really wanted to keep the blanket, but in this place, it didn't much matter what she wanted. She let it fall into the metal chair and stood.

"Step into the hallway."

She kept her hands at her sides and did as she was told.

"This way." He held her arm and guided her. They walked side by side to the end of the hallway, turned right, and kept walking. "Stop here." He scanned his ID, and she heard the familiar buzz followed by the click. He pushed the door open. "Step inside."

She stepped into another small interview room. The door closed behind her. Once again, she was all alone. At least this room was warmer. Something clicked above her head, and the whirl of the air-conditioner blower ramped up to speed. Freezing cold air saturated the room. Great. She didn't even have the blanket to fend off the chill. She walked in circles around the table and tried to stay warm.

There was no way of knowing how long they kept her waiting. She lost count of her laps. It could have been ten minutes or countless hours. Finally, she heard the buzz and click, and Agent Palmer walked into the room holding a large cardboard box.

Chase followed him with a manilla envelope. "You're being released. I'll work with a judge to get a relief order signed so we can get the arrest expunged from your record, and you're free to go."

Sam felt like she was being punked. "It's over? But who did it? Who stole the money? Who set me up?"

"A statement was released to the press a few minutes ago," Agent Palmer said. "The person responsible for the theft was the owner, Michael Walsh. Everything that pointed to you and the other suspect, a Mr. Brent Olsen, was nothing more than smoke and mirrors. I'm sorry it took this long to sort it all out. We believe that he set it up that way, hoping he'd have enough time to disappear. We had a big break in the case this morning, and he confessed to everything. He's been attempting to clean up the code so that the evidence would be gone by the time Ms. Delgado got to the claims module. He thought she'd cancel the contract on her first day, but apparently, you interfered. What he didn't know was that we had started our investigation long before she was hired and had the code from an ex-client's servers."

An ex-client's servers. Of course. It was all starting to make sense now. "The Eastman account. They hosted their own software. I remember that being an issue and from that point on, Mike insisted that all future clients use our cloud-based servers. I didn't understand the big deal back then, but if it was him, it makes more sense now." Sam rubbed her eyes. Her head was pounding. "Mike did this? He set me up to take the fall? I've been to their house for cookouts. Why would he do this?"

"He hasn't yet shared the why of it all. Our search warrant was unexpected. He had no choice but to come in for questioning. We've had him in custody for as long as you've been here. That's all I can say without jeopardizing the case. Your attorney has a nondisclosure form for you to sign. It's valid until after the trial. We'll need you to testify."

A sense of betrayal overtook the sleep-deprived numbness. Mike was responsible. Never in a million years would she have thought it was him. Her money had been on Brent, but he'd been set up just like she had. It was a good thing she hadn't been running the investigation. She wouldn't have been easily swayed to his innocence. She might have done to him what the FBI had done to her.

It was probably best she stick to technology. There was simple logic to follow there, instead of dealing with human nature. "Was Kelly arrested too? What happens to the company and all the employees and the existing clients?"

"At this point, Mrs. Walsh has not been taken into custody. However, it's still an ongoing investigation. The company is closed indefinitely." Agent Palmer pushed the box across the table. "Here's everything belonging to you that we removed from your home. Your attorney has a copy of the search inventory list to compare to what's in the box. All electronic devices that belonged to Walsh Software Design are now evidence and will not be returned. Ms. Phillips, you are free to go."

Sam looked at the contents of the box, plucked out her wallet, verified its contents, and stuffed it into the back pocket of her jeans. She picked up her belt and put it on. Next, she searched for her wedding ring. Not wearing it felt weird. Part of her knew it was time to put it away. She spotted it, plucked it out of the bag and slid it on her finger. She'd remove it for good another day. Right now, it helped her feel somewhat normal, somewhat human.

One last item was missing. She dug through the box. "Where's my phone? It's not here."

Special Agent Palmer opened the folder in his hands. "It was an employer provided phone."

"Yeah, they paid for it because I was on call twenty-four-seven, but it's my only phone. My pictures are on it. There are voice mail messages on there that I don't want to lose. They ported in my personal number. It's the phone number that I've had forever."

"Let me see what I can do," Chase said.

"I'll work with our tech people," Agent Palmer said.

Sam sighed. She looked at Chase. "Thank you for everything."

Chase set a white shopping bag on top of the banker box. "Jennifer sent you a change of clothes, although I'm sure you'd like a steaming hot shower first. Come on, I'll walk you out. She's waiting outside. She's been here all day, determined to take you home."

Chase's words warmed Sam's heart. Jennifer had been there all day, waiting. It reaffirmed everything she'd thought about while sitting all alone in the cell and was just one more reason Sam was in love with her.

Agent Palmer scanned his badge, and for the first time since she'd entered the building, Sam wasn't instructed with a guiding grip on the back of her arm. She walked next to Chase as a free woman. She hastened her pace. She wanted out of this building. More than that, she couldn't wait to hold Jennifer in her arms.

"What time is it?" Sam asked, carrying her box. "Typically, I'd check my phone, but ya know."

Chase looked over to her and smiled. "It's almost six o'clock in the evening."

The bright sunshine was blinding. Sam blinked several times until her eyes adjusted. She felt like a mole coming to the surface for the first time in weeks. She heard the fast-approaching footfalls of high-heeled shoes. Her heart skipped a beat. Jennifer. Walking out of the FBI building gave Sam a sense of a new lease on life. She was going to make the most of it.

"Sam! I was getting worried that you weren't going to be released."

Sam set the box down and wrapped Jennifer in her arms. "Are you ever a sight for sore eyes. I'm so glad you're here. I've missed you. It feels so good to hold you. I don't want to let go."

"I'll be in touch about expunging your arrest. I think you two have some catching up to do." Chase patted Sam's shoulder and walked away.

Sam just stood there, holding Jennifer because it was what she wanted to do, and for the first time in two days, she could do exactly what she wanted. "Thank you for believing in me and for hiring

Chase. I don't know what I'd do without you," Sam whispered into her neck.

"Of course I believe in you. There was never a doubt in my mind." Jennifer held her tightly. "I've missed you too."

"Will you stay with me tonight? I want to hold you. I want to be with you." Sam kissed her with all the appreciation and affection overflowing in her heart.

"Try to stop me." Jennifer snuggled close. "We can get a hotel if you want a shower and clean clothes, or we can just go home. Tell me what you want. I'll do whatever you need," Jennifer said when Sam released her tight hold.

"I know it's late, but I'd like to go home." Exhaustion hit and hit hard. Now that she was with Jennifer, she wanted nothing more than to curl up and sleep.

"How about you stay with me tonight? If your house looks anything like my apartment did, it's going to be a mess. We can tackle it tomorrow once you've had some sleep. What do you say?"

She was probably right. Sam was so tired that she was nauseated. "I don't care which house, as long as I'm with you." She picked up her box of belongings and followed Jennifer to the car.

❖

Even with Jennifer's warning, Sam wasn't prepared for what she saw when she walked into her house. Her organized and orderly world had been tossed into a box and shaken violently until nothing was anywhere close to where it belonged.

Everything had been touched, and everything was out of place. The dinner plates were on the wrong side of the cabinet. Cups were scattered across the counter and not above the coffee maker. The silverware tray was sitting on the island. Everything had been inspected and rearranged to make room for the next section of inspection. What on earth had they been looking for that required the removal of the lids from the flour and sugar canisters? Even if they wore gloves, she was tossing both into the trash and starting over.

"I can start putting this room back together," Jennifer said from behind her. "I have an idea of how you like it."

"Sure, we can start in here, but I'd like to take a look around."
The living room looked just as bad. The couch cushions were tossed
about, and the drawers in the side tables had been removed and were
sitting on the coffee table. The books in the small library had all
been rifled. Some were stacked on the floor.

She turned and noticed that the chair blocking her bedroom
door had been moved, and the door to the primary bedroom was
open. Did she even dare look? She hadn't expected to deal with that
room today. One thing at a time had always been her motto. One
crisis, one problem, one life altering event at a time. Her methodical
nature insisted on that. It was why her career had always been such
a good fit. Technology involved process, procedure, and an order of
execution. Today, it seemed, chaos prevailed.

Sam walked up the short hallway. The door leading into the
basement was open too, and the laundry room looked as bad as the
kitchen. Sam stepped into the primary bedroom, looked to her right,
and froze.

Kara. Why would they open the urn? It had been sealed with
melted wax. Now, her ashes were scattered and sprinkled all over
the top of the dresser. How could the agents be so callous? What
did they think she was hiding in a sealed urn? She gulped down
the flood of emotion that threated to knock her to her knees. Sam
planted her hand on the wall for support. She covered her mouth
with her other hand and clenched her jaw. Somehow, she'd survived
the past couple of days, and she'd find a way to survive this too. She
just had to get past the shock.

She looked past the urn and took in the rest of the room. The
dresser drawers were open, and much of the contents had been
dumped on the floor and bed. Jesus, they'd dumped out the sex toy
drawer for all to see. Harnesses, dildos, and vibrators in all sorts of
sizes and colors. She couldn't easily recall the last time she'd been
in that drawer. Life had taken over, and she'd forgotten all about
it. How embarrassing. The bed had been stripped. The pillows had
been removed from the pillowcases, and the mattress was askew.
Both side tables were open and empty. Seeing the bedroom like this
felt every bit as violating as she imagined a cavity search would.

The closet door was open. Why wouldn't it be? Of course
they'd been in there because Kara's urn had been in there. She

willed her feet to move. Kara's clothes and shoes were scattered everywhere. Some were still on hangers, but most were crumpled heaps on the floor. The framed photographs that Jennifer had placed on the shelf had been disassembled. The frames in one stack and the photographs were on the floor, piled in a heap. Discarded like trash.

All of a sudden, the reality of it all came crashing down, and it was just too overwhelming. One sucker punch too many in the last few days. Like a pinched twig, she was on the edge of snapping. She'd seen enough. She walked out through the screened-in porch and continued to the back deck. The sun felt good on her skin. She hadn't completely thawed from her time in the holding cell. It was still hard to believe that she'd spent the better part of two days in custody. She flopped into a chair and stared at the meadow.

After a while, she heard the door open from the dining room and the sound of footsteps on the deck. Jennifer placed two cups of coffee on the table. She stood behind Sam and rested a hand on each shoulder. Sam leaned back until her head was resting against Jennifer's body.

"How are you holding up?"

Sam continued to stare at the meadow. "Not too well at the moment."

"Care to talk? You've been so quiet since you were released. Not two words on the drive back or at the apartment last night."

Sam reached up and squeezed one hand, then let it fall back into her lap. "I'm sorry. It's all been a bit too much."

"You have nothing to apologize for." Jennifer bent and wrapped her arms around Sam's neck. "What can I do to help? I'm worried about you."

"I'm not sure I ever shared this, but I don't do well in chaos. It's the main reason that I don't go to visit my mom or my sisters. We have nothing in common. Their houses look like that." Sam waved toward her house. "All the time, on purpose." She literally shuddered at the thought. "I was always more like my dad. There's a place for everything, and everything has a place. It makes life easier if things are where they belong."

"I know. It's one of the many things I admire about you. It won't take us long to put things away. You'll see."

The overwhelming emotion from moments ago in the primary

bedroom rose right back to the surface. She drew in a deep breath and tried to keep it under control. "They opened the urn. Kara's scattered all over the dresser." Sam picked at the hem of her new shirt.

"I saw."

Sam leaned her head back until her cheek was touching Jennifer's. The contact was comforting. "I don't know what to do. Do I just put it back?"

"We can have the urn resealed."

"It's not just the urn. It's all of it. Everything. How do I put it all back and pretend like nothing happened?" She huffed out an exhale.

"Well, that depends on what you want. If you put everything back the way it was, it doesn't leave much room for anything new." Jennifer squeezed her shoulders. "It's been an insane couple of days. You don't have to do everything right this minute. You can close the door like before and tackle that room another time."

"They pulled the rug out from under me and flipped my world upside down. They went through my life with a fine-tooth comb. Tossed my treasures on the floor like they were trash." Anger flared. Her stomach clenched along with her fists. She'd need a solid week at the gym to work off the frustration. "I gave Mike everything I had, even when I had nothing to give, and he repays me for my loyalty by setting me up to take the fall for his crimes? Why? I don't understand. The whole year after Kara died, that job was all I had left. He *knew* that! I just want to know why." Sam leaned forward and rubbed her face. She wanted to scream. She wanted to throw something, break something, smash something into a thousand pieces, rip it apart like they had done to her life. The one thing that kept her from completely losing her mind was Jennifer. She was the anchor keeping Sam from being lost at sea.

"Oh, sweetheart, I wish I had answers for you. I can't imagine how hurt and angry and betrayed you must feel." Jennifer rested a hand on Sam's back.

"I'm furious! I was handcuffed. I was chained to a bench. I was fingerprinted. I had mugshots taken. Left profile, right profile, face forward. They locked me in a room that was freezing cold. I had no idea what time of the day it was or how long I'd been there. No coffee. Periodically, I'd get a stale tray of food out of a vending machine. And all I want from Mike is to know why. Why me? What did I do to deserve that? I gave him twelve years. No one deserved to be treated like that. Look at my house! I'm guessing your place looked just as bad. Why would he do this to any of us?" Sam leaned forward and cupped her hands behind her neck. She had to try something to maintain the last thread of control.

Jennifer walked around and stood in front of her, and Sam rested her head against Jennifer's stomach. She just sat there, wrapped in Jennifer's arms. Tears fell. Tears of anger. Tears of betrayal. Tears because she'd been hurt and then tears because she was loved. It was so confusing to feel all of that at once.

She couldn't get over how comforting Jennifer's touch was. She didn't want her to let go. Ever. She wrapped her arms around Jennifer's waist and held her close. "I saw the eviction notice on your counter this morning. Probably not what you expected when you accepted this contract."

"Definitely another first for me. Minnesota's been chock-full of firsts."

"I'm sorry you were dragged into this mess."

"Oh, my sweet, sweet Sam, you have nothing to apologize for. Mike's actions and the last few days aside, I wouldn't change a single thing. I couldn't be more grateful that I took this contract. I couldn't be more grateful for the Lonely Blonde that introduced us that first day at Talley's. Taking this job brought you into my life, and I am eternally thanking—"

Boom, boom, boom.

The sound of a fist on the front door radiated all the way to the back deck. Sam froze. She was beginning to hate the sound of someone knocking on the front door, let alone pounding. If she ignored it, maybe they'd leave. Then the memory of the FBI's words shot to the front of her mind: Open up or we'll enter with force. Fuck. She stood and walked through the living room. The pounding started again. She looked out the side window but didn't see a car in the driveway or a body by the door. As if attached to someone else's body, Sam watched her hand turn the knob and pull the front door open. She expected the worst but was surprised to see the stoop completely empty.

"Hello?" She stepped out of the front door and looked up the driveway. She could barely make out the bumper of a car parked on the far side of Jennifer's. At least it wasn't law enforcement. Sam heard a car door close, and the sound of footsteps grew louder. Slowly, the shadow of two people appeared on the sidewalk right before the bodies that had created the shadows turned the corner.

Pat and Angie. Filled with dread, Sam's stomach dropped to the floor. She wasn't entirely sure she was up for this today. She didn't have the energy to hear how much they missed Kara.

"Sammy! Oh my God, you are home. Are you okay? I'm so happy to see you. We were about to give up and head back to town." Angie ran up and engulfed Sam in a hug. "We've been texting and calling like crazy."

"It's really good to see you, pal." Pat wrapped her arms around both Sam and Angie and squeezed.

Sam couldn't move. She went numb. Like her past and present were about to collide in a glorious explosion. She wasn't ready for the two vastly different worlds to meld. She needed to find her balance before she could deal with one more thing, and Pat and Angie wouldn't add a little thing to her upside-down world. No, it would be a big, over the top, booming, boisterous thing. She thought about brushing them off and asking them to leave. Then she caught a whiff of Pat's cologne and Angie's perfume. The familiarity brought back memories of a lifetime of friendship. They had been there for everything. College graduation, celebrating her first professional job, closing on the first house. Sam had always enjoyed their friendship until after the funeral, when she couldn't enjoy anything. Even then, whether she welcomed it or not, they'd been there. A fresh wave of emotion threatened to take her down. She breathed through it as best she could.

Finally, after what seemed like forever, Pat released them from the bear hug and stepped back. "We've been worried sick. The FBI raid has been the talk of the town. It was all over the evening news, and you went dark. You haven't answered your phone for the last three days. I even used the emergency code. You always answer the emergency code. What the hell happened? Are you okay? What's going on?"

The expression on their faces conveyed their sincerity and genuine concern. Sam had pushed them away and avoided them long enough. It was time to deal with everything. All of it, and apparently, today was the day. "I couldn't answer because the FBI took my phone. In fact, they still have it."

Pat's eyebrow shot up in that quirky, questioning expression that Sam envied. A much younger version of herself had spent way too long in front of the mirror, trying to get her eyebrow to do that, without any success. "Why does the FBI have your phone?" Her arm wrapped around Angie's shoulder; Angie's wrapped around her waist, the other hand planted on Pat's stomach as if bracing her to keep her from falling forward.

If Sam didn't know any better, she would have sworn that they were propping each other up. It occurred to her that they had been through a lot too. They'd lost not just one but two of their best friends for the better part of a year and a half.

Sam let her folded arms drop to her sides and softened her stance. "Because technically, Walsh Software Design paid the bill. It was logged into evidence when I was arrested."

"Wait, what? *You* were arrested?" The concern that flashed across their faces made Sam feel good. Like they'd maybe get through this and be okay.

"Yes, and released last night with no charges filed. Trust me, it's been a crazy few days." Jennifer had kept her balanced in much the same way that it seemed they were doing for each other. A basis. Something in common.

"Were you in jail?" Angie asked.

"Not really jail. They called it a holding cell, but yeah, it was kinda jail. I wasn't allowed to leave. That's about all I can say about it." Sam stepped back and opened the door fully. "Come on inside. Don't mind the mess. The FBI redecorated when they searched the house, and we haven't really started to put it back together yet."

Pat and Angie stayed on the stoop. "We? Well, that explains the mystery car in the driveway. I was wondering who you knew from New Mexico, or is it a rental?"

Sam waved them into the house. "Yes, we. There's someone I'd like you two to meet." Pat nodded and followed Angie inside. The sounds of items being put away drifted out of the kitchen.

"Holy shit, your house really was tossed. Do all of the rooms look like this?" Angie's eyes darted back and forth.

"I'm not sure. I haven't had a chance to check out all the rooms." She led them into the kitchen, which was, for the most part, back to normal. Jennifer must have worked on it while Sam was out on the deck. She was a treasure beyond the definition of the word. The coffee pot was full, and the two cups that Jennifer had taken out to the deck were now on the island next to two empty cups, along with cream, sugar, and two spoons at the ready. Sam looked at Jennifer and mouthed the words *thank you*. Jennifer nodded and smiled.

"Pat, Angie, this is Jennifer. Jennifer, this is Pat and Angie." Sam stood next to Jennifer and wrapped her arm around her shoulders. "She's very, very important to me. Please be kind."

Pat stepped forward first. Her typical gruff exterior softened a bit. She held out a hand in greeting. "It's nice to meet you. I'm Pat, and this is my wife, Angie." Angie stepped up next to her. "I'm going to guess that it's you we should thank for getting my pal here to a hair salon. The new cut looks good, Sam."

Sam stood next to Jennifer and watched as her old world interacted with her new one. She held her breath with awkward anticipation, but at the moment, it wasn't as bad as she'd expected.

Chapter Twenty

Jennifer drew in a deep breath and smiled her best smile. She wasn't at all prepared to meet friends from Sam's previous life with Kara. How would Sam introduce her? They hadn't had a chance to discuss what might be next for them, given that their first time together had been interrupted by a search warrant, handcuffs, and an arrest. Just as the nervous butterflies took hold, Sam revealed to her, once again, what an amazing person she was. She led her friends into the kitchen and walked around the island and stood at Jennifer's side with her arm wrapped protectively around her shoulders.

"Pat, Angie, this is Jennifer. Jennifer, this is Pat and Angie." Sam gave her a little squeeze. "She's very, very important to me. Please be kind."

One of the women was easily a head taller than Sam. She had broad shoulders, a crew cut, and a stocky build. She wore khaki slacks and a polo shirt. The other was just a tad taller than Jennifer. She was more feminine, wearing a short-sleeved summer dress and with shoulder-length strawberry-blond hair and a fair complexion.

The taller woman stepped forward and held out a hand in greeting. "It's nice to meet you. I'm Pat, and this is my wife, Angie." Angie stepped up and smiled. "I'm going to guess that it's you we should thank for getting my pal here to a hair salon. The new cut looks good, Sam."

Jennifer relaxed and released her held breath as she shook their hands.

"It's very nice to meet you," Angie said.

Jennifer smiled. "It's very nice to meet both of you. I've heard wonderful things."

"You look good, Sam. Not quite the old Sam yet but much better than the last time I saw you. Different but good," Pat said.

"Thanks. I don't know how I could ever be the old Sam again. Too much has changed. I like this version of me just fine. Hopefully, you will too. I'm coming out the other side."

Jennifer looked from Sam to Pat. So few words and yet, it seemed as though they had a moment of deep understanding. Pat nodded and smiled. Sam returned both gestures.

"Coffee?" Sam stepped away to fill the two empty cups on the counter.

Jennifer instantly missed the feeling of her protective shield. What she wouldn't give to be out on the back deck with Sam, continuing their conversation. She remained quiet and watched, and before she knew it, Sam was back.

Pat picked up her coffee. "It's kinda weird to see you standing in this house, in this kitchen, with your arm wrapped around someone who isn't…well, someone new. I'll get used to it, but it's weird. There, I said it. Now I can get past it."

When Pat and Angie had first arrived, Jennifer had a momentary fantasy that they could be couple friends. She couldn't believe how much things had shifted for her in Minnesota. She found herself craving things she'd once run away from. Anymore, she dreamed of a future with Sam and friends to hang out with. And now, Pat's words caused her to bristle. Was this what it was going to be like? Not so long ago, she'd worried about coming second to Kara in Sam's heart, but something had shifted between them, and she no longer felt that way. Pat's words, however, had her wondering if it would be that way with all of Sam's friends. Would she forever be seen as Sam's second choice? She tried not to rush to judgment and instead strived for a wait-and-see approach.

"If you don't mind me asking, how'd you two meet?" Angie asked while pouring cream into her coffee.

"In a roundabout way, I have Pat to thank for that," Sam said and squeezed Jennifer's shoulder.

"Yeah, how's that?" Pat set down her cup.

"Do you remember when we bumped into each other at the

grocery store several months back? Angie was off somewhere buying up the rest of the store."

"Uh, yeah, if you're referring to the time you ditched your cart of stuff and bolted."

Jennifer felt Sam stiffen. She'd been so caught up in how much Pat's words affected her, she hadn't stopped to think how awkward this must be for Sam. Protectiveness flared. She wrapped an arm around Sam's lower back and squeezed gently.

"Yeah, that's the time I'm talking about. You told me that I was stuck. Called it tumbling down the rabbit hole and that I needed to snap out of it and move on. You told me to go to grief group or counseling. The conversation stuck with me, and a week or so later, I actually tried grief group."

"So you two met at grief group?" Angie asked. "That's oddly romantic."

"No." Sam shook her head. "Grief group was an epic fail. I bolted pretty quick. There was way too much grief. Anyway, on my way back to my truck, I caught a whiff of burgers and fries from Talley's. I found a seat at the bar and ordered my usual. Jennifer walked in and climbed onto the stool next to me. She's snappy and has a quick wit, but more than that, there was something about her that drew me in. I hadn't felt that comfortable in a long, long time. We chatted. We ate. She beat me at darts. And the next day, she showed up at work as the consultant programmer. That first day, she talked her way into my office and, over the past few months, into my heart. It might sound weird, but spending time with her and getting to know her has helped me get to know myself more than I could ever put into words. Like I said earlier, she's very important to me."

Jennifer wanted to jump up into her arms and kiss her right there. She decided to resist the urge until they no longer had visitors. Instead, she settled for a subtle squeeze and leaned into Sam's shoulder. There was no denying how much the words touched her heart. Someone started talking and pulled her out of her swoon-worthy moment.

Pat looked directly at Sam. "Can I ask you something?"

Sam nodded. Jennifer felt her tense again. This had to be so difficult, especially after the last few days.

"Why'd you pull away from us? I'm not talking about the big

group. Hell, there's times I need a break from them. I'm talking about me and Angie. We've been friends since college. But after the accident, you totally ghosted us. You declined invites. You stopped answering calls. You disappeared, and I don't understand what we did wrong."

Jennifer looked at all of them. Never before had she felt like such an outsider. She wasn't part of this group. She was an intruder. "I should go so you three can talk."

Sam held on a little tighter. "I'd rather you stay. Please? For me?"

Her words were soft and spoken with such sincerity that Jennifer couldn't imagine leaving her side, ever. "Okay."

Sam picked up her coffee. Her hand was shaking. She took a sip and set it back on the counter and stared at it. "In the days right after Kara's accident, before my family showed up, all of you came over to be with me, but every time someone knocked on the front door, the conversations quickly became a loop of 'remember when Kara did this,' or 'remember when we all did this,' or 'we all did that.' It never failed. I know you were dealing with the loss and the grief too, but hearing those stories over and over and over did nothing but rip my heart out and kept reminding me that there would never be a new story. There would never be another memory. It was as if you all had accepted the accident, accepted her death, before I did. I wasn't there yet. I was still waiting for her to come home."

Sam gulped in air, and then her breath caught. She leaned her head down, and Jennifer could see her jaw clench. She knew Sam was trying to hold back her emotions. She'd seen it before during intense conversations. She felt helpless. Sam had to express this in her own way, but it broke Jennifer's heart to see her hurting all over again.

Sam buried her face in her hands for a few moments before she finally lowered them. Jennifer rested a hand on her back and felt her draw in a deep breath and let it out slowly. "After the funeral, I began to wonder if all we'd ever had in common was Kara. Like, maybe without her, I'd kind of lost my place with all of you." She wiped at the tears streaming down her cheeks. "You didn't do anything wrong. You didn't deserve to be ghosted. All I can say is that I needed time. I needed time to accept and process her death.

I needed to let go and have a chance to say good-bye so that when I saw you, I didn't instantly look for her. You weren't wrong at the grocery store when you said I was stuck. I was. I see that now. Mind you, it's taken the last three months and countless conversations with Jennifer to put any of that into words."

Jennifer was so focused on her and the steady stream of tears that ran down her cheeks that she didn't realize Pat and Angie had migrated from the far side of the island until arms engulfed both her and Sam as if they were one. Angie was closest, and her body shook with sobs. Jennifer could feel the same from Pat's massive arms that were wrapped around all of them.

"You're my best fr…friend. I've missed you so much." Pat's voice boomed above her head. "I had no idea what you were really going through. I am so sorry."

"Oh, Sammy, we've missed you so much. Yes, we miss Kara, but we've missed you too." Angie's voice was muffled by Jennifer's hair.

"I've missed both of you too. I hadn't realized how much until you showed up today," Sam said between sobs.

The four of them huddled there for quite some time. It was such an emotional moment about a time in their lives that Jennifer hadn't even been there for, and yet, tears streamed down her cheeks as if she'd experienced it all too. She felt so much empathy for all three of them but especially for Sam and all she'd endured.

Pat released her grip, pulled a paper towel free, and blew her nose. "Big jerk, you made me cry, and now snot is running down my face." She tugged on Sam's arm until they faced each other and pulled her in into an even tighter hug. "Can you look at me yet? You know, without expecting Kara to walk in the room? I want my friend back. I miss hanging out with you."

"Yeah, I think so, now that I understand what I was even feeling." Sam held her tightly. "We never stopped being friends, you big oaf. I'm sorry it took me so long to work through it. I've missed hanging out with you too."

Jennifer felt a tap on her arm and turned to Angie. Mascara streaked down her round wet face. "Thank you for being there for her and bringing our Sammy back." She pulled Jennifer into a hug. "I look forward to getting to know you."

"I look forward to getting to know you too," Jennifer said and realized that she meant it. There was so much more on the tip of her tongue, but it needed to be said to Sam, not Angie. The right time would come.

Angie released Jennifer from the hug, turned and slapped Pat's arm. "Quit hogging Sammy. It's my turn for a hug."

"We're good?" Pat asked.

"We're better than good." Sam smiled. "Thanks for opening up the conversation. I don't know that I would have."

"I'm kinda glad you were arrested and that the company was on the news because it made this happen. I'm glad to have you back, pal."

"I could have gone without the being arrested part," Sam said.

Pat turned to Angie. "Okay, now you can smother her with your love and affection."

Angie slapped her arm again and stepped into Sam's embrace. "I love you, Sammy, and I've missed you so much."

"I love you too. I love both of you." Sam held Angie close.

Jennifer longed to be in Sam's arms and to hear those same words but in a slightly different context. There was no doubt in her mind that she was in love with Sam. There was no doubt that she wanted to share a future with Sam. Something told her that Sam felt the same way. Her fears of playing second chair to a ghost were fading with each step Sam took forward.

Pat's voice shook her out of her thoughts. "Okay, we've solved the world's problems. Time for a change of topic."

Sam laughed and wiped the tears off her face. Angie did the same and returned to a seat next to her wife.

"Will the office get to reopen, or are the two of you now unemployed loafers?" Pat asked. "Weren't you supposed to retire soon anyway?"

"Yeah, good memory, the retirement thing was last summer, but after the accident, I kicked the can on that. I couldn't see doing all the trips alone or not doing the trips and sitting here all alone. Anyway, I think it's fair to say that we're both unemployed, but honestly, I haven't had two minutes to think about any of that. Today, I'd like to focus on putting the house back together, and quite honestly, I'd like to take a moment to catch my breath before thinking about what might be next."

"Jennifer, how far did you travel for this work? We noticed New Mexico plates on the car. Is it a rental, or do you live there?" Angie asked.

She wasn't at all surprised by the question. "That's my car. When this opportunity came up, I decided to take a leap of faith. I am very glad that I did." She reached for Sam's hand, very glad indeed. She could tell by both Pat and Angie's expressions that the topic wasn't dropped. Nope, not even close. The gears had clearly started to churn the moment they'd heard that she lived in New Mexico. She had a feeling where this was heading and hoped she was wrong. She didn't want to be cornered. It was like Sam had said. She really wanted a moment to catch her breath before she approached what might be next. More than anything, she wanted a chance to talk with Sam.

"If you live in New Mexico, when will you go home? I imagine you have feelers out for the next consulting gig?" Pat was to the point, that was for sure.

"That's not a conversation for today, all right? Please? It's been an intense week," Sam said. "We haven't had two minutes to consider what might be next."

Jennifer could have said the same thing, but she was certain that it carried more weight coming from Sam. She was right. Pat's stance softened. Her shoulders relaxed. She smiled and nodded. Angie did the same. They were protective of their friend. There was no doubt about that. Maybe someday, they'd feel that protection for her too.

"Yeah, okay, just so you don't move to New Mexico, Sam. Well, we've taken up enough of your time." Pat set down her empty cup.

"Or…" Angie started and looked from Jennifer to Sam. "We could pull out something a bit stronger, crank up some tunes, and put this house back together. Four sets of hands are better than two, and bonus, we kinda know where most everything goes or used to go, anyway."

"Give us a second?" Sam asked and tugged on Jennifer's hand.

Jennifer followed her out to the garage.

"How are you feeling about all of this?" Sam asked. Something about her expression begged for honesty.

Another swoon-worthy moment. Sam had known her friends for more than thirty years and had every right to make any decisions about the afternoon, but instead, she wanted to know how Jennifer was feeling. The best part was that she felt good and could answer honestly. "Sam, I like them. I'd like to get to know them better, but none of that matters if you're not ready. You tell me. How are you feeling?"

"I think it would be fun to crank up some tunes, have a few cocktails, and put this house back together." She smiled. "I'm ready."

"I'm all in. You should probably clean a few items off the primary bed before any help arrives in that room." Jennifer wiggled her eyebrows and smiled. "Full disclosure, I know those items were purchased with and for your wife, but if we tried them or purchased some of our own someday, I'd be open to all of it."

"How'd I get so lucky to have you walk into my life?" Sam hugged her. "Our talk was interrupted. There's so much I want to say to you."

"There's so much I want to say to you but not while you have company waiting inside. I'm not going anywhere." She gave Sam another squeeze and stepped back.

"Thank you for being open to all of this. I'm sure it wasn't easy, especially after the past few days."

The last few days had been crazy and unbelievable, but everything with Sam was effortless and easy. "So you're not surprised, I've already cleaned up the dresser. Kara's urn is in the sewing room closet. We can have it resealed. I hope I didn't overstep. I took care of it while you were all outside."

"Not an overstep at all. I appreciate it more than you know. Thank you." Sam kissed her forehead. "We should get back inside."

She nodded and followed Sam into the house. She and Sam could have easily tackled the cleanup, but she knew this was more about repairing friendship and less about many hands and all that. Still, she found herself eager to get at it. The sooner they finished, the sooner she could have Sam all to herself again. There really was so much that she wanted to say.

"Okay, there's two-day-old pizza in the fridge if anyone gets hungry. Let's make some cocktails, crank some music, and put a house back together," Sam said.

Pat and Angie whooped out in celebration. Pat clapped Sam on the back. Two old friends had stopped by and helped turn a dark, troubled day into something fun and possibly healing. It might even turn out to be something fun for all of them. Jennifer welcomed the potential for new friendships.

CHAPTER TWENTY-ONE

The last of the books were returned to their proper place in the freshly dusted bookcase. Sam turned and took in the space. The main living area was, for the most part, back to normal.

"Sammy, can I borrow you for a moment?" Angie asked. She was standing in the hallway leading to the laundry room and the primary bedroom.

Sam squinted and wondered which of the two rooms she was going to be pulled into. She had a hunch and walked in her direction.

Angie hooked her arm in Sam's and led her to the primary bedroom. "Where's Jennifer?"

"On the other side of the house, working on one of the spare bedrooms." Sam wasn't about to tell her that Jennifer was working on the bedroom she'd called her own for the last few months. "Why, do you need her?"

"Nope. I'm glad she's occupied for the moment. This is a conversation for just the two of us." She let go of Sam's arm.

Sam looked around. Jennifer had done a nice job cleaning up. There was no evidence of Kara on the dresser or the floor. Angie had already straightened out the mattress and made the bed with clean sheets, evident by the pile of sheets in front of the big dresser.

"Sweetie, come here and sit with me for a minute." Angie patted a spot on the edge of the bed. "I can see how much Jennifer means to you, or at least, I can see how much she's helped you so far, but are you sure you're ready to start a new relationship?"

Not this. "Ang, I know you and Kara were best—"

Angie held up her hands. "That's not what this is about. It's not about me being protective or my friendship with Kara. It's about you and your inability to let Kara go." She stood and walked into the closet. "Sweetie, the house, especially this room, still looks as if Kara just ran to the store. Everything is exactly how she left it. It's been over a year, and you still have all her stuff. Her clothes, her shoes, her makeup, and other stuff in the bathroom. If you can't let this stuff go, how can you look at Jennifer the way you do?"

Sam looked around and saw what Angie saw. In the days after the accident, she'd felt paralyzed by grief. She'd needed everything to remain in place and stay the same. It was the only way she could function. She hadn't been ready to say good-bye to Kara or her clothes or the scent of her that lingered around the house. Days had turned into weeks, and weeks had turned into months and on it went. Deputy Jones hadn't helped. It had been difficult to escape her relentless torment. She'd truly been stuck. Tumbling down the rabbit hole into a quagmire of loss. She hadn't seen a way out of it, certain that the best of what her life had to offer was already in the past.

Then Jennifer had walked into her life and ignited a flicker of hope. The time they'd spent together had helped to chase away the relentless darkness. She'd thought outside the box and found ways to help Sam heal. As time went on and the feelings between them grew stronger, Sam had started to see that she didn't have to be limited by what was gone because the future held the promise of something more.

Yes, it was time. There was no reason to hang on to all of this stuff. "One thing has nothing to do with the other. Truth be told, I haven't been in this room in a couple months. I've been staying in one of the guest bedrooms. Yeah, right after the accident, it was comforting to be surrounded by her scent and her stuff, and the thought of going through it was overwhelming. I know it's time to let it go. Take anything you want. Hell, I'm open to boxing it all up. I'm just not sure what to do with it. It seemed wrong to fill a dumpster with her treasures."

"I'm happy to hear you say that." Angie patted her hand. "It just so happens that I've been working at a shelter for abused women for most of the past year. Some of them show up with nothing but the clothes on their backs. Kara's wardrobe could be put to good use. There's room in the back of our Cherokee if you're really ready."

Sam stood and walked into the bathroom. Kara's jewelry box was open on the counter. It had been rummaged through, but everything she expected to see was there. She picked up the box and returned to her seat. "Do you remember back in college when you and Kara had those friendship rings made? When worn together, they formed a knot or something, but worn separate, the design looked completely different?"

Angie smiled sadly, wiggled her fingers, and Sam spotted the ring right away.

"Yep, that's the one. For the longest time, Kara thought she'd lost hers. Well, I found it when I was going through some stuff in the bathroom. I think you should have it. I know it's what Kara would want." She lifted the tricolored gold ring from the jewelry box and set it in Angie's hand.

Angie removed her ring, slid Kara's on first and put her half on top. The two linked together and looked every bit as perfect as that day at the jewelry store. "Thank you for this, Sam. I can't tell you how much it means to me."

Sam picked up Kara's wedding band and the emerald and diamond bracelet she had given her for their thirtieth wedding anniversary. She held on to those two items and passed the box to Angie. "You two always had similar taste in jewelry. These two are special to me, but you're welcome to anything else in that box, or take the entire thing," Sam said. "Same goes for her clothes. Certainly, we can take everything to the shelter, but if there's something you'd like, anything that means something to you, by all means, keep it for yourself."

"Thank you. This means more than you could possibly know." She hugged Sam tightly. "There have been a few things, but it felt weird to ask for them when we weren't speaking."

Sam nodded in understanding. This private time spent with Angie was just what she'd been needing. It felt good, almost therapeutic, to share Kara's treasures with someone who would treasure them every bit as much. Sam looked at her left hand and slid her wedding ring off, then put it onto the bracelet with Kara's ring. She clasped the bracelet and tucked the three items in her side table drawer. "I have some boxes in the garage. My mom bought a bunch while she was here for the funeral. She said that I needed to make space for a new roommate."

"Jesus, your mom has always been so out of touch."

"Right?" Sam rolled her eyes. "I'll be right back."

Sam made her way to the garage and realized that the idea of clearing out Kara's clothes was, in a weird way, freeing. It was like Jennifer had said earlier. If she put everything back the way it was, there'd be no room for anything new. It was time to make room. It was time to move forward, and bonus if it would help someone in need. It was time to embrace the next chapter of her life.

She thought about her conversation with Bill at Talley's. She finally felt like she wasn't forgetting Kara by moving on. She was honoring her memory and could finally look back on their time together with appreciation instead of deep sorrow. She found the boxes and the packing tape in the front corner of the garage, right where she'd tossed it all more than a year ago. She picked up as many boxes as she could manage and the tape wheel and made her way back into the house.

"That stack is one I'd like to keep." Angie pointed at a small pile of clothes folded on the bed next to the jewelry box.

There was no flood of memories when Sam looked at it. She wasn't consumed with sadness. Instead, she was filled with reassurance that it was all going to be okay. She opened a box, folded in the flaps, and sealed the bottom before flipping it over and filling it with countless pairs of shoes.

A few hours later, she carried the last box out to her truck and put it in the last pocket of open space and closed the tailgate. Pat and Angie's car had been stuffed to the gills an hour earlier. She could have stopped when their car was full, but for some reason, tonight was the night, and she wanted to finish. She returned to the house and flopped on the couch next to Jennifer, Pat, and Angie. "I can't thank you all enough. This is huge, and it feels good," Sam said.

"You're very welcome. I can't think of a better way to spend a Friday night than helping friends." Pat pushed out of the couch and held out her hand for Angie. "Well, my love, I think we should be going. Sam looks like she's going to crash right here."

"We'll bring the stuff in the truck over tomorrow. Just let me know when you're at the shelter." Sam stood and held out a hand for Jennifer.

"Sounds great. Jennifer gave me her cell number. Hey, Sam, go all in and get a new phone, would ya? Maybe a new number too, since you're starting over and all." Angie smiled and pulled her into a hug, then stepped to the side and hugged Jennifer too.

"You have a point." Sam knew exactly what she was talking about. The last four digits of her old number—5272—had been picked out because it spelled *Kara*. Yeah, it was probably time to get a new one.

"So we're on for next Friday night?" Pat did that eyebrow thing again.

"Yes. Your house, just the four of us." Sam smiled and hugged her tightly. "It's good to have you two back. Again, I'm sorry it took me so long to work through it all."

"What's one lost year when you have almost thirty-five years of friendship? You can't get rid of us that easily. Love you, friend." Pat squeezed her tightly. She turned and engulfed Jennifer in a hug too. "Thank you. I don't say that lightly."

Sam smiled. Pat didn't do anything lightly. She was happy that the three of them were getting along so well. They walked Pat and Angie out to their car and waved as the taillights disappeared off in the distance.

"Well, if that wasn't a day of unexpected events," Sam said.

"Oh, just a day?" Jennifer nudged her with her elbow. "More like a week. How are you feeling? I hope you didn't feel pressured to box up Kara's things."

"Surprisingly, I feel good. Exhausted but good. It felt right. It was time. How about you? It's been a crazy week for you too, not to mention that Pat and Angie can be a little intense."

"I'm feeling much like you in the exhausted but good category. Pat and Angie are nice. I like them. When they first arrived, I think it was a little awkward, but it seemed like their visit was just what you all needed to clear the air and reconnect. I'm glad they stopped by."

Sam wrapped her arms around Jennifer and squeezed gently. The light inside the garage timed out, and everything went dark. It was a moonless night, at least so far. In the darkness, she was content to hold Jennifer in her arms. She could feel each breath. It was exciting, relaxing, and comforting all at once. Her eyes adjusted to the low light, and the stars sparkled above like a distant firefly show. Sam thought about the fireflies from the other night and made no effort to head inside. The stillness and togetherness were, in their own way, pure perfection.

She'd told Pat and Angie how she felt about them, about Kara, and about Jennifer. Now the time seemed right to say the three words that had been on the tip of her tongue.

"I love you." Sam tilted her head down until her forehead touched Jennifer's. "Heart, body, and soul, I love you."

She felt Jennifer's breath catch. Even in this dim light, she could see Jennifer's eyes sparkle as she leaned back. Her smiling expression said all Sam needed to know. "I love you too, Sam. Heart, body, and soul, I love you too. I have never felt like this before. I'm totally in love with you."

Sam kissed her tenderly on the lips.

Jennifer pulled back to look at her. "Say it again. Please, say it again."

"I love you, Jen. Head over heels in love with you." Sam kissed her. "I love you, and I want to share a future with you."

"Oh, sweetheart, that sounds like heaven." Jennifer stepped back and tugged on Sam's hand. "Hey, where's your ring?"

"It's with Kara's in a drawer. It felt right. It was time."

Jennifer cupped her cheek. "Come on, love. Let's go inside."

Sam held her hand and walked with her into the house. Everything felt good. Everything felt right. With Jennifer at her side, she had a future to look forward to.

CHAPTER TWENTY-TWO

Jennifer felt like she was floating on a cloud. She'd certainly wanted to give Sam all the time she needed but couldn't deny how incredible it was to hear Sam express her feelings using those three little words. The look in her eyes and the tone of her voice made her profession of love mean all that much more. Sam was in love with her. Really in love with her.

Jennifer held her hand and led her into what she considered their bedroom, at least for now.

Sam stood behind her, hot breath next to her ear. "Jen, I love you."

"I'll never tire of hearing you say that." She turned her head slightly. "Sam, I love you too."

Sam's hands rested briefly on her hips, then lifted her blouse over her head. After just one time together, she craved Sam's touch, and her body buzzed with excitement. She kept her eyes closed and enjoyed the sensation of each caress and teasing touch. Not knowing where Sam would touch or kiss next added to the excitement and the arousal. She felt her hair lift from her neck. Sam's lips were warm on the delicate skin behind her ear. Kisses trailed down along the side of her neck. Warm fingertips touched her back where her bra clasped. She felt it release, then Sam's hands were on her shoulders, guiding the straps down her arms. She drew in a sharp breath and held it in anticipation of where Sam would touch her next.

A faint whoosh of cool air teased the skin on her back, and she heard clothing land on the floor. She leaned back against Sam's now bare chest. Her skin was so warm. She swayed slightly and smiled when she felt Sam's hardened nipples brush her back. Sam's hands glided around her waist toward her belly button. The button on her jeans released, and the zipper lowered. Sam explored her stomach and waist with the slightest touch. Goose bumps erupted along Jennifer's skin with each teasing caress. She reached up and clasped her hands behind Sam's neck. Warm hands teased her cheeks and along her neck and the outside of her breasts.

"You're absolutely beautiful. I love how you respond to my touch," Sam whispered in her ear.

"Hmm, I love the way you touch me. It makes me tingle all over, and I ache for more."

Sam leaned forward and slid one hand into the waist of her jeans. She enjoyed the way Sam savored her body. She'd never had anyone want to please her the way Sam wanted to, as if her needs were the only focus.

Sam slid a warm hand beneath her lace panties. She was already so wet. She kept her eyes closed and leaned back as Sam's other hand cupped her breast and teased her nipple. "Oh, that feels so good," she whispered.

She parted her legs slightly. This was seductive torture. She rocked her hips forward and moaned when Sam added a bit more pressure. Her legs quivered, and she wasn't sure how long they'd support her. She wanted to feel Sam inside her and reached to pull her even closer. She was already so close, and they hadn't even made it to the bed.

Sam slid her fingers inside.

"Oh yeah, baby, just like that."

Sam moaned in her ear, and it sent shivers through her body. She reached up again and buried her fingers in Sam's hair. Sam pushed with her hips and matched the rhythm of her fingers deep inside. Another first and it felt incredible.

"Don't stop. Feels...so...good." The rhythmic pressure from Sam's hips and the heel of her hand tipped Jennifer over the edge. "Oh, yes. Oh, yes. *Oh...*" She quivered and shook. She couldn't recall orgasms quite so powerful with anyone else. She shivered with aftershocks while rocking her hips in a tiny circle on top of

Sam's hand. She wanted to turn and smother Sam with kisses, but she wasn't sure she could stand on her own quite yet.

Sam kissed her shoulder and neck and held her close while her body recovered. Then she pulled her hand back and pushed Jennifer's jeans down her shaky legs. She stepped out as Sam's fingertips caressed up the outside of each calf, then across the back of her legs, over her butt cheeks and up her back. She shivered from head to toe until Sam's touch once again disappeared.

Jennifer turned and stepped into Sam's embrace, wrapping her arms around Sam's neck. She pulled her close and kissed her with all of the passion and emotion she felt. She unbuckled Sam's belt and slowly unbuttoned and unzipped her jeans. She pushed both jeans and boxers down Sam's hips and smiled when she heard the belt buckle thud on the carpet. She tried to pull the bedspread back without breaking their kiss, but it was just out of reach, so she gave up on the covers and guided Sam on top, then slid onto the cool covers next to her. "I can't get over how good it feels to be with you."

Sam ran her fingertips along Jennifer's arm. "I feel the same way."

Jennifer rolled Sam onto her back and straddled her. Everything with Sam felt amazing and effortless. They fit together perfectly. "Tell me what you like," Jennifer said, trailing kisses down Sam's neck. "I want to make you feel as good as you make me feel."

Sam stroked her back. "Believe me, you do."

"Do you like it when I do this?" She slid down and wrapped her lips around Sam's nipple. She carefully grazed it with her teeth and swirled her tongue around it.

Sam moaned and buried her fingers in Jennifer's hair. Jennifer smiled. She shifted slightly to the side and explored Sam's body with her fingertips. Her skin was smooth as silk. Sam lifted her hips into Jennifer's touch. She was so wet. Jennifer traced her folds. It was so erotic to see her bite her lip and thrust her head back into the pillow in the faint light from the hall. Jennifer slid two fingers inside her, loving how it felt to experience her this way. She still felt inept about how best to please a woman, but she was a quick study and wanted more than anything to please Sam.

Sam rolled the two of them over with Jennifer's fingers still inside. She straddled Jennifer's hips and pushed into her hand. Hot and sexy, Sam rocked on top of her and started to tighten inside. Her legs shook, and her muscles tensed. She thrust her hips in short, jerky movements before she fell forward into Jennifer's arms. Her body quivered and pulsed. Incredible.

Breathless, Sam kissed Jennifer, then lifted off her hand and lay on top of her. Even the weight of her body felt good. Jennifer spread her legs and loosely wrapped them around Sam's hips. "Wow," Sam whispered in her ear.

"Wow indeed." Jennifer trailed a finger across her cheek. "I love you."

"I love you too." Sam rolled over with Jennifer wrapped in her arms.

Jennifer slid down and rested her head on Sam's chest. "I can feel your heartbeat."

"I think it's still on double time."

"It feels so good to be in your arms. I know I keep saying that I've never felt like this before, but I've really never felt like this before. Being with you just feels so right."

"It feels amazing to hold you. I'm so grateful to have you in my life."

"Can I ask you something?" She wasn't sure how Sam would feel about her question, but for some reason, she needed to hear her answer.

"Anything."

"Earlier today, Pat said it was weird to see you in the kitchen with your arm around my shoulders, and I wondered how it feels to you. Is it weird to have me in a space that you shared with Kara for so many years?"

"Wow, that's a doozy. I could ask you the same thing. Is it weird for you to be here?"

"No, because I've only ever known you in this house. I mean, I've seen all of the pictures. But I never knew her or experienced Kara here, so I don't have the memories that you have inside these walls. I hadn't thought about it like that until Pat mentioned it. It kind of stuck with me all day." She hoped the conversation wasn't too much. She certainly didn't want to dampen the mood.

Sam was quiet for a few moments. Her heartbeat slowed to normal, and her breathing hadn't changed. That had to be a good sign. "No, it hasn't been weird to have you here. You brought light and life back into this house. Having you here makes it feel like a home again." She grew quiet again and gently ran her fingers through Jennifer's hair. "You asked me the other day if there was room in my heart for you."

Jennifer propped herself up on her forearms. Hearing the words was one thing, but seeing Sam's expressions granted access to her soul.

"Little did you know, you'd already captured my heart, but I understood what you were asking. I thought about it a lot in the holding cell. And it was like this light bulb went off, and I finally understood that I don't have to choose. I don't have to forget about Kara so I can make room in my heart to love you. I can have both. I realized that it was okay to love Kara and the lifetime of memories that we shared. *And* it's okay that I've completely fallen in love with you. There's room in my heart for the past, the present, and the future. I sat there in that holding cell and dreamed about a future... with you. It sounds crazy when I say it out loud. Does that make sense? The walls don't matter as long as we're together."

Tears of happiness welled in Jennifer's eyes. She nodded. "You couldn't make me any happier than I am right now."

Sam pulled her closer for a kiss. "I'd like to try." She rolled them over again and trailed kisses and nibbles down Jennifer's neck.

She leaned into the pillow and closed her eyes. Sam cupped her breasts, and the warmth of her mouth surrounded Jennifer's nipple and slowly pulled away. She couldn't believe how erotic it felt to be teased by warm breath on wet skin. Sam took her nipple and sucked with the perfect amount of pressure while stimulating her even more with delicate flicks from the tip of her tongue. She caressed, savored, and teased one breast before focusing on the other and left Jennifer wanting more when she pulled away and kissed down her stomach. Jennifer buried her fingers into Sam's short hair as Sam kissed the delicate skin on one hip, then the other, then slid down her body.

Jennifer's breath caught in anticipation.

"Is this okay?" Sam asked and kissed each leg, close to the inner thigh, where they joined the rest of her body.

"Yes," Jennifer said in a raspy whisper.

Sam slid her arms beneath Jennifer's legs and wrapped them around her hips. Jennifer bent her quivering knees and welcomed Sam's lips on her right thigh, then the left. The way she took her time was blissful torture. Any concern Jennifer might have had about competing with Kara for Sam's love had already melted away. She immersed herself now in the love they shared for each other.

CHAPTER TWENTY-THREE

Bright sunlight filtered into the room. Sam turned her head and focused on the alarm clock. Seven thirteen in the morning. She'd only been out of a job for two weeks and was surprised by how quickly her body had adjusted to the ability to sleep in. Although it was more likely the fact that she and Jennifer had been staying up late each night making love. Each passionate night had been more intense and adventurous than the one before. Sam shivered with the thought.

She pulled on some clothes and shuffled out to the kitchen for a cup of coffee. There was a note on the counter: "Good morning, love. I ran over to the apartment to pick up the last few things and drop off my keys. I'll be home soon, Jen."

Sam smiled. *I'll be home soon, Jen.* She liked the sound of that. She ate a breakfast bar and carried her coffee into the primary bedroom. The colors they'd picked out together looked great. It was amazing how some paint and carpeting gave the room an entirely new feel. The remodeling smells were finally fading. It was moving day, and Sam was excited to once again occupy the entire house, especially this room…with Jennifer. She no longer felt the need to close the door on the memories of Kara. Every day, it was easier and easier to acknowledge the past as a life well lived and look forward to the new memories that had yet to be made.

A quick request to the smart speaker and Sam had the company of her morning DJ for a couple of hours while she worked.

There was an extra bounce in her step today. Not only would Jennifer be officially moved in, but it was their first evening out since the arrest. A dress-up evening of dinner and dancing with Pat and Angie. They had reservations at a restaurant on the lake, and with it being the Fourth of July weekend, there would most likely be several fireworks shows over the water. The homeowners who lived on the lake put on some of the most spectacular private shows every year. Another first for Jennifer. She hadn't seen fireworks in person for as long as she could remember. Sam loved sharing all the Minnesota firsts with her. It kept reminding her why she loved the area so much.

She arranged the drawers in the dresser and did a best guess on where Jennifer would like things based on what she could remember from packing up the apartment. When that was finished, she started moving clothes from the closet. While the guest room had certainly helped her reset, she was excited to be back in the space she'd designed so long ago. The more time she'd spent in this end of the house, preparing for today, the more she'd realized that she wouldn't change a thing given the chance to build somewhere else. Jennifer couldn't think of any changes either, and that made Sam smile with pride.

A knock on the front door pulled her out of her thoughts. It could be Jennifer. Although her car had been programmed to open any of the three garage doors, and she had her own bay to park in. Sam took a quick glance at her reflection in the dresser mirror. Her hair wasn't too crazy.

She walked through the house and peeked out the side window. Kelly stood on the stoop, shifting her weight from one foot to the other. Wow. That was the last person Sam expected to see. What on earth was she doing here? Anger flared. She had a lot of gall. But she hadn't been charged. And she'd been betrayed by her own husband. Sam unlocked the door, pulled it open, and feigned her best smile.

"Hey, Sam, I'm sorry to show up out of the blue. I tried to call, but there was no answer." Kelly appeared to have aged ten years in the few weeks since the arrests. She'd lost weight and had dark circles under her eyes. All of which was easier to see since she wasn't wearing any makeup.

"The FBI confiscated my phone. I had to get a new one." Sam wasn't sure whether she should invite her inside. Even though it had been Mike and not Kelly, she couldn't squash the anger of being set up to take the fall.

"They took mine too." Kelly's chin quivered. "Anyway, I had to empty out the office so the building can be put on the market. I thought you might want your personal stuff. I know these prints are pictures from your property. I also grabbed your diffuser and some books from your shelf. I think I got it all." She held out the box.

"Thank you." Sam opened the screen door and took the box. Suddenly, her heart ached for all that Kelly had been through. She'd seen the coverage on the news. Kelly had been hit from all directions. The toll that it had taken on her appearance likely paled in comparison to what it had done to her spirit. Sam had been able to walk away. Kelly hadn't been so lucky. She held the door open. "Would you like to come inside and have a cup of coffee?"

"I appreciate the invite, but I should go." Kelly touched her arm. "I'm sorry." Her chin quivered again, and tears welled in her eyes. "I'm sorry I doubted you. I'm sorry that you were pulled into this, and I'm sorry for everything you went through while in custody. I filed for divorce. I'm leaving. I'm going to stay with my sister in Oregon until I can figure out what to do. I can't stay here. I can't even go to the grocery store without whispers and finger pointing. I went from adoring him to hating him. I can't even look at him. He destroyed my life."

"Do you know why he did it?"

"Gambling. I guess he got in over his head in some online gambling thing. I had no idea. I thought he was just playing stupid free games on the internet like I did. He said he wrote the code and stole the money so he could hide how much he had spent since I paid the credit card bills. Said that he thought he'd strike it big and he'd pay it all back. Had these dreams that we'd retire in the Bahamas. When he saw how quickly the money added up, he got greedy and kept the code active. At least, that's what he said. I don't know what the truth is anymore. I haven't gone to see him. He's ruined my ability to trust anyone like that ever again. I've lost everything. I'm almost sixty, and I'm starting over."

The remnants of Sam's anger subsided. Empathy washed over her because she understood how overwhelming it felt to have to start over. "It may take some time, but you'll come out the other side. I did." She smiled.

Kelly nodded and backed up a few steps. "Thanks for that and for not slamming the door in my face. You're the one who was charged for his crime and the only one who didn't chase me off the property. Thank you."

"I wish you the best. Take care, Kelly." Sam wasn't sure what else she could say. She couldn't think of anything that would help Kelly feel better about what had happened.

"You too, Sam." Kelly smiled, turned, and walked away.

Sam set the box down and watched the car head up the driveway. She was glad that Kelly had stopped by. As brief as their chat was, it gave Sam the answers she'd been looking for. Kelly's car pulled out onto the road just as Jennifer was pulling in.

Jennifer was home. Sam liked the sound of that. The silliest things made her feel giddy these days, like the fact that Jennifer's car now had Minnesota license plates. She was really staying. She was home. Sam walked around the house to see if she needed any help carrying the last of her belongings inside.

"Was that Kelly?"

"Yeah, she dropped off the stuff from my office. She's divorcing Mike and moving to Oregon." She held out her arms for the clothes Jennifer was lifting out of the back seat.

"I feel so bad for her. I can't imagine what she's going through. Did she say why Mike stole the money?" Jennifer pulled the last few things from her car and pushed the car door closed with her hip.

"I guess it all started to hide a gambling problem. I can't believe he threw his life away thinking he'd hit it big." Sam balanced the clothes in her arms and pushed the button to close the garage door.

"How sad."

"Agreed. I can't believe that Mike let himself get caught up in that." Sam walked toward the primary bedroom. Jennifer followed her into the closet, and she smiled when Jennifer squealed in delight.

"Sam, I love it! What a wonderful surprise. I thought we were going to wait a few more days."

"Well, I came in here this morning, and the fumes were all but gone."

"Thank you for doing this." Jennifer hung her clothes on the rod and lifted the others from Sam's arms. "I've consumed all the closet space at the other end of the house and thought I'd lay this load on the bed in the sewing room."

"Not anymore. There're just a few more things to get from the guest room, and we'll be all moved into our new space. Welcome home." She'd been thrilled when Jennifer had agreed to move in. She couldn't imagine waking up and not having Jennifer snuggled up next to her. Being with Jennifer felt wonderful. It felt right. They'd been inseparable since the arrest.

Jennifer stepped into her arms. "Do you realize that you're the first person I've lived with in twenty-seven years?"

"Luckily, you've been here so much that I feel like we've had a few months of practice." Sam bent and touched their foreheads together.

"Based on those few months, I think we're quite compatible."

"Me too," Sam said and kissed her tenderly. "I've moved everything from the small bathroom to this one too." Sam lifted her shirt and bra over her head. She unbuckled her belt and undid her jeans. Jennifer watched and stepped closer, but Sam stepped into the bathroom. "Care to join me in the shower?"

❖

Three hours later, Jennifer stood in front of the mirror. Her hair and makeup were perfect. She considered a necklace but decided to leave her neck bare and let the dress be the focal point.

Sam hadn't seen this one before. She'd only asked to know the color. The gown was an asymmetric midnight blue metallic ruffle designed by Mac Duggal. The elegant design left her right shoulder bare, and the slit in the left front of the dress came up to mid-thigh. It was sexy as hell, if she did say so herself. She loved the design and had ordered it a couple of years earlier, but until this evening, she hadn't had a reason to wear it. The dress hugged her in all of the right places. She couldn't wait to see Sam's expression. For a finishing touch, she slid her feet into stiletto sandals that matched the color of her dress perfectly. She twirled in front of the mirror. Nice. Very nice indeed.

She stepped onto the wooden floor of the hallway. She loved

the click of her heels. At the living room, her breath caught, and she stopped dead in her tracks. Holy sexy. Sam looked amazing in a three-piece black suit with a white shirt beneath. Her perfectly knotted necktie and crisp pocket square were midnight blue to match Jennifer's dress.

"You look stunning." Sam held out her hand.

Jennifer loved how her expression said so much more than her words. She hoped hers did as well. "You're the one who looks stunning. Wow. I love that suit on you."

Sam smiled. "Do we have to go out, or can I talk you into staying in?"

"You promised me fireworks." Jennifer kissed her lips and wiped away the trace of lipstick she'd left behind.

"I bet I can honor that promise even if we stay in." Sam walked in a circle around her. The admiration in her eyes said everything Jennifer had wished for.

Sam held out an arm, and Jennifer tucked hers in the crook. Already, the evening was perfect. Sam led her out the front door to where a Lincoln Town Car was outside waiting. The driver stepped out and held the back door open. "A treat for our first official date night so you'll have my full attention." Sam held her hand while she sat and slid into the center seat.

She wasn't scooching all the way across. She planned to snuggle in Sam's arms on the ride, especially since neither one of them had to drive. She felt like Cinderella going to a ball with her Prince Charming. Sam couldn't have planned a more romantic evening. She picked up two rocks glasses from a small console in front of them. Jennifer sniffed hers: a touch of her favorite whiskey on the rocks.

"To us and whatever our future holds." Sam held up her glass.

A perfect toast. "To us and whatever our future holds." Jennifer carefully tapped her glass to Sam's and took a sip. Ice-cold, warm, smooth perfection greeted her taste buds. "You certainly know how to make a woman feel special."

"You are special. I love you." Sam leaned over and kissed her cheek.

"I love you too."

Within ten minutes, they pulled into the restaurant parking lot.

The driver stepped out and opened their door. Sam slid out and held her hand out. It was a perfectly romantic moment. Jennifer thought back to the recruiter who'd talked about her time in Minnesota being right out of a Hallmark movie. Her time with Sam was just that, the loving romance she'd only ever seen on TV, only now she was enjoying it in person. How had she become so lucky?

Sam walked her into the restaurant. Pat and Angie were standing just inside the doors. Pat looked good in black trousers and a jacket. She wore a white shirt underneath and had a black necktie. Angie looked stunning in a dark green evening gown. Her strawberry-blond hair had almost a 1920s finger wave to it. Their expressions when they turned were priceless.

"You two look like models. Holy sexy," Angie said and stepped forward for a hug.

"I love your dress and your hair, wow," Jennifer said. "You look stunning."

Angie beamed. Pat leaned down for a hug too. "Hello, beautiful."

"Hello, handsome. Don't you look dashing."

Pat kissed her cheek and turned, then hugged Sam. "New suit?"

"Yeah. It was time for something that fit."

Jennifer smiled. She'd thought it was new but didn't want to assume she'd seen all of Sam's clothes. It made her feel special that Sam had ordered something just for their first night out.

The hostess stepped into their circle. "Your table is ready."

Sam held out an arm for Jennifer. She accepted it with a happy heart. Such a simple gesture meant the world to her. Their table was in a nook beneath an awning but open to the outside on three sides. She could smell the lake. It was perfect. The sun was just dropping in the sky. Boats cruised past, some pulling kids on tubes or bright orange and yellow floating couches. She could hear the squeals of excitement. It was quite picturesque.

They ordered their drinks and appetizers and sat like four old friends catching up on the events of the week. Jennifer felt comfortable and welcome. Just as their food arrived, brilliant fireworks lit up the sky. To hear the boom and see the spray of fiery color both in the sky and mirrored in the water was an experience she'd cherish for the rest of her life.

She leaned close to Sam. "This is the second most magical evening I've ever experienced."

"The second?"

"Yes. Nothing beats a first kiss in a field of fireflies." She cupped Sam's cheek.

Sam leaned over and kissed her. "I love you."

"I love you too."

Jennifer thought about their conversation at the nursery while sitting on the tailgate enjoying a cinnamon roll and each other's company. Sam had asked if she'd found happiness in being single. Once upon a time, she had. Then Sam had walked into her life and swept her off her feet. Now she felt complete. She couldn't imagine a future without Sam. Every day with her was filled with memories she'd treasure forever.

About the Author

Nance Sparks is a Goldie Award–winning author of lesbian romance. She lives in south central Wisconsin with her spouse. Her passion for photography, homesteading, hiking, gardening, and most anything outdoors comes through in her stories. When the sun is out and the sky is blue, especially during the golden hour, Nance can be found on the Wisconsin River with a camera in hand, capturing shots of large birds in flight.

Books Available From Bold Strokes Books

The Accidental Bride by Jane Walsh. Spinsters Miss Grace Linfield and Miss Thea Martin travel to Gretna Green to prevent a wedding, only to discover a scandalous passion—for each other. (978-1-63679-345-0)

Broken Fences by Jo Hemmingwood. Former army sergeant Seneca Twist has difficulty adjusting to civilian life until she meets psychologist Robyn Mason and has a place to call home. (978-1-63679-414-3)

Never Kiss a Cowgirl by Ali Vali. Asher Evans dreams of winning the National Finals Rodeo in Vegas, and Reagan Wilson wants no part of something that brings back the memory of what killed her father. (978-1-63679-106-7)

Pantheon Girls by Jean Copeland. Cassie Burke never anticipated the detour life is about to take when a meeting with a prospective client reunites her with a past love and reignites the star-crossed passion they shared twenty years earlier. (978-1-63679-337-5)

Roux for Two by Aurora Rey. For TV chef Chelsea Boudreaux and hometown boy Bryce Cormier, love proves as tricky as making a good pot of gumbo. (978-1-63679-376-4)

Starting Over by Nance Sparks. Jennifer has no idea if she can mend Sam's broken soul after the sudden loss of her wife, but it's never too late for starting over. (978-1-63679-409-9)

Three Wishes by Anne Shade. A magic lamp, a beautiful Jinni, and a cursed princess make for one unbelievable story. (978-1-63679-349-8)

Undiscovered Treasures by MJ Williamz. For Cyl and her friends Luna and Martinique, life's best treasures often appear when they're not looking. (978-1-63679-449-5)

Curse of the Gorgon by Tanai Walker. Cass will do anything to ensure Elle's safety, but is she willing to embrace the curse of the Gorgon? (978-1-63679-395-5)

Dance with Me by Georgia Beers. Scottie Templeton mixes it up on and off the dance floor with sexy salsa instructor Marisa Reyes. But can Scottie get past Marisa's connection to her ex? (978-1-63679-359-7)

Gin and Bear It by Joy Argento. Opposites really can attract, and as Kelly and Logan work together to create a loving home for rescue cat Bear, they just might find one for themselves as well. (978-1-63679-351-1)

Harvest Dreams by Jacqueline Fein-Zachary. Planting the vineyard of their dreams, Kate Bauer and Sydney Barrett must resist their attraction while battling nature and their families, who oppose both the venture and their relationship. (978-1-63679-380-1)

The No Kiss Contract by Nan Campbell. Workaholic Davy believes she can get the top spot at her firm if the senior partners think she's settling down and about to start a family, but she needs the delightful yet dubious Anna to help by pretending to be her fiancée. (978-1-63679-372-6)

Outside the Lines by Melissa Sky. If you had the chance to live forever, would you take it? Amara Rodriguez did, and it sets her on a journey to find her missing mother and unravel the mystery of her own heart. (978-1-63679-403-7)

The Value of Sylver and Gold by Michelle Larkin. When word gets out that former Boston homicide detective Reid Sylver can talk to the dead, the FBI solicits her help on a serial murder case, prompting Reid to assemble forces once again with Detective London Gold. (978-1-63679-093-0)

When It Feels Right by Tagan Shepard. Freshly out of the closet Marlene hasn't been lucky in love, but when it comes to her quirky new roommate Abby, everything just feels right. (978-1-63679-367-2)

The Fall Line by Kelly Wacker. When Jordan Burroughs arrives in the Deep South to paint a local endangered aquatic flower, she doesn't expect to become friends with a mischievous gin-drinking ghost who complicates her budding romance and leads her to an awful discovery and danger. (978-1-63679-205-7)

Lucky in Lace by Melissa Brayden. Straitlaced stationery store owner Juliette Jennings's predictable life unravels when a sexy lingerie shop and its alluring owner move in next door. (978-1-63679-434-1)

Made for Her by Carsen Taite. Neal Walsh is a newly made member of the Mancuso crime family, but will her undeniable attraction to Anastasia Petrov, the wife of her boss's sworn enemy, be the ultimate test of her loyalty? (978-1-63679-265-1)

Off the Menu by Alaina Erdell. Reality TV sensation Restaurant Redo and its gorgeous host Erin Rasmussen will arrive to film in chef Taylor Mobley's kitchen. As the cameras roll, will they make the jump from enemies to lovers? (978-1-63679-295-8)

Pack of Her Own by Elena Abbott. When things heat up in a small town, steamy secrets are revealed between Alpha werewolf Wren Carne and her human mate, Natalie Donovan. (978-1-63679-370-2)

Return to McCall by Patricia Evans. Lily isn't looking for romance—not until she meets Alex, the gorgeous Cuban dance instructor at La Haven, a newly opened lesbian retreat. (978-1-63679-386-3)

So It Went Like This by C. Spencer. A candid and deeply personal exploration of fate, chosen family, and the vulnerability intrinsic in life's uncertainties. (978-1-63555-971-2)

Stolen Kiss by Spencer Greene. Anna and Louise share a stolen kiss, only to discover that Louise is dating Anna's brother. Surely, one kiss can't change everything…Can it? (978-1-63679-364-1)

To Meet Again by Kadyan. When the stark reality of WW II separates cabaret singer Evelyn and Australian doctor Joan in Singapore, they must overcome all odds to find one another again. (978-1-63679-398-6)